Snow Globe Magic

By

Cara Marsi

Published by The Painted Lady Press
United States of America
Electronic Edition: May, 2016

This book is a work of fiction and all characters exist solely in the author's imagination. Any resemblance to persons, living or dead, is purely coincidental. Any references to places, events or locales are used in a fictitious manner.

Cover by Harris Channing
Formatting by Aileen Fish

The gift of love…

A mysterious matchmaker alters the destiny of three women when she offers each the gift of a magical snow globe. Is the elderly stranger simply eccentric? Or is there enchantment in her gifts?

Her Snow White Christmas…

A Christmas snow globe swirls holiday magic for a sophisticated New York woman with a broken heart and a handsome Iraq War vet with a secret. It's Christmas in Vermont, and magic swirls in the air like glitter in a snow globe.

Her Frog Prince Holiday…

The gift of a magical snow globe paints the scene for romance between a Manhattan art gallery manager and a sexy man who isn't what he seems. It's Halloween in Manhattan. Can a woman who thought she wanted a frog learn to love a prince?

Her Red Riding Hood Valentine…

A magical snow globe sets the stage for romance between a drama teacher who no longer believes in love and an enticing photographer picturing a different life. It's the season of love in Manhattan. Can a feisty redhead and a wolf in an Armani suit picture a new life together?

Her Snow White Christmas

By

Cara Marsi

A Christmas snow globe from a mysterious stranger swirls holiday magic for a sophisticated New York woman with a broken heart and a handsome Iraq War vet with a secret.

As a child, Avery Coleman loved Snow White and dreamed of Prince Charming. The adult Avery no longer believes in fairy tales. She'd settle for a handsome prince as ambitious for success as she is. Then an eccentric woman gives Avery a Christmas snow globe, advising her that princes come in many disguises. But when family obligations call Avery from Manhattan back to her small hometown in Vermont, she finds there aren't many princes to be found in the forest of her family's Christmas tree lot. At least it's a vacation from her wicked witch of a boss.

Iraq War veteran Josh Huntsman always did what was expected of him. Believing there had to be more to life than chasing money and prestige, he'd left the corporate world for life in the Army. But his stint in the military cost him more than expected. Back from Iraq, Josh hides his past, volunteering at the homeless shelter and working at a Christmas tree lot. He isn't ready to rejoin the rat race, and definitely has no use for a bright-lights-big-city girl like the ambitious fiancée who dumped him.

Leaving New York to spend the holidays selling Christmas trees in Vermont might sound magical to some, but for Avery, it's a return to the place she worked hard to escape. But it's Christmas and magic swirls in the air like glitter in a snow globe. And a single kiss might awaken a lifetime of happily ever after.

CHAPTER ONE

Avery Coleman stepped off the elevator into the reception center of the Manhattan offices that housed the fashion magazine where she worked. She drew a calming breath. *You can do this, Avery.*

It was two weeks before Christmas and she had to convince her boss, the formidable Edie Queensland, senior editor, to give her time off for the holidays. Her parents and her sister needed her in Vermont. But the icy Edie Queensland could freeze those plans.

In her three years with the magazine, Avery hadn't been able to convince Edie to let her write articles with her own byline. Edie said she'd hired Avery as her assistant not as a writer.

"Morning, Tiff," she said to the receptionist.

"Hey, Avery." Tiffany grimaced and nodded toward Edie's office. "She wants to see you."

Of course she does, Avery thought, resisting the urge to roll her eyes. As she strode toward her boss's office, she unbuttoned her coat, feeling suddenly overheated.

"Avery, wait up."

She turned to see Molly, one of the secretaries, hurrying toward her. Smiling, Molly handed Avery a flyer.

Avery glanced down at the bright green paper. "What's this?"

"My community on Long Island is having a Christmas craft fair this Saturday to benefit one of the no-kill shelters. I hope you can come and please bring some friends. The shelter really needs the money."

"I'll try, Molly. Sounds like a worthy cause."

"Thanks." With a small wave, Molly walked away.

Avery stuck the flyer in her purse and continued to Edie's office. Steeling herself, she knocked on the door, then opened it at Edie's strident, "Come in."

Her boss, blond hair in a sleek bob, looked up when Avery entered. Edie glanced at the wall clock. "You're late."

"It's seven twenty. I'm forty minutes early."

"I don't have time for excuses." Edie grabbed some papers from her desk and held them out to Avery. "Here are the points I need to cover for my April editor's letter. Write it and have it back to me by January second."

Avery took the proffered papers and met Edie's pale blue gaze. "I'll get writing credit this time, won't I?"

"Of course not. It's *my* letter. And you're my assistant, not a writer."

"But I'm a good writer. You know that."

"That's beside the point."

Don't argue, Avery. You need this job and you need that vacation.

When Avery didn't move, Edie looked at her over the top of her half glasses. "Do you want something?"

"I do." Avery straightened her shoulders and went into the speech she'd rehearsed.

"I didn't take all my vacation days last year and I've got some left for this year. I need time off to go to Vermont and help my family. With my parents unavoidably away and my sister seven months' pregnant, I have to help out at our

Christmas tree lot. I'd like to start my vacation a few days before Christmas. I'll be back after the New Year."

Edie took off her glasses and gave Avery one of her stony looks that made grown men quake. Avery stood her ground.

Finally, Edie waved a hand. "Take the damn vacation. But I want that letter tomorrow. I'll be gone over the holidays anyway. Greg's invited me to Aspen."

Greg was Edie's new boyfriend, a Wall Street trader. Since she'd started dating him five months ago, she'd grown a little softer, treating her staff with kindness they'd not known from her before. Just now, saying his name, Edie's face seemed to glow.

Thank you, Greg. Avery wanted to punch a fist in the air, but settled for smiling.

"Thank you, Edie. I'll have that letter for you today."

"Look! Fairy-tale ornaments." Avery Coleman waved a hand toward a booth in the center of the cavernous school gym housing the Christmas craft fair. "Let's go see."

With her friends Bella and Carlyn following in her wake, Avery, like a laser finding its target, homed in on the booth. She'd needed this outing with her friends, needed to forget the heartache of the past four months. And now that Edie had given her the vacation she wanted, maybe she could finally get into the Christmas spirit.

When they reached the booth, her gaze landed on a delicate Snow White ornament suspended from a silver ribbon. She picked it up and ran her hand over the brightly painted ceramic figurine.

"That's cute," Carlyn said.

"It is." Bella wrinkled her nose. "But I still can't believe you dragged us all the way out to Long Island for a craft show."

"Lighten up," Avery said. "It's good to get out of Manhattan once in a while to see how 'real' people live."

"The only time I leave Manhattan is in the summer to go to the Hamptons," Bella said.

Carlyn rolled her eyes. "You're such a snob."

"Stop it, both of you," Avery said. "I promised my co-worker Molly I'd be here. The proceeds go to a no-kill shelter."

Bella held up a hand in resignation. "I agree it's for a good cause, but I love Manhattan during the holidays."

"I'm glad to be out of the city on a Saturday." Carlyn put her hand over her heart. "All those frantic Christmas shoppers give me *agita*." She nodded toward the figure Avery held. "You always had a thing for Snow White."

Avery dangled the shining ornament in front of her. It glinted in the weak sunlight streaming through the high windows, sending out tiny sparks of cheer. "When I was little, I used to dream that Prince Charming would kiss me and awaken me to life and then whisk me off to the big city." She chuckled. "I stopped believing in fairy tales and princes a long time ago."

Bella snorted. "I never did believe in all that fairy tale hocus pocus. You buying that ornament?"

Avery nodded. "I'll buy this one for myself. It's ten days to Christmas and I still haven't bought gifts for my cousins' daughters. I think I'll buy fairy-tale ornaments for them, too."

As Avery waited for the clerk to wrap the eight ornaments she'd purchased, she turned to her friends. "When I was a teenager, I thought Prince Charming's kiss to Snow

White was a metaphor for a guy awakening a woman's sexuality."

Her friends burst out laughing. "Awakening sexuality?" Bella said when she could talk again. "So who woke you up sexually?"

Avery shrugged. "Hasn't really happened yet."

"You mean Mitch didn't ring your sexual alarm clock?" Carlyn asked.

"Mitch and I had a nice sex life," Avery answered.

"*Nice* sex life!" Bella widened her eyes. "Girl, you *needed* to dump that guy."

"Technically he dumped me when he decided to cheat on me." The familiar pain of hurt and betrayal tightened a knot in Avery's chest. "Mitch and I might have had a comfortable sex life, but it sure looked like he and that casting agent I found him in bed with were having a grand time." Mitch had accused Avery of being inadequate in bed, of not fulfilling him sexually, but she'd never told that to her friends. They'd understand, but she couldn't risk the humiliation.

"You're better off without him," Carlyn said. "Especially if he wasn't so great in bed."

Frowning, Bella studied Avery. "If Mitch didn't awaken you sexually, what about Ethan? You and he dated all through college. Or Ryan? You seemed really into each other for a while before Mitch."

Avery took her package and thanked the clerk. Giving her friends a wry smile, she said, "Those other guys were okay. I don't want to talk about men now or that cheating rat bastard Mitch."

"Wonder how long before he cheats on the new girlfriend," Carlyn said.

"Who cares?" Bella said. "Avery's right. Forget him. There's a decent guy out there for Avery." She grinned. "Someone who will *awaken* her."

"I hope we each meet a guy who will *awaken* us," Carlyn said with a laugh.

Bella sniffed the air. "I don't need a guy, but I need one of those cinnamon cookies. They're calling to me. Let's eat."

A few minutes later, they sat at one of the small tables set up in the gym, drinking lattes and eating homemade Christmas cookies.

Avery moaned softly and licked her lips. "Yum, these cookies are delicious. Almost as good as the ones my mother bakes. My cousins' wives are all great cooks too. If I have to spend the holidays selling Christmas trees in Vermont, I know I'll be eating well. Except for my parents, the whole family is having Christmas dinner together."

"I can't believe you have to sell trees at your family's lot," Bella said.

Carlyn chuckled. "I can't believe your witch of a boss gave you vacation until after the New Year."

"I know," Avery said. "Edie has a new boyfriend so she's been in a good mood since she started dating him. The whole staff is grateful to Greg, the boyfriend."

Carlyn daintily wiped her mouth with her napkin. "Everyone needs love, even your witch of a boss."

"Love!" Bella said. "I don't need it, don't want it."

Avery laughed. "One of these days you'll meet a guy who will knock you on your ass."

Carlyn smirked. "I can't wait until that day."

Bella waved a hand in dismissal and bit into another cookie.

Pushing aside her empty plate, Avery sighed and said,

"I like my job, but I wish Edie would reconsider and give me a regular column in the magazine."

Carlyn patted her hand. "You'll get your column. At least your fashion blog is gaining popularity."

"I'm happy about that," Avery said. "Not happy I have to spend my first real vacation in three years selling Christmas trees. Growing up, my sister and I helped my parents out at the lot every year. I couldn't wait to get away from the trees, the family farm, and the town. But I'm glad my parents won that cruise, even if it means they're away during the holidays and I have to sell trees. They tried to reschedule the cruise and couldn't, and they were going to give it up, but Addison and I insisted they go. My parents work hard and they deserve a break."

Carlyn held up her mug. "Here's to cruises, Christmas trees, and bosses who suddenly have the Christmas spirit." She glanced around, then pointed to a booth in the far corner of the room. "Oh! Snow globes. I want one."

They cleared away their empty cups and dishes and crossed to the booth draped in a shimmering gold cloth, unlike the others that were decorated in reds and greens.

"Hello, dearies," the elderly woman manning the booth said as they approached. The woman's hair was orange, in a shade not found in nature, and piled high in a sixties beehive style. She peered at Avery through green-framed cats-eye glasses. Her bright red sweater bore appliqués of Christmas scenes.

Avery smiled. The woman was as festive as her booth. Maybe more so. Avery reached for a globe with a small cottage nestled inside. "How beautiful!" Before she could touch it, the elderly woman held out another to her.

"This one is for you," the woman said.

Glistening flakes of white and silver fell inside the globe the woman handed to Avery. The flakes settled to reveal a tiny Christmas tree adorned with a single gold star. Avery squinted to see the minuscule figure standing next to the tree—Santa Claus

"This is lovely." The globe was warm, and as Avery cradled it, contentment rolled through her and filled her with optimism. She felt happier than she had since finding Mitch with... She refused to go there. "I'll take it."

As she handed the globe to the orange-haired woman to wrap, their hands touched. Heat seemed to flow from the woman's hand up Avery's arm.

Brown eyes behind the cats-eye spectacles looked deeply into Avery's. "Princes come in many disguises. You'll find yours where you least expect him."

Avery laughed. "I'm not looking for a prince."

"That which you don't seek will find you." The elderly woman gave her a sly smile and proceeded to wrap Avery's purchase.

"You're going to find your Prince Charming," Bella said, laughing.

"No way," Avery said. "I may see Santa, but, trust me, Prince Charming doesn't live in Lorewood, Vermont."

CHAPTER TWO

Avery stepped out of the bakery and sniffed the clean air, inhaling the scent of pine from the forest that surrounded Lorewood. Along Main Street, multicolored Christmas lights, strung from the lampposts, twinkled in the winter sunshine and reflected on the light covering of snow, giving the place an other-worldly air.

They had the new manufacturing plant to thank for the town coming back to life after decades of bleeding jobs and people. The company had recently renovated an abandoned factory outside of town and moved their operations from overseas, providing jobs to hundreds of people, including all seven of her male cousins.

Holding a bag filled with pastries and a carrier with two Styrofoam cups of coffee, Avery strolled to her parents' car which she was using while they were away. A commotion at one end of the street caught her attention. Focusing on the young mother trying to calm her toddler's tantrum, Avery didn't watch where she walked. She slipped on the icy sidewalk and slammed her head into a pole. The last thing she remembered as she passed out was thinking she'd have to buy more coffee to replace the ones she spilled.

"Are you okay, miss?" A deep male voice penetrated through the fog in her brain.

As she tried to open her eyes, it felt like she was fighting her way out of a snow bank. Avery finally met the concerned deep green eyes of—Santa Claus? He bent over her, only inches from her face.

"An ambulance is on the way," he said.

She touched her forehead. "I'm okay." She was going to have one hell of a bump and she must be hallucinating. Santa Claus?

When she tried to sit up, a wave of dizziness overtook her and she sank back to the ground.

Santa put his hand on her shoulder, proving he was very real. "Don't try to move."

He smiled. His white beard and mustache framed his perfect white teeth and full, enticing lips. If she leaned up a little, she could taste that delectable mouth. What was wrong with her? The knock on the head must have made her crazy. She was fantasying about kissing Santa Claus.

A siren rent the air.

"Here's the ambulance now," green-eyed Santa said.

◇◇◇

Two days later

"It's about time you showed up." Avery's breath hovered in the cold air, and she rubbed her gloved hands together as she walked up to the guy her sister had hired to help out at the Christmas tree lot. Frustration and worry, tight as the ropes they used to tie up the trees, coiled in her chest. Her sister, Addison, feeling sick, had gone home thirty minutes ago at Avery's urging, leaving Avery to wait for the guy. And he was late.

"Sorry," the guy said, a trace of humor in his deep voice, a familiar voice that reminded Avery of rich, hot chocolate.

She met his eyes, deep green, the color of a pine tree,

and shining with amusement. His smile brought out the dimple in his cheek and showed his perfect white teeth. She knew those teeth and those tempting lips. Her insides warmed. She took a step back.

"Santa Claus?" she blurted.

He laughed. "Not today. I was doing a party at the women's shelter the other day." Concern softened his eyes and he closed the space between them. "How are you feeling?"

Avery touched the lump on her forehead. It had gone down considerably since her accident. "I'm fine. No concussion. They didn't keep me long at the hospital."

"I'm glad. You took quite a hit."

"Thanks for helping."

While they stared at each other, not speaking, Avery studied him. He looked to be in his mid-thirties and wore a faded Army jacket that stretched across his broad chest and wide shoulders. His ripped jeans showcased long legs that went on forever. The name stitched onto his jacket said Huntsman.

She cleared her throat. He must be down on his luck if selling Christmas trees was the only work he could get. Maybe after his stint in the military, he'd come into hard times. A sad story repeated too often. At least she could do her small part to help. With a smile, she said, "I'm glad you made it. Have you ever sold trees before?"

He furrowed his brow. "Uh—yes. But it's been a few years." He looked around. "Nice selection of trees. Is this your first year at this location?"

"My parents have sold trees on this lot every Christmas for over thirty years. In the summer they sell fresh produce from their farm here."

"Good spot," he said.

Despite the way he was dressed, he didn't have the look of someone beaten down by life. His eyes gleamed with intelligence, and his features were strong, with a straight nose and firm chin. Dark blond hair peeked from the back and sides of his black knit cap. He stood a foot taller than she did.

His stunning good looks made her heart beat a rapid tattoo. First, she'd wanted to kiss Santa, and now she was getting hot over a guy who sold Christmas trees. Okay, the same guy, but still, this was so not like her. The men she got involved with were successful and ambitious—like Ryan, owner of a string of high-end accessories boutiques, and Mitch, who acted on and off Broadway and was beginning to make a name for himself in Hollywood. Trying to get control of the situation and her rising libido, she said, "Business is starting to pick up." She nodded toward a couple looking at some fir trees. "They've been here awhile. The prices are on the trees."

"I'll take care of it, ma'am," he said, with that trace of laughter back in his voice. He loped away toward the couple.

Despite her annoyance at her reaction to him, Avery couldn't stop herself from admiring his animal-like grace. Two days selling trees and one bump on the noggin, combined with the overpowering scent of pine, had all gone to her head.

As he walked away, Josh Huntsman grinned at Miss City Girl's take-charge attitude. He'd seen the pity in her eyes before she became all business. She'd pegged him for a down-on-his-luck vet. He might be out of work at the moment, but the truth was a little more complicated. Let her think what she wanted, but she was sure easy on the eyes— petite and slim, with that long, thick black hair and big brown eyes, and a luscious mouth begging to be kissed. He turned to watch her stroll toward the trailer at the end of the lot, her hips swaying seductively.

Down, boy. Miss City Girl wasn't for him. She might be selling trees in this little backwater town, but despite her worn jeans and bulky down jacket, her looks and attitude shouted city sophisticate. He'd had his fill of city life and women like her. That wasn't what he wanted, not anymore. But what did he want? The thought nagged him as he approached the couple examining a Douglas fir.

CHAPTER THREE

Settled into the trailer a short while later, Avery poured boiling water into her mug and let her tea steep. Wind whistled through the old trailer they had used for years as an office for the Christmas tree lot and their summer produce. She remembered sitting here drinking hot chocolate when she was eight, twenty-four years ago. Her parents had let the trailer fall into a state of disrepair, like the old farmhouse where she'd grown up.

Her tea ready, she carried the mug to the scarred oak table and sank onto one of the chairs rimming it. Despite her desire to escape this town, she'd had a great childhood. Her parents, hard-working and poor, had lavished love on her and Addison. Her sister had never had ambition to live anywhere else, but Avery had studied hard in school, earning a scholarship to the town's elite private high school, and plotted her escape. She'd worked her way through college, graduating with an English degree.

Now, she was living her dream in New York City, the greatest city in the world. If her long work hours didn't leave her much time to enjoy all New York offered, life there was better than anywhere else. Her magazine job might not be the glamorous career she'd envisioned, and her drop-dead gorgeous actor boyfriend might have betrayed her, but her life was everything she'd ever wanted. And yet…

19

Shaking away any negative thoughts, she focused on the here and now. She'd get a chance to work on her blog while she was here. After all, nothing much happened in this town.

Her cell phone rang and she pulled it from her jacket pocket. Seeing her sister's name come up, she connected the call. "Hey, Addy. How are you feeling?"

"I'm better. Thanks. I hated to leave you there alone. I just got a call from Chris. He's not going to be able to work for us after all. He got a better offer from the drugstore."

"Who's Chris?"

"The teenager I hired to help out at the lot. He was supposed to start today."

Avery almost choked on the tea she'd just drunk. Slamming the mug onto the table, she jumped up. "Gotta go, Addy." She disconnected the call and rushed outside.

Had she allowed a stranger, maybe a homeless guy, to walk away with money that belonged to her family?

At the end of the lot, she saw Santa Claus/Mr. Tattered Army Jacket hoisting a tied-up tree over his shoulder. With his powerful build, and the ease with which he lifted the tree, he reminded her of a lumberjack, a sexy lumberjack. Or a hunter who was good with a bow and arrow. Where had that come from? Oh, right. The name stitched on his Army jacket said Huntsman.

Whatever his name, he was a guy who might be stealing from them. Almost running to catch up to him, she slowed down when she realized he was helping a middle-aged couple with the tree. He set the tree into the back of their truck. They handed him cash, then got into their pickup and drove away.

Avery strode up to him. "That belongs to me." She held out her hand.

He placed bills into her open palm. "I sold two trees. Here's the money." His eyes sparkling, he leaned closer. "Do you want my tips, too?"

Clutching the money, she stepped back. "No, you keep the tips. I thought you were the guy my sister and her husband hired."

Laughing, he pulled his cap off and ran his fingers through his longish hair. "Come clean. You thought I was some tramp who was going to steal your money."

Avery swallowed. "You can't be too careful nowadays." She put a hand on her hip. "If you knew I thought you were someone else, why didn't you set me straight?"

"I could see you needed help and I figured while I was here, I might as well give you a hand."

"Why are you here?" She hadn't meant to sound so accusatory. "Sorry. Did you come to buy a tree?"

"Let's start over." He removed one of his gloves and thrust out his hand. "Josh Huntsman."

She placed her bare hand in his large, strong one. "Avery Coleman." Warmth, like a hundred Christmas lights, shot through her as they stood holding hands. She quickly withdrew hers. "Did you want a tree?" she asked again.

He nodded. "I'm volunteering over at the men's shelter. We'd like some trees to help give the guys a nice Christmas. We'd appreciate a donation of a few trees, but if you can't do that, I can work for them. You're obviously short-handed."

Disappointment mixed with relief in Avery. Relief that the hot guy wasn't a thief, but disappointment that he probably wasn't too far removed from homeless himself.

"We'd be glad to donate some trees and you don't have to work for them. We like to give back to the community."

His gaze met hers. "That's great. We'll take the trees, but you need help here. I live outside town and I'm between jobs. I'd be glad to work for you." He grinned. "And I've had some very recent experience selling trees."

Avery chewed her lip. With Addison pregnant, her sister couldn't help out much at the lot. And this close to Christmas, it might be hard to find someone. "Uh. Okay. You're hired."

He gave her another dimpled smile. "I'd better get to work. I see more customers. What time should I report tomorrow morning?"

"We open at ten."

"I'll be here."

Avery watched his long-legged gait as he strolled toward the family shopping for a tree. Josh Huntsman. Out of work. Definitely hot. And she'd be seeing him every day.

CHAPTER FOUR

Avery stared at her laptop, as if the mere act of staring would bring forth the words. But they wouldn't come. She slid back from the table in frustration. At the knock on the trailer door, she shouted, "Come in."

Josh entered, brushing snow off his coat. He pulled off his knit cap and ran his fingers through his hair. He'd been working at the lot five days, and Avery had fought to keep their relationship on a professional level, despite the warmth that settled in her every time she was near him.

"We have no customers at the moment," he said in that rich, deep voice that slid over her like melted chocolate. "I thought I'd come in to warm up."

"Have some coffee. It's a fresh pot."

He poured a cup and sat across from her at the oak table. "What are you working on?" He nodded toward her computer.

"I write a fashion blog, but I'm having trouble today. It could be that I'm out of the city and not getting my usual inspiration."

"Don't you write for that magazine you work for?"

As they'd worked side by side at the lot, they'd talked a little. Actually, she'd talked a lot. Josh, not so much. She'd told him about her job in Manhattan, but he hadn't been forthcoming about his life, other than working at the men's shelter.

"As assistant to the senior editor, my duties don't include writing."

"So you write a blog?"

She suppressed her rising doubts about her career. So what if writing a blog wasn't as fulfilling to her as writing a regular column for the magazine would be? "I love my job. I'm living in the city and doing what I've always wanted." She wondered why she felt compelled to explain herself.

"So growing up here, your dream was to escape to the big city?"

Josh had figured her out in five days. In the three years she'd been with Mitch, he'd never really gotten her, or never really cared to understand her.

She leaned her elbows on the table. "From an early age, I plotted my escape. How did you guess?"

He shrugged. "You're different from your sister. She seems content with her life here, but you must have been looking for something more." His gaze locked with hers. "You're living your dream. How's that working for you?"

Avery bristled. "Who are you? Dr. Phil?" As soon as the words were out, she wanted to bite them back.

He held up both hands. "Whoa! I'm just making conversation."

She settled back in her chair. "I'm sorry. That didn't come out right. I do love my life." She sounded unconvincing, even to herself.

"There's a 'but' in there somewhere." He sipped his coffee and watched her over the rim of the mug.

She squirmed in her seat. The man really did "get" her. "I want to write a column for the magazine, but I can't convince my boss. Writing my blog gets some of that need to write out of my system."

"Maybe you should look for a job at another magazine."

"Quitting a well-paying job for another with maybe less money isn't easy, even if I could find one."

"No, it's not easy at all."

A muscle worked in his jaw and his voice had taken on a hard edge. She suspected she'd touched a nerve with the job remark.

"No man in your life?" he asked.

Surprised by his change of topic, she could only stare at him for a moment. "Not anymore." She didn't understand why she was telling Josh so much about herself. Maybe with Carlyn and Bella so far away and Addison totally involved with impending motherhood, Avery needed someone to talk to. Josh was a good listener.

"So, what happened?" He finished his coffee and went to the pot to pour another cup.

Avery watched him, admiring his strong profile and long, lean, graceful body. Josh carried an air of confidence despite the fact he'd apparently fallen on hard times. Mitch had been confident too, but in a brash way that said he knew he was gorgeous and he expected others to fawn all over him. And they did, especially the women.

As Josh walked back to the table, she shook away her thoughts and decided to turn the conversation to him. She'd said enough. "Did you do a tour in Iraq or Afghanistan when you were in the military?" she asked as he sat down. He'd mentioned he'd served time in the military but he didn't elaborate.

A shadow came over his eyes and he looked away. Finally, he turned back to her, but focused on a spot over her shoulder. "Two tours in Iraq."

"That must have been rough."

"I survived."

He'd closed down. With a twinge of regret, Avery sighed. She'd enjoyed their conversation, even if it made her uncomfortable at times.

A knock at the door propelled Josh from his seat, as if he was suddenly glad to get away. He opened the door to a customer. "Coming right out," he said. Without a backward glance, he left.

CHAPTER FIVE

That evening, Josh shouldered his way through the crowd assembled in the town square for the annual Christmas caroling. He scanned the throngs of people as he walked. He didn't want to admit it, but he was looking for Avery.

His attraction to her had sucker punched him. He hadn't felt this drawn to a woman in a long time. When he went to the tree lot that first day, he hadn't planned to ask for a job. But Avery needed help, and he could donate his wages to the shelter. A win-win for everyone.

And if he were honest with himself, spending every day with Avery was an added bonus.

Maybe he was finally healing. Could he learn to trust again after Jennifer?

His tours in Iraq hadn't torn his heart apart the way she had. He'd been too blinded by Jennifer's beauty to see her for what she was—a woman more in love with his family's wealth and what that wealth could do for her than she was with him. And now, once again, he was attracted to a woman who preferred the glitz and glamour of life in the big city. He'd had it with the whole rat race thing. The military had freed him, had allowed him to see the truth. He'd never looked back.

He could be setting himself up for more heartache if he

pursued his interest in Avery. He should have told her the truth about himself. But a perverse part of him needed her to accept him for the man he was, not for his family's prestige. He needed a woman who could understand why he'd walked away from privilege and forged a new life. When his old Army buddy Neil asked him to help out at the shelter over the holidays, he'd jumped at it. Working with the men there fulfilled him the same way working with the poor kids in Iraq had. The guys at the shelter took him for what he was— a vet who cared about them.

His thoughts were interrupted when he spotted Avery with her sister and her brother-in-law. Josh's heartbeat quickened as he made his way toward them.

As if she'd felt his approach, Avery turned. Their gazes met, and once again he felt the connection, an awareness that went beyond the physical. Her brown eyes widened before she turned away.

He wanted to grab her and kiss her senseless. He knew someone had hurt her, and he wanted to make her forget that guy, to make her want him, Josh Huntsman, and no one else. He was a damn fool.

"Glad you made it, Josh," Addison said when he joined them.

"Wouldn't miss it for the world." He smiled at Addison and shook hands with her husband Barry.

"Hi, Avery," he said, looking down at her. He'd last seen her ninety minutes ago when they'd closed the lot. Despite the long hours there, she looked fresh and sweet. With her thick hair pulled back in a ponytail, she appeared less the New York sophisticate and more the small-town girl. He grinned, knowing she'd likely haul off and hit him for thinking that.

She slowly raised her gaze to his. "Hey, Josh."

With a knowing grin, Addison moved over to give him room to stand next to Avery. He slipped in between the sisters, moving closer to Avery. Warmth radiated from her, heating him. Damn, but he had it bad.

He was only Josh, Avery told herself. Plain Josh who volunteered at the homeless shelter and worked at the Christmas tree lot. *Yeah, right.* There was nothing plain about Josh Huntsman. Standing close to him, her insides heated up like the roasted chestnuts one of the vendors sold along the square. The fresh scent of Josh's soap enveloped her, mingling with the aromas of pine and chestnut that wafted over the crowd. A Christmas memory in the making, one she suspected she'd remember for a long time.

The person behind Avery jostled her, pushing her into Josh. He slid his arm around her waist, steadying her. "You okay?"

"I'm fine." But she wasn't. He was too close, too tempting, too everything, for her peace of mind. Her mouth went dry as yearning pulsed through her.

He kept his arm around her. She knew she should pull away, but she didn't want to. Besides, the crowd had gotten larger. Restless bodies pressed against each other. Anticipation whipped through the air like a zip line as they waited for the caroling to begin.

"Josh, what are you doing Christmas day?" Addison asked.

"I'm helping serve lunch at the shelter."

"If you're not doing anything afterwards, would you like to have dinner with our family? We always have room for one more. One of our cousins is hosting this year. I promise great food, especially desserts."

Avery stiffened. What was her sister up to?

"That would be great. I'd like that. Thanks," Josh said.

"And could you pick up Avery and drive her? Barry and I would do it, but I'm afraid I'll have to leave early and I'd hate for Avery to miss anything."

"I can drive myself," Avery said in a tight voice.

Addison shook her head and gave Avery a sly smile that would make the wicked queen in Snow White proud. "With all this snow and ice on the roads, I'd feel better if you weren't alone."

Avery felt Josh's stare and lifted her head.

His lips tilted in a grin. "I'd be happy to drive you, Avery. It's all set."

Avery glanced at Addison, but her sister wouldn't look at her. Wait until she got her scheming sister alone.

Christmas was in two days. Avery had thought once Christmas Eve was over, she wouldn't have to see Josh again. He disturbed her in ways that made her long for something unnamed, something a little wild. Now, she'd have to spend Christmas Day with him. Josh was not her type. But she couldn't ignore the joy that bubbled up at the thought of spending more time with him.

"Princes come in many disguises. You'll find yours where you least expect him."

Unbidden, the words of the old woman who'd sold her the snow globe played in Avery's mind. Don't be ridiculous, she told herself. The woman was merely someone trying to sell her wares, nothing more.

CHAPTER SIX

Much later, as the caroling ended and the crowd began to disperse, Avery couldn't deny that the uplifting music had sounded more beautiful and vibrant than she'd ever heard. Somehow, when she was with Josh, everything around her took on a new life and vitality, even her small hometown.

She shook her head impatiently. Josh had nothing to do with it. She hadn't been home for Christmas in years. That was why everything seemed new.

As she and Josh walked away from the square, others began to push against them and he took her hand. Holding onto him gave her a feeling of security and comfort she hadn't known in a long while.

Addison had left earlier, claiming fatigue, but she'd insisted Avery stay for the entire show. Josh had offered to drive her home. Now, plowing through the swarm of people with Josh, Avery wondered if her sister was truly ill. Addison's attempt at matchmaking was too obvious. She needed that talk with her sister.

When they got to Josh's truck, an ancient rattletrap of a vehicle that had seen better days, he helped her in, then went around to the driver's side and climbed in. He carefully pulled away from the curb and headed out of town.

"How do I get to your parents' place?" he asked.

"It's off this road about five miles. I'll tell you where to turn." Avery settled into her seat. The truck bumped along the country road and she grasped the armrest to steady herself.

Snow had begun falling, covering the trees and ground in shimmering white.

"It's pretty here," Josh said. "Especially with the snow."

"It is. One thing, the only thing, I miss about living in Manhattan is not having a white Christmas. Christmases here in the mountains are special."

He chuckled. "You've got big city written all over you. If I hadn't met you here I'd never have guessed you were raised in a small town."

"Thank you. That was a compliment, wasn't it?"

"Take it any way you want."

The amused tone in his voice told her it hadn't been a compliment. "Where were you raised?" she asked. A place like this, she'd be willing to bet.

"Boston."

"You grew up in Boston?" Avery winced at her shocked tone. Sure hadn't been expecting his answer.

He turned to her with a wry look. "Hard to believe, huh? A guy like me living in a big city."

"No, I didn't mean that."

His attention on the road again, he laughed and said, "Sure, you did. But that's okay."

"You don't have a Boston accent."

"I worked hard to get rid of it."

"Really? Why? I like their accent."

"Reminded me of too many things I want to forget."

What things? She wanted to ask, but suspected he wouldn't tell her. "You don't want to live in Boston now?"

He shrugged. "After Iraq, I wanted peace and quiet. I

like the small town atmosphere, like tonight. Everyone coming together to enjoy the music and the camaraderie."

"You can't hide forever," she blurted. Where had that come from?

His hands on the steering wheel tightened, but he didn't look at her. "What makes you think that's what I'm doing?"

"Are you?"

"Hell, no." His jaw clenched.

She folded her arms and looked ahead as the truck ate up the road. Josh Huntsman was definitely hiding something. Part of her wanted to find out what, and another part told her it was none of her business. She'd be gone after the holidays, anyway.

The turnoff to her parents' house was coming up, saving her from further thought. "Turn right on the next road."

Josh turned down the long driveway to her parents' rambling farmhouse.

He pulled in front and cut the engine, then turned to her. "Nice house. With the snow, it looks like a picture on a Christmas card."

"I suppose so. I never thought of the old house like that." She stared through the window at the gently falling snow. Josh was right. "It was fun when I was a kid, sledding and ice skating." Like candy canes, the memories wound through her, familiar and sweet.

With a sigh, she pushed aside thoughts of childhood and unhooked her seatbelt. Josh did the same, but neither of them moved. She should go into the house, but sitting in the close confines of the truck with Josh filled her with comforting warmth edged with anticipation.

He slid closer and reached out to brush strands of her hair away from her face. His gentle, sensuous touch made her insides melt like marshmallows in hot chocolate.

"What is it you want, Avery?" he asked in a thick voice.

"What do you mean?"

"I sense unhappiness in you, as if you're searching for something."

She pulled away from him. "You don't even know me."

"I feel like I've been looking for you all my life."

"What kind of line is that?"

He laughed softly. "Didn't mean for it to sound that way. I can't explain it, but I feel a connection to you."

She wouldn't admit it to herself or him, but she felt a bond with him too. And it scared her to death.

He moved back to his side of the seat and faced her. "Tell me about the man who hurt you."

"How do you…?"

"I can tell you're carrying hurt around. Let it go. He wasn't good enough for you."

She quirked an eyebrow. "Let me say it again. You barely know me."

This was crazy. Sexual tension swirled heavily in the air around them. And Josh was asking her about Mitch.

"He was an actor, a very good one. He acted as if he cared about me," she heard herself say. She could see Josh's eyes in the light from the front porch. The intensity in his gaze made her want to go on, to bare her soul to this man she hardly knew. "Mitch had gotten jobs doing commercials and some shows on and off Broadway. His career in New York was taking off. Every few months his agent would send him on a casting call to Los Angeles."

Leaning against the door, she clasped her hands on her lap and took a deep, cleansing breath. "During one of those trips, he met a casting agent who said she could open doors for him out there." Avery rolled her eyes. "She opened doors, all right, straight into her bedroom. He started to get small roles in movies and began to spend most of his time in Los Angeles. A few months ago, my boss sent me to L.A. on business. I didn't tell Mitch. I wanted to surprise him. I went to his hotel room and found him doing a little after-hours acting with the casting agent, in bed."

Josh sat straighter, his features tight. "That jerk! Avery, I'm sorry."

She waved a hand. "Don't be. Taught me a lesson. I'll be careful who I trust from now on."

"You deserve better than that."

His eyes darkened and he slid closer again. Her pulse quadrupled.

Avery raised her head. Josh kissed her tenderly. He curved a hand around her nape and pulled her closer. His tongue teased her lips apart. She welcomed his hot invasion.

Passion ignited in her, burning through her defenses. She pressed closer to him as their tongues mated and danced. A low moan escaped her. Josh left her mouth to trail a line of kisses down her throat. She threw back her head, giving herself to him. When he began unbuttoning her coat, she moaned again.

"Avery," he whispered. "So beautiful."

The raw need in his whispered words made anxiety and good sense rear their collective heads, freezing her. She pushed away, her breathing ragged. "I've gotta go. Thanks for driving me home. I've gotta go." She was babbling.

He put out a hand as if to touch her arm, then pulled back. "Stay. Let's talk."

"I really do need to go." She fumbled for the door handle, jumped out of the truck and ran across the porch to her front door. With shaking fingers, she unlocked the door and slid inside. Leaning against the closed door, she heard Josh drive away.

Her hormones were acting crazy. Josh wasn't right for her. But his kiss had awakened something inside her, a sizzling heat she'd never felt before. She touched her lips.

Prince Charming waking Snow White.

CHAPTER SEVEN

What was wrong with him? Josh pounded a fist on the steering wheel as he drove away. He didn't need any complications in his life. Jennifer had supplied all the drama and heartache he would ever need.

As he turned onto the main road, he thought of that kiss, the feel of Avery's lips, her responsiveness. She wanted him as much as he wanted her.

He had to put Avery and that kiss out of his mind. *Like that could happen.* Since the day he'd seen her lying on the sidewalk, passed out, spilled coffee next to her, he hadn't been able to stop thinking about her. She might have a sophisticated veneer, but he'd glimpsed the caring woman beneath, the woman who worried over her pregnant sister, the woman who put aside her own Christmas plans to help her family.

He had to figure out a way to make her accept him for the man he was, even if she thought he was a down-on-his luck vet.

◇◇◇

On Christmas Eve morning, when Josh showed up wearing his Santa outfit, Avery burst out laughing. Thankfully, the suit took away some of the tension that might have been between them since that kiss the night before.

The toe-curling kiss had awakened a long dormant part of her. She hadn't been able to forget it. But she had to. On New Year's Day she'd head back to Manhattan and her job. Her real life. Where she belonged. Not this tiny town stuck in a last-century time warp. She knew she was being unfair to her hometown. Lorewood had come back to life and into the twenty-first century when the manufacturing plant opened.

She waited by the trailer door for Josh, smiling as he headed toward her. Even wearing a Santa suit, he walked with a sexy grace that made her heart pound.

Pine needles crunched under his black boots as he walked. She had always hated the sound of the needles and the scent of pine, but she suspected after this Christmas, they'd always remind her of Josh. The sap from the trees was another matter. It had ruined more than one pair of gloves and some old jeans.

"Merry Christmas, Santa," she said when he reached her. "Shouldn't you be at the North Pole? Don't you have something to do tonight?"

His rich laugh rang through the frosty air. "I have staff for that. I think the kids will enjoy seeing Santa today. Maybe it'll help sell more trees."

"Can't argue with that. Come in and have some coffee before the Christmas Eve frenzy starts."

He followed her into the trailer and shut the door behind them. He filled the small space, especially in his Santa suit. Avery inhaled the strangely comforting scent of Josh's soap mingled with the pine fragrance all around them.

She poured two mugs of coffee, handing him one, black, the way he liked it. Damn, she even knew how he liked his coffee. She never would have thought selling Christmas trees could be so intimate.

She put distance between them by moving to the table but didn't sit.

"Do I make you nervous, Avery?"

"Of course not."

"Maybe it's Santa you don't like."

"Who doesn't like Santa?"

"Who indeed?" He set his mug on the counter and walked slowly toward her. When he reached her, he took her mug and set it on the table.

He gripped her shoulders and pulled her close. "Ever been kissed by Santa?"

Unable to speak, she shook her head.

He bent and kissed her lightly on the lips. His beard tickled, but she didn't pull away. Instead, she pressed closer and returned the kiss.

Despite his beard and the padding under his suit, his kiss set fire to her insides.

The door opened, bringing in a rush of cold air.

"I saw Avery kissing Santa Claus," Addison sang to the tune of "I Saw Mommy Kissing Santa Claus."

Avery and Josh jumped apart. Avery's face burned hotter than her coffee.

"Uh, we, uh," she stammered.

Addison waved a hand. "Don't mind me. I came in for some coffee. There are a few people looking at trees. I'll take care of them while you two carry on." Giggling, she headed for the coffee.

"I'll take care of the customers." Josh rushed out the door.

Avery sank onto a chair. "Oh. My. God. I can't believe I kissed him and I can't believe you saw us." She narrowed her eyes at her sister. "Why didn't you knock?"

Addison's eyes glinted with amusement. "And miss all the fun?"

"It was nothing. Just a kiss." *Sure.*

"Hey, you don't have to make excuses to me." Addison sat opposite Avery. "I know you and Josh have a thing for each other. He's a nice guy." She wriggled her eyebrows. "Smokin', too."

"Sure, he's hot, but he's not my type. He doesn't have a real job, for Pete's sake. He told me he lives outside town, but I suspect he lives at the shelter."

Addison plunked her mug down on the table and leaned closer. "Listen to you, Ms. Snob. The big city has changed you, and not in a good way. Snobbery isn't a fashion statement and it doesn't become you. Josh is decent and a hard worker. So what if he doesn't make a lot of money? Or have a 'real job,' as you put it?"

"Is it a bad thing to aim high, to want a man with the same work ethic and ambition I have? I don't mean to be snobbish, but you know how important it is to me that any guy I date is as career-minded as I am. I don't understand people who don't strive to be all they can be."

Addison laughed. "You sound like an Army recruiting poster." Her features sobered. "Maybe Josh is happy doing what he's doing. Since we were little, you always had to have everything, even people, perfect. Remember Donny from high school? He crushed bad on you, but you wouldn't give him a chance because he wanted to help run his dad's auto body shop after graduation. You thought he should go to college and be a doctor."

Putting a hand over her swollen stomach, Addison moved back in her chair. "Setting your sights so high hasn't gotten you much, has it? Mitch wasn't the dream guy you thought. And other than your blog, you're not doing any writing."

Avery bristled. "I have a terrific life, an exciting life. I work for one of the best magazines in the country, doing what I love."

Addison's brown eyes softened. "Sorry I was so harsh. Your words say you're happy, but your eyes say something different. You're overworked and you're not doing what you really want." She reached out to tug on Avery's hand. "Listen to your big sister. Maybe you need to make some changes in your life. Grab that brass ring and let it rip."

"You're giving me advice?" Avery's voice was sharper than she'd intended. "You've never wanted anything more than to stay here and live the same lives as our parents."

Hurt flashed across Addison's face. "You can't put down others because they don't share your idea of success. You think Barry isn't good enough for me, that I should have escaped this town after school. But I love this place and I love my husband. He's a good man. So what if he works at the plant? He likes it there, he loves me, he provides well for me. And he'll be a great father."

Regret and contrition gathered in Avery's chest, tightening in a knot. She almost envied her sister's contentment. From the time she was twelve, Avery had dreamt of being a writer, of traveling the world, of having a thrilling lifestyle. She couldn't understand why others didn't have big dreams, why her sister and parents were happy staying in one place, doing the same things over and over, with the occasional holiday thrown in to relieve the boredom. Maybe Addison was right and Avery needed to accept others' differences.

Avery squeezed her sister's hand. "I'm sorry. I really am. I shouldn't have said that. I know you're happy. And Barry loves you very much. You're a lucky woman."

"You've always been different from the rest of the family," Addison said. "I hope someday you get what you're looking for. That you find what it is you truly need."

The sisters sat quietly for a few minutes. Then Addison sighed and slid her hand from Avery's. "This is like old times. I miss Mom and Dad, but I'm happy they're having a good time." She smiled. "And I'm glad you and I are spending the holidays together. It used to hurt Mom and Dad when you didn't come home for Christmas."

As if on cue, Bing Crosby crooning "I'll be Home for Christmas" played on the radio.

The sisters looked at each other and laughed.

"Old Bing knew what he was talking about," Avery said. "I didn't realize I'd hurt our parents. Mitch always wanted to stay in the city, and he had such a wide circle of friends from the theater that we went to a round of parties starting in early December through New Year's Day."

Addison studied Avery with narrowed eyes. "Did you love Mitch? The one time I met him, I thought he was a conceited ass and couldn't figure out what you saw in him." She rolled her eyes. "Other than his looks, that is."

Avery laughed. "Conceited ass? I suspect you're not the first one to think that. I thought I loved him, but now I'm wondering if I was in love with the whole glamorous life we led."

"And you had no idea he had a girlfriend in California?"

"Of course not." Anger sparked anew through Avery at the memory of Mitch's cheating. "I understood why it was important to his career that he take frequent trips to L.A. If I hadn't gone to California myself, I might still be blissfully unaware of his deception."

"I feel so bad that happened to you. Maybe you've been looking in the wrong places. You might find the right guy for you where you don't expect him."

A chill ran over Avery. The orange-haired woman had said almost the same thing.

CHAPTER EIGHT

"Merry Christmas!" Avery waved at the young couple as they drove away from the lot with their Christmas tree tied to the roof of their car.

She must have said the holiday greeting thirty times today. She was getting sick of it, just as she was sick of the scent of pine. Now, she remembered why she'd hated helping out at the lot once she'd become a teen. That, plus the mean-spirited teasing from the cool girls at school who made fun of her for selling trees.

Finally, time came to close for the season. Addison had left an hour ago. The surge of customers had trickled to a few, and Avery and Josh could handle them. They'd sold most of the trees. A recycling group would take away the unsold ones after Christmas. With a heavy sigh, Avery started toward the trailer. The crunch of pine needles behind her made her turn.

Josh walked up to her, pulling off his Santa hat, wig and beard. He shook his head and raked his fingers through his hair.

"You've got hat hair," Avery said with a laugh.

"That I do."

As they faced each other, his green eyes gleamed with awareness, matching an answering awareness in her. She shifted from one foot to another.

Clearing his throat, he said, "I'll help you close up."

"You don't have to. I'm used to it."

He took her elbow and turned her in the direction of the trailer. "I'll help."

When they'd locked up and stood outside again, Josh said, "Have dinner with me? That home-style restaurant outside of town has good food. It's been a rough day, and it's Christmas Eve. Let's relax a little."

She frowned. "I like that place, but Addison invited me to her house for dinner."

"Call her. I'm sure she'll understand."

Avery knew she should say no. It wasn't fair to let Josh think she was interested in him. But when he looked at her with those green eyes, and smiled with that dimple, her resolve dissipated into the crisp air.

"Okay," she said. "I'd like that."

Avery followed Josh's truck in her car to the festive-looking restaurant on the outskirts of town. Christmas lights were strung along the porch of the large wooden structure. The parking lot wasn't full and they found spots near the front. He put his hand on the small of her back as they entered the restaurant. It wasn't crowded, yet laughter and loud talk greeted them. Everyone appeared to be in a Christmas mood. People she didn't know waved to them as they stepped inside.

Things were sure different from the trendy bars and restaurants she and Mitch used to frequent in Manhattan. Rather than the jeans and sweaters favored by the patrons here, the places she was used to were filled with men and women dressed in the latest fashion, most of them trying to impress the others. That had been her life for the past several years. And she missed it.

Or did she? Truth be told, something about this small homey restaurant with its joyous atmosphere, as sweet and familiar as spiced hot cider, touched a chord deep within her. Even the gaudy Christmas decorations and the brightly lit artificial tree in one corner lent a happy air. No one appeared to be trying to impress anyone, only have a good time with friends and neighbors.

They found a table and placed their orders—meatloaf, mashed potatoes, vegetables, and red wine. Hometown comfort food. Back in Manhattan, she would never have eaten such a fattening meal, but it felt right here.

Avery really relaxed for the first time since she'd come home. She didn't need to make an impression on anyone or worry what they thought of her. And Josh seemed happy to be with her. Maybe small-town life wasn't so bad after all.

Dinner over, they said goodbye to some of the other patrons. As they walked to the parking lot, Josh put his hand on the small of her back again. His touch scorched her through her heavy jacket. Inhaling the pine-scented air, she looked up into a cloudless black sky. The stars strewn across it looked like diamonds thrown onto velvet. She could almost see Santa in his sleigh pulled by reindeer. She let out a contented sigh.

When they reached her car and his truck, Josh cupped her shoulders and turned her to face him. His eyes were dark and mysterious in the muted overhead lights. "Thanks for coming with me. I had a good time."

"Me too. Thanks for dinner."

"Avery," he whispered and lowered his head.

Unable to stop herself, she raised her face.

Their lips met. She melted against him, boneless. Dropping her purse, she pressed closer, winding her arms around his neck.

He deepened the kiss and his tongue demanded entry. She opened to him, wanting and needing more, needing him.

She hardly recognized her low moans of pleasure as they stood, wrapped in each other's arms, their tongues exploring.

After several passion-filled minutes, they pulled apart.

The look of wonder on his face mirrored her own. She didn't want the night to end, didn't want to leave him. But she had to. Josh had danger written all over him—danger to her peace of mind, to her well-ordered life, the life she'd thought she'd figured out. Now she wasn't so sure.

"I—I have to go," she stammered. She picked up her purse, not caring that it was wet from the icy ground. Unlocking her car, she slid in. As she drove away, she looked through her rearview mirror to see him watching her.

On the short ride home, her mind reeled. She lusted after a guy with no permanent job, a guy who might drift from town to town for all she knew. Yet, she sensed there was much more to Josh, so much more, that lay just below the surface.

"No!" she shouted in the empty car. "No more." No more kissing him, as hot as he was and as much as she wanted him.

With Josh still on her mind, she pulled into her driveway, turned off the car, and entered the house. The light from the floor lamp reflected on her small snow globe on the corner table. Snow fell in the globe, covering the tree and Santa. She hadn't touched the globe. She must be hallucinating, but she'd had only one glass of wine. Avery blinked her eyes and looked again. No snow fell inside the glass ball. It had been her imagination.

CHAPTER NINE

Nervous as a teen going on her first date, Avery paced the living room. Josh would be here soon to drive her to her cousin's house for Christmas dinner. She could have insisted on driving herself, but she'd gone along with her sister's clumsy attempt at matchmaking. Because, even though she shouldn't, she wanted to spend more time with Josh.

The doorbell rang and her heart stuttered. Smoothing her hands down the sides of her slacks, she marched to the door and opened it.

Josh gave her one of his dimpled smiles that made the air leave her lungs. She knew she fought a losing battle against her own desires. Stepping aside to let him in, she willed herself to remain in control.

"You look good," he said as he scanned her.

"Thanks." She'd dressed in black slacks that had cost two weeks' salary, a pale yellow cashmere sweater, and sky-high black stiletto boots.

She let her gaze wander his tall, muscular form. Dressed in a well-tailored gray suit, white shirt unbuttoned at the neck to reveal a scattering of fine golden hairs, and polished black shoes, he made her pulse do a little jig.

"You look great, too," she said, unable to keep the surprise out of her voice. "Stylish."

"Are you saying I clean up good?"

His words broke the tension and she laughed. "You clean up real good."

Still laughing, she grabbed her coat and purse from the chair. Today might not be so bad after all. She'd enjoy Josh's company, but nothing more. She could control her libido around him. Of course she could.

As they turned to leave, Josh looked over at the snow globe. "Pretty globe. Do your parents collect them?"

"It's mine." She hustled toward the door. "We'd better get going." She glanced back as she slipped out. Snow fell lightly inside the globe. Convinced she was imagining things again, she slammed the door shut.

A half hour later, they arrived at her cousin Stevie's house. Soon, they were enveloped in bear hugs by her seven cousins and their wives and kids. Avery introduced Josh to the others.

"I don't know if I can remember all the names," Josh said.

"Don't worry about it," Stevie's wife said. "Come have some appetizers. Dinner will be ready in an hour."

A short time later, drinking a beer and sitting on the large, comfortable sectional in the family room, Josh felt as if he'd stumbled into a twisted fairytale. Avery's seven cousins were shorter than average, and they all worked in the new manufacturing plant. If they worked in a mine, things would certainly have taken a turn for the bizarre.

Avery's family was friendly and boisterous and made him feel welcome. Seeing the happiness on the faces of the children, a sudden surge of regret pulsed through him. He'd never felt this kind of joy with his wealthy, influential family. His parents used holidays to throw lavish parties meant to impress. He'd broken free of their constraints and expectations by doing the only thing he could—quitting his well-paying job and joining the military where he finally had the opportunity to do some good.

Across the room, Avery sat on the floor, engrossed in a boisterous board game with some of the older kids. When she scored a point, she high-fived the kids and laughed. Her joyful laughter took Josh from his melancholy mood. He smiled. Unbidden, a picture of Avery holding their child, her face blissful, floated into his mind. He didn't know where that had come from, but rather than scaring the crap out of him, the image filled him with pleasure, chasing away the hurt that was his constant companion. She might think she belonged in the big city, but the delight she took in her family told Josh she was a small-town girl at heart. His job was to convince her of that.

Hours later, filled with great food, Avery and Josh said their goodbyes. Josh had to admit his Christmas with the seven cousins was one of his best ever.

CHAPTER TEN

When they got to Avery's parents' house, Josh insisted on seeing her inside. Once in, Avery closed the door and leaned against it, facing him. "Thanks for driving me."

His smile made her pulse jump, and she nervously began to unbutton her coat.

"I know your sister blindsided you by asking me to drive you," he said, "but I'm glad she did. I had a great time with your family."

She returned his smile and moved away from the door, throwing her coat over a chair. "My cousins are pretty cool. I always enjoy being with them. Would you like something to eat or drink?"

Josh patted his stomach. "I've eaten too much." He stepped closer. "But I don't want to say goodnight yet. Maybe a glass of water?"

Avery swallowed, sure he could hear the rapid beating of her heart in the quiet room. "I'll make some herbal tea. How about that?"

"Sounds good."

Settled comfortably on the overstuffed sofa fifteen minutes later, Avery and Josh sipped their tea. The lights from the large Christmas tree by the living room window reflected on the white walls. The melancholy sounds of "Silent Night" filled the room from the CD of Christmas

51

songs she'd put on. Avery hadn't felt this contented in a very long time, since she was a child in this same house.

"This is nice," Josh said, turning to her and setting his mug on the coffee table. "It must have been fun growing up on a farm."

"As a kid, farm life *was* fun. But when I got older, it bored me and I wanted to live in the city. We always want what we don't have."

He moved closer and slid his arm over the back of the sofa. "What do you want now, Avery, that you don't have?"

Sighing, she stared at the glittering tree and fought a war with herself. A year ago she would have said she had everything thing she'd ever wanted. But now, not so much. She'd kept up the façade for her family, but she suspected Josh would see through her lies.

Turning, she met his gaze. "I thought I had the life I wanted. Living in New York, the job at a major magazine." She shot him wry smile. "The actor boyfriend who made other women green with envy."

"I don't know how to compete with an actor boyfriend."

Unsure how to respond, she gulped a huge sip of tea. The liquid burned its way down her throat and she coughed.

"You okay?"

She nodded. "You're competing for me?" she managed.

He reached out and touched strands of her hair that lay over her shoulder, twisting them around his finger. "You haven't figured out I want you?"

"No. I don't know." Avery slid away from him and the temptation he offered.

He settled back in the sofa. "What is it you really want?"

"I'm not sure. My job consumes me, leaving little time for myself. At first, I liked it, but not as much now. My boss treats me like her personal servant. I'm earning writing creds with my blog so that helps ease the fact that I don't have my own column."

"You're smart," he said. "And obviously talented to get a job with a big magazine. I know it's hard to give that up, but you should find a magazine that appreciates you."

"I'm afraid." The words slipped out, but she felt a huge relief. She'd gone and said it. She was scared.

He leaned toward her and skimmed his knuckles over her cheekbone. "You'd be surprised how freeing it is to overcome your fears."

Avery squirmed and slid back, uncomfortable under his knowing gaze and his touch. "What about you, Josh? Are you free, volunteering at a shelter? Is that all you want?"

"I'm good." Steel sharpened his voice.

"You're a smart guy and a hard worker. Don't you want to do more with your life?"

"What if I'm happy with my life as it is?"

"Are you?"

He didn't answer, but glanced away from her.

"I don't get why you wouldn't want more," she finally said.

His eyes sparked green fire as his gaze met hers. "There are a lot of things I want." His voice had thickened.

At the hungry look in his eyes, she set her mug onto the table with a shaking hand. He grasped her shoulders and pulled her closer. His lips met hers in an urgent kiss that electrified every cell of her body.

Thoughts jumbled through her mind. He was kissing her to avoid talking about himself. But she didn't care. His kisses unleashed a part of her she hadn't known she possessed—a wild, passionate side. Being with Josh was so wrong, yet felt so right. Desire for him overwhelmed her and pushed aside her doubts. She wound her arms around his neck and kissed him back.

They sank down together on the sofa. His tongue filled her mouth. Passion, hot and demanding, seared her, a raging inferno she'd never before experienced.

His lips seduced, teasing her into submission. Her whole body inflamed, she pressed closer to his taut frame, needing to possess all of him. She felt hot, restless, her breasts tight, her nipples pushing against her bra. Whimpers of need came from deep inside her throat as her world spiraled out of control. Like Snow White's Prince, Josh had awakened her sexually.

He trailed scorching kisses down her throat. When he slipped a hand beneath her sweater to cup one of her breasts, she melted into him. Pulling her sweater up, he slid down her body to suckle her nipple under the lacy bra. Avery moaned and arched her hips, demanding more. He pushed her bra up and turned his attention to her other breast. Her flesh tingled from his sensual attention.

He lifted his head and looked at her with dark eyes, bedroom eyes. "I want you, Avery."

Her thoughts a dizzying whirl, she looked away. She wanted him more than she'd ever wanted another man. He was too warm, too sexy, too appealing. And too decent and kind. Not a man she wanted to hurt, and she would have to leave him. As if an outside force drew her, her attention went to the snow globe. Snow began falling inside the small orb.

Like ice thrown at her face, Avery pushed away from Josh and he released her. She sat up and hastily pulled her bra and sweater down. "I can't do this."

He moved back. "I thought...I guess I got my signals

wrong."

"No, Josh. I wanted it too, but it's not right. We're not right. I want to be friends, only friends."

His features tightened. "I understand. You want a big-city, successful guy and all that comes with him."

She placed a hand on his arm. His muscles tensed under his jacket. "Josh."

His eyes softened and he put his hand over hers. "I'm not ready to give up on you. I think you like it here more than you want to admit. You could move back to Lorewood, work on your blog. The community college is looking for a creative writing instructor." His gaze locked with hers. "I'm falling for you, Avery. Stay here. Let's see where this goes."

The tenderness shining from his eyes and his softly spoken words tempted her. She swayed toward him, then stopped. "I can't, Josh. I have a job and a life in Manhattan. Lorewood isn't the life I want. I'm sorry."

"Then I know where I stand." He rose slowly and strode to the door. With his hand on the doorknob, he looked back at her. "Goodbye, Avery."

After he left, she sat on the sofa and blinked back tears. She'd been right to send him away. Her feelings for him frightened the dickens out of her. She couldn't move back to Lorewood, couldn't give up all she'd worked for. But she'd never see Josh again.

She glanced over at the small snow globe, bright and shiny, as if mocking her. Quick strides brought her to the table. She snatched up the globe. Anger and frustration propelled her to throw it across the room. It hit the wall and fell to the carpeted floor, unbroken.

CHAPTER ELEVEN

Avery had been back in Manhattan a week. She'd spent a quiet New Year's Eve with Addison and Barry. Her parents had arrived home early New Year's Day. Time enough to hear all about their cruise. Not enough time for probing questions from them, to Avery's relief. She'd been glad to get out of that small town, to escape again.

But she couldn't escape her thoughts. They were filled with images of Josh, with the feel of him, his laugh, his dimpled smile. She wondered what he was doing. Did he miss her? Was he still at the shelter?

Jamming her hands in her pockets, she walked down Fifth Avenue, too used to the city to bother looking into the store windows. Funny how she'd begun thinking of Lorewood as home again. Maybe Josh had something to do with that.

The city was as busy and loud as always. Snow lay in dirty piles by the curbs. No one on the street made eye contact with her. Back home, people had nodded to her as she'd walked down Main Street. Even her job felt empty. Her boss was more demanding than ever, working Avery long hours. Like tonight. It was close to eight, and Avery had just left work. Increasingly, her dream job was becoming a nightmare.

She'd met Bella and Carlyn for dinner a few nights ago

and told them about Josh. Carlyn, always the romantic, thought Avery should go back to Vermont to see him again. Bella, the practical one, scoffed at any long-term romance between Avery and Josh. She said because Avery was out of her comfort zone, Josh appealed to her. Once Avery got back into her fast-paced Manhattan lifestyle, Josh would be only a pleasant memory.

Pleasant memory? Josh? Avery would never forget him.

A while later, she entered her apartment, locked the door, and strolled to the kitchen to set the takeout from the Chinese restaurant and her purse onto the counter. As she shrugged off her coat and headed to the living room, her gaze fell on the snow globe on her side table. Next to it was the Snow White ornament.

She froze. Like the sun emerging from the clouds, it was all clear now. Throwing her coat over a chair, she walked to the table and picked up the globe, shaking it until the snow began to fall. Prince Charming hadn't only awakened Snow White sexually. He'd also awakened her to life, to being true to herself, to following her dream and her heart, to stop hiding.

Much like the Prince, Josh had freed Avery's sexuality. Even now, she warmed all over thinking about his kisses, his heat, his passion. He starred in her fantasies and erotic dreams. But he'd done more. He'd forced her to question herself, to step out of her comfort zone, to stop hiding behind her fears.

Clutching the small globe with one hand and the Snow White ornament with the other, Avery sank onto the sofa. Damn it all! She'd let others cause her to fall asleep, to abandon her dreams. She'd been seduced by Mitch's looks and glamorous lifestyle. She'd let her boss, the witch in designer clothes, rule her. And she'd become complacent, too accustomed to her familiar life to assert herself. She'd come so close to realizing her dream, yet had backed off. It was time she woke up and took charge of her life and her future.

The next morning, when Avery stepped off the elevator into the magazine's reception center, resolve and a new sense of freedom quickened her stride.

Tiffany smiled at Avery. "Morning, Avery."

"Morning, Tiff. Is she in?" Avery nodded toward Edie's closed door.

Tiffany winced. "She is, and she's already asking for you."

What new demands did Edie have today? It didn't matter. Avery had a few of her own.

Edie looked up from her computer when Avery entered. "Good. You're here. I just emailed you Stacey's column. Her interview with that bimbo Kasey Kapeheart is a mess. Fix it."

"And I'll get a byline, of course."

"Wrong. You're not a columnist."

Taking a deep breath to dispel her rising anxiety, Avery plunged in. "I can't do this, Edie. Any of this. I quit." She clutched her purse and met Edie's steady gaze. "I'll give two weeks' notice, though, to give you time to find my replacement."

Edie stood slowly, her face a stony mask. "You'll leave now."

Thirty minutes later, pumped up on adrenaline shot with a heady dose of fear, Avery waited by the elevator, the large box containing her personal effects in her arms. Once the adrenaline left, fear would take over, but she wouldn't think about that now.

When the elevator doors opened, her co-worker Molly stepped out.

Sadness flitted across Molly's face. "I heard what happened, Avery. I'm so sorry. The witch doesn't appreciate talent when it's staring her in the face. We'll all miss you."

Avery let the elevator go without her and smiled at Molly. "Thanks, but I'll be fine, probably better than I've been in a long time."

Stepping closer to Molly, she said, "I haven't had a chance to talk to you since I got back, but I meant to tell you how much my friends and I enjoyed the craft show on Long Island before Christmas."

"I appreciated your coming."

"I especially like the snow globe I bought from the strange orange-haired lady."

Molly frowned. "She *was* eccentric. Came in the morning of the fair and insisted she'd reserved a spot weeks before, but we didn't have any record of her." Molly shrugged. "We let her stay, but she didn't stay long. Sold three globes according to the slip she filled out, then left."

Another elevator opened. Avery said goodbye to Molly and slipped in, thoughts tumbling in her mind. The orange-haired lady had sold snow globes to Avery and her two friends, then closed up? Strange, indeed.

Almost from the day she bought the snow globe, Avery's life had taken on twists she couldn't have imagined. Would the same thing happen to Bella and Carlyn?

◇◇◇

The next ten days were a whirl of activity. To Avery's utter amazement, Edie had called her two days after she quit and begged her to come back. Stacey had quit, but Edie confided she'd been ready to fire the other woman. They needed someone to fill Stacey's job, and Avery had the writing ability to do it. Edie also revealed she'd held Avery back because she hadn't wanted to lose the best assistant she'd ever had. She promised Avery not only Stacey's column but the job as features editor. And she offered Avery a huge raise.

With Edie making her a dream offer she couldn't refuse, Avery gladly accepted. Using her newfound confidence, she told Edie she wanted to work from home. Surprisingly, Edie had agreed. Edie also took Avery's suggestion that she use Molly as her temporary assistant.

Still trying to grasp all that had happened, Avery sat at her desk in her Manhattan apartment, working on her latest article. She couldn't believe she'd asserted herself to Edie. Being back in Lorewood with Addison, and especially Josh, had given her a new perspective on life. Made her realize where a person lived wasn't as important as finding a life that satisfied.

She'd been harsh in her judgments. What was in a man's heart was more important than what he did for a living.

Josh. He was always on her mind. It seemed she missed him more every day. He'd wanted her to stay in Lorewood, to see where their relationship took them.

Sighing, she stood up and strode to the window, looking out at the clogged traffic and the pedestrians hurrying along the sidewalks. Everyone busy, involved with their own lives. But despite its tarnish, she still loved the city and couldn't imagine living anywhere else. Yet, there was Josh.

Avery picked up the snow globe. She shook it, then rubbed the glass orb as the tiny flakes fell over the tree and

Santa. "What should I do about Josh?" she asked the globe, as if it were a genie, or a fairy godmother, ready to grant her wishes. "I miss him. I've got to see him, to know if we have a chance together." The Santa in the globe remained silent. With a wry laugh at her own silliness, she set the globe down and watched the last of the sparkling flakes drop.

Calmness stole over her. She knew what she had to do. When she emailed her latest column to Edie today, she'd pack a bag and head up to Lorewood for the weekend. She couldn't give up on Josh. If the sparks still flared between them, they'd figure out a way to make things work.

Her cell phone rang and she grabbed it from the desk. When she saw Josh's number on the ID, her insides trembled. "Josh," she said when she'd connected the call. "I've been thinking about you." She glanced at the snow globe and a chill ran over her.

"I've been thinking a lot about you, too," he said, his voice husky. "I'm in your lobby. May I come up?"

"You're here?" She pressed a palm to her stomach. Wish something and it happens. She looked at the snow globe again while more chills made the fine hairs on her nape stand at attention.

Snapping back to reality, she said, "Of course. I'll let you in." She went to the callbox on the wall and pushed the button that would open the outside door.

Too nervous to sit, she paced until she heard the knock on her door. She smoothed her hands down the sides of her jeans and opened the door to Josh.

His hair was shorter, a tad longer than military style, and he was dressed in dark jeans and a heavy wool jacket. But it was his green eyes, soft and shining with tenderness, that held her.

61

"Come in." Her voice sounded shaky. She stood aside to let him enter.

When he'd shed his coat, they stood unmoving and stared at each other for long minutes. With his pale blue sweater that looked like cashmere, and his designer jeans, he could fit in with the sophisticated New Yorkers she knew. She swallowed, fighting her nervousness, and blurted the first thing that came to mind. "How about some coffee?"

"Sounds great."

As she made the coffee, Josh stood at the granite-topped center island watching her. When she glanced at him, his eyes flashed with a sure determination. *What?* She almost dropped the carafe.

When Avery handed Josh his mug of coffee, their fingers touched and flames seemed to shoot up her arm. Yup. Sparks were still there. Hope bubbled up in her.

He lifted his mug in a salute. "To Avery, the woman who turned my life upside down."

Avery froze with her mug halfway to her mouth. "What do you mean?"

He drew an audible breath. "I have a story to tell you."

"Let's go into the living room." Her stomach in knots, she gripped her mug as she led him into the other room.

CHAPTER TWELVE

When they'd settled on the sofa, their coffee mugs on the low table in front of them, Josh took one of her hands in his. His touch warmed her like the hottest coffee.

Stroking her hand, he began. "You know I grew up in Boston. What you don't know is my family is influential, wealthy, and politically connected. It was ground into me from childhood that I'd be a lawyer and work in my father's firm. And I did that. Even managed to get myself engaged along the way."

Avery widened her eyes. "You're engaged?"

He squeezed her hand. "Not anymore."

Relief swirled through her. "You're a lawyer?"

He chuckled. "Shocking, huh? And here you thought I was a nearly homeless vet with no prospects."

"Was I that unfeeling, Josh? Did I really come off as elitist?" But she knew the answer. She'd been quick to judge Josh by what she thought he did, quick to put a label on him as a slacker, a man with no ambition. Humbled, she lowered her head.

Releasing her hand, he touched her chin with his fingers until their eyes met. "I never thought of you as a snob. You're a big-city woman with a small-town heart."

"I like that. 'Big-city woman with a small-town heart.' Tell me the rest of your story."

He settled onto the sofa. "Jennifer, my fiancée, had grown up solidly middle class, but she wanted more. She loved my family's wealth and influence. And she loved that I'd someday inherit a large, moneyed law firm. But I was unhappy. I wanted to do something worthwhile. Patent law didn't do it for me. I finally got to the point where I had to make a change."

"I can relate." Avery sipped her coffee and watched the play of emotions on his chiseled features—relief, sincerity, and a little bit of doubt.

He drank some coffee and set the mug down again. "I quit my job and joined the Army. My parents, especially my father, were livid. I thought Jennifer loved me enough to want me to be happy, that she'd support me in whatever I did. But she was furious. Broke our engagement immediately. She didn't want to marry someone she felt had taken a job beneath him. It turned out she didn't love me, only the life I could give her. A year later she was engaged to another lawyer, one richer and more influential than I was."

Avery touched his arm. "Josh, I'm sorry."

"Don't be. It all worked out. The Army and my tours in Iraq changed me, for the better. I was finally free to be my own man. I was doing something worthwhile at last. I helped my country and I helped a lot of people over there. I liked the feeling. When I got stateside, I bought a house near Lorewood. An Army buddy was raised there and always talked about the quiet. I needed quiet after Iraq."

Josh's gaze locked with hers. "You accused me once of hiding. And you were right. I was hiding from the world and from myself. I didn't know what I wanted to do. I was conflicted. After knowing you, I realized I had to come out

of hiding and do something meaningful with my life."
She smiled. "Funny how that works."
"What?"
"I have something to tell you too, but later. You told me
once you had a place outside Lorewood, and I'm ashamed to
admit this, but I suspected you lived at the shelter. I didn't
want to embarrass you by asking. I'm sorry, Josh."
He held up a hand. "You have nothing to apologize for.
I wasn't real forthcoming with information. I was an officer
in the military and I have a trust fund from my grandmother."
He gave her a tender smile. "Not the down-on-his-luck vet
you thought I was."
Her insides trembling, not able to drink any more coffee,
she put aside her mug. "Why didn't you tell me who you
really were, Josh?" Hurt washed over her. "You didn't trust
me with the truth?"
He took her hand again and held it tightly as if afraid
she'd bolt away. "That wasn't it. I liked you from the first,
when I saw you lying on the sidewalk. I wanted to kiss you
to wake you up." He gave a self-deprecating laugh. "But I'm
no Prince Charming."
"The Prince would have told me he was a prince. He
would have been honest."
"I'm a mere mortal and I make mistakes. I should have
told you, but an obstinate part of me wanted you to know the
real man behind the Santa suit, the man who worked at a
homeless shelter and a Christmas tree lot. I wanted you to
care for me, not the rich guy from Boston, not Santa, not
Prince Charming, but me, Josh Huntsman, combat vet."
He grasped her upper arms and pulled her closer. Their
faces were a whisper apart. "Don't you see, Avery? You
were special to me from the beginning, but after Jennifer, I

wanted a woman who could love me. Plus, I was still working through who I was, what I really wanted. I couldn't explain all that then. I didn't understand it myself. Can you forgive me?"

She touched his face. "I understand. It hurts a little that you weren't totally honest with me, but we'd just met. I've missed you, Josh. I was planning to come to Lorewood this weekend and talk to you."

"Talk about what?"

Gathering her thoughts, she slid away to the corner of the sofa. "Talk about us, if we have a future together."

"Even thinking I was out of work, you were willing to take a chance on me?"

She nodded and blinked away tears.

"What do *you* think about our future?" The intensity in his eyes held her.

"I think we should see where this is taking us."

Josh slid closer and framed her face between his hands. He kissed her softly. "There's more," he said when he'd pulled away.

"Really?"

He nodded. "When you made me realize I was hiding from the world, I decided to put my fancy education to use. I joined a law firm near Lorewood, one that specializes in helping disadvantaged vets. Right now, I'm doing paralegal work until I pass the Vermont bar."

Avery grabbed one of his hands and held it tightly. "Josh, that's great. I'm happy for you, and for the people you'll represent."

His features sobered. "I know you love Manhattan and your work is here, but I need to stay in Lorewood. I can't ask you to move up there, but I can't let you go either."

Avery smiled. "I have news too. Because of you, I found the courage to go after what I really wanted. I quit my job."

He jerked his head back. "You quit? You're out of work?"

She laughed. "I was out of work for less than forty-eight hours. Two days after I quit, my boss called and offered me my own column plus the position of features editor. You helped me, Josh. I'd stopped being happy a long time ago, but didn't realize it until I spent time with you. You taught me that where you live isn't as important as doing something that makes you happy."

Releasing his hand, she leaned closer and skimmed fingers over his full lips. "And I know what's in a man's heart means more than what job he has."

"I'm happy you've gotten everything you wanted," he said. "But where does that leave us?"

"I don't have everything, not yet."

His eyes darkened. "What else do you want?"

"I want a future with you."

"Avery." He pulled her to him and kissed her, a kiss filled with tenderness.

When they pulled apart, he looked at her with love shining from his eyes. Her pulse soared.

"We have a little problem, though," he said. "You live here. I live in Vermont."

"It's not as much of a problem as you think." Smiling she ran her hand over his arm, needing to touch him. "I work from home now, but I have to go into the office once a week. I can work from anywhere."

He smiled. "We'll figure it out. All I care about is that we're together."

"I have something to show you." She stood, strode to

the snow globe, and grabbed it off the table. She walked back to Josh and held the globe out to him. "I got this from a very wise woman. She told me, 'Princes come in many disguises. You'll find yours where you least expect him.' She was right. I found you." Avery set the snow globe on the coffee table and sat on the sofa close to Josh. The snow fell in the glass orb, cloaking the miniature tree and the figure of Santa in white.

"Kiss me again," she said, turning to Josh.

With a small laugh, he took her into his arms. His kiss promised passionate nights and loving days. And a life filled with romance.

EPILOGUE

The following Christmas Eve

"Merry Christmas, Mrs. Huntsman." Josh tapped his champagne flute against Avery's.

"Merry Christmas, Mr. Huntsman."

Married a few hours, they sat at their reception at Lorewood's best hotel. The party was in full swing. The DJ played music that had most of the guests dancing. Across the room, Bella and Carlyn, her bridesmaids, laughed and talked with Avery's and Josh's parents. Avery's mother cradled Addison and Barry's ten-month-old, Maggie. Josh's parents may have had their differences with their son, but they'd been gracious and warm to Avery and her family. They were trying to heal the rift that had torn their family apart.

The most wonderful day of Avery's life was almost over. She looked at her husband, so handsome in his tux. Their life together was just starting. And it promised to be a life filled with love and happiness. And dreams come true.

Avery's column at the magazine was gaining popularity, and her blog had gone viral. She and Josh divided their time between their new house in Lorewood and her apartment in Manhattan. She knew when they started a family, there would be other decisions to make, but she and Josh would handle whatever life threw at them.

She sighed and lifted her face to her husband's to give him a tender kiss. "I love you, Josh."

"I love you, Avery. More than I can say."

He slid his arm around her shoulders and drew her close.

Snuggled against her husband, Avery looked out over the crowd and bolted upright. Across the room, an elderly woman with orange hair in a shade not found in nature stood by the door. She gave Avery a knowing grin and a thumbs-up.

Smiling, Avery picked up her champagne flute and saluted the other woman. Slipping through the door, the woman was gone.

"Who was that?" Josh asked.

"A very wise woman." Avery pressed closer to her husband. She'd found her Prince. Snow White would always have her happy ending.

***

Her Frog Prince Holiday

By

Cara Marsi

The gift of a magical snow globe from a mysterious stranger paints the scene for romance between a Manhattan art gallery manager and a sexy man who isn't what he seems.

At a Halloween party, uptight gallery manager Bella Cassani lets her friends goad her into kissing a handsome stranger. Yes, a girl has to kiss a lot of frogs to find her prince, but Bella prefers "frogs." They're safer than the sexy-but-unfaithful kind. When fate brings the knock-her-hat-off-with-a-kiss guy back into her life, things get complicated.

Chad Prince likes his life just as it is. Working in art galleries, he travels the world with no complicated relationships or family entanglements. There's more to life than the money and success that were so important to his father, and no woman will betray him again like the last one did. Falling for sexy Bella Cassani is the last thing he wants.

Bella thinks Chad is just too good looking. Handsome men remind her of her ne'er-do- well father and a childhood that often left her hungry and insecure. But Chad's kiss awakens a whole new kind of hunger in Bella. Can a woman who thought she wanted a frog learn to love a prince?

PROLOGUE

Ten days before Christmas, Long Island, New York

Isabella Cassani reached for the snow globe with the grinning snowman inside. "I like this one."

"No, dearie, this is for you." The eccentric elderly woman with orange hair in a shade not found in nature and piled high in a sixties beehive style, squinted at Bella through green-framed-cats-eye glasses. The red sequins on the woman's Christmas-themed sweater sparkled in the overhead lights as she handed Bella a snow globe.

When Bella took the globe from the woman, their hands touched. A shock ran up Bella's arm and a wave of dizziness hit her. The happy babel of voices in the cavernous school gym that housed the Christmas craft show faded. Even her two friends, Avery and Carlyn, standing next to her, seemed to disappear.

Bella stared down at the small snow globe in her hand. "A frog?" Inside the glass orb, a smiling frog wearing a golden crown sat atop a rock. Glittering flakes fell on him, coating his green body in sparkling white.

"Your true love will find you. So it is fated," the elderly woman said in a sing-song voice.

The strange woman had already chosen a snow globe for Avery, with the words, "That which you don't seek will

73

find you." And now she handed a globe to Bella with equally enigmatic words. Bella shivered.

"What a cute frog!" Carlyn's words snapped Bella out of her strange spell. The noises in the gym reappeared again.

Clutching her snow globe with a Christmas tree and Santa encased in the glass, Avery peered at the one in Bella's hand. "It's different."

"Why a frog?" Bella mused.

Carlyn shrugged. "Why not a frog? You have to kiss a lot of them before you find your prince."

Bella snorted. "You know I don't believe in any of that fairy-tale stuff."

CHAPTER ONE

Halloween, the following year, Manhattan

His lips softened over Bella's—teasing, cajoling, seductive. He tasted of wine and passion. Lost in his heat, wanting more, she curled her arms around his neck. Tiny sounds of pleasure she barely recognized escaped her lips. A slow ache began to build inside her, and she forgot everything but the feel of his lips and his body, hot and demanding. He cradled the back of her head, burying his fingers in her hair. Her cone-shaped witch's hat slipped off her head, brushing her shoulders on its way to the floor. She'd never been kissed like this before, with an urgency and expertise that turned her insides to liquid. He did more than kiss her. He possessed her.

The thunderous sounds of clapping and shouts of "more, more," rose around them, releasing Bella from her delicious haze and bringing her back to Earth like a witch who'd fallen off her broom. Embarrassment swirled through her and she jumped back.

Her breathing harsh, she stared at the man in front of her. His ragged breathing matched hers. The intensity in his blue eyes behind the black half-mask made her shift uncomfortably. With his black cowboy hat pulled low over his head, she had a glimpse of dark hair brushing the collar of his western shirt.

"What's your name?" he asked.

She held up her hand and shook her head. Face burning, with all the composure she could summon, she adjusted her own half-mask and picked up her hat. Then she strolled slowly away, fighting the urge to grab her long black skirt and run through the open door of the bar.

She headed across the room toward Carlyn, Avery, and Josh, Avery's fiancé, who were clapping their hands and inciting the crowd into even louder claps and cheers. Calls for more reverberated throughout the raucous bar, filled with patrons celebrating Halloween.

"Wait!"

She turned to see the cowboy striding toward her, his long legs eating up the distance.

"Don't go," he said. "Tell me your name."

"The Mad Witch of Manhattan."

He threw back his head and laughed.

The absurdity of the whole thing hit Bella and she laughed too. Isabella Cassani, uptight art gallery manager, had let her friends goad her into kissing a stranger. Too much wine, celibacy, loneliness, and seeing Avery so happy with Josh, had all burned past Bella's natural reticence, and she'd accepted her friends' silly dare.

No big deal. On Halloween, everyone pretended to be someone else, and inhibitions flew out the door.

With her mortification beginning to dissipate into the alcohol-laden air, she couldn't help but once again appreciate the stranger's blatant sex appeal. His black leather vest fit snugly over a tan western shirt that stretched across his broad chest. Black jeans hugged his long legs. He looked like every woman's fantasy of the gunslinger come to town.

His blue eyes held a teasing glint. She fought the sudden urge to whip the mask from his face and lean in for another kiss.

As if he read her thoughts, his full lips tilted in a sexy grin and he moved closer to whisper in her ear. "I've always found mad witches very sexy, especially ones from Manhattan. This cowboy's already under your spell."

Bella put her hand on her hip. "I'll undo the spell because this mad witch isn't interested in any cowboy."

"Say that like you mean it."

"Arrogant male." With a toss of her head, she strode back to the table where her friends waited. The cowboy's deep laugh followed her.

"Bella, that was great." Carlyn wiped tears from her eyes. "I can't remember when I laughed so hard."

"Wipe those grins off your faces." Bella plopped down on her chair and grabbed her glass of wine, taking a long swallow as if it could wash away the last of her embarrassment. Nothing could flush away the memory of that kiss. Even now, thinking about those delectable lips on hers made her toes curl. "I can't believe you made me kiss a stranger in a bar."

Avery waved a hand. "You were ogling the sexy cowboy from the minute he walked in. It's Halloween, and about time you let loose."

Bella frowned in mock outrage. "I'll get all of you for this."

Josh put up his hands. "Hey, leave me out of it. They did it."

"Coward," Avery said, punching him in the arm.

Grinning, Carlyn said, "The sexy cowboy is hot. Don't pretend you're sorry you kissed him."

"He's probably a frog under that mask." Bella slid a

glance to the stranger. He seemed to sense her stare, because he turned. His intense blue eyes met hers.

Something told her he wasn't a frog at all.

CHAPTER TWO

"How was the Halloween party Friday night?" Gwen, the art gallery's receptionist, asked Bella the following Monday morning.

Bella adjusted her purse over her shoulder while juggling her briefcase and her large Styrofoam cup of vanilla latte. "Okay. Lots of drinking. Good music."

Gwen, middle-aged, her short blonde hair highlighted with pink streaks, studied Bella over the rim of her pink-framed half-glasses. "No hot men there?"

"I couldn't tell. They all wore masks." *Liar*, a little voice inside said. Even wearing a mask, Kissing Cowboy, as she now called him, was smokin'. All weekend, Kissing Cowboy had dominated her thoughts. She'd even had an erotic dream about him. The dream still made her blush. If she told Gwen about Kissing Cowboy, Gwen would try to play matchmaker and encourage Bella to find out who he was.

"Too bad you didn't meet anyone," Gwen said. The older woman, who devoured romance novels, knew Bella had hopes of more than an employer-employee relationship with their boss, the wealthy, cultured, and talented photographer Hugo Lancashire. Maybe Hugo wasn't scorching like Kissing Cowboy, but he was solid and stable. Bella wanted solid and stable.

Gwen called Hugo a stick-in-the-mud and told Bella she should find herself someone hot, a man with real passion. Kissing Cowboy had the passion part down, and Bella could tell he was good-looking. After the heartbreak her gorgeous father inflicted on her mother and her, Bella refused to date great-looking men. She didn't want to worry about women hitting on her guy all the time.

"Anything I should be aware of today?" Bella asked Gwen, anxious to change the subject.

"Not much. That new assistant Hugo hired is coming in today."

"I forgot about him. I hope he has the computer skills to better organize our catalog after the mess Leon made."

A few minutes later, Bella sat at her desk and turned on her computer, ready to start her day by going through her copious emails.

"Got a minute?" Hugo stuck his head in her doorway. With his thinning dark hair expertly styled, and wearing an exquisitely tailored gray pinstriped suit with a blinding white shirt and a lavender tie, Hugo always looked like he'd stepped out of a men's fashion magazine. Though with his pug nose and close-set gray eyes, he didn't qualify as model material.

Bella smiled. "What's up?"

"Chad's here, my new assistant. He's in my office. When you get a chance, I'd like you to meet him."

"Let me look at some of these emails and I'll be right there." When Hugo left, Bella scanned a few of the more important emails while she drained her coffee, then headed to his office down the short hallway.

When she entered his office, she found Hugo conversing with a tall man who had his back to Bella. The man's pale blue cotton shirt strained across his broad back. His tailored black pants showcased long legs and a nicely rounded butt. Dark hair brushed the collar of his shirt.

Bella put a hand to her throat. If the stranger's front matched his back, she thought she might swoon. And she wasn't the swooning type.

"There you are, Bella," Hugo said. "I want you to meet my new assistant, Chad Prince."

The other man turned around with a smile. His blue eyes locked with Bella's. She recognized those eyes. Her gaze strayed to his mouth. She recognized those sensuous lips.

She opened her mouth but no words came. Her feet seemed rooted to the spot. No, it couldn't be. What were the chances?

"Bella?" Hugo's confused-sounding voice brought her back to Earth.

Chad had his hand out. Forcing her lips into a smile, she placed her hand in his. His large hand, roughened and strong, swallowed her much smaller one.

"I'm Isabella Cassani, the gallery manager. Everyone calls me Bella." Thank God her voice sounded normal.

"Nice to meet you, Bella." His smoky voice, the same as Kissing Cowboy's, rolled over her like the light stroke of a paint brush over canvas. He held her hand a little longer than necessary.

She pulled free. "Nice to meet you too, Chad."

Hugo glanced down at his Rolex. "I have an appointment in a few minutes with one of our serious collectors. Bella, why don't you take Chad to your office and go over the catalog with him?"

"Sure." She pivoted on her heel and marched out of the room, with Chad close behind her. She had to be wrong, but if he and Kissing Cowboy were one and the same, that didn't mean he'd recognize her. She worried over nothing.

When they got to her office, she headed to her desk, putting heavy oak between her and Chad.

With a sexy grin, he approached her desk. Leaning over until they were a whisper apart, he, said, "Hello, Mad Witch. Where's your hat?"

CHAPTER THREE

"You recognize me?" Great, she sounded like an idiot. Bella took a calming breath and gathered her professionalism around her like a heavy coat of varnish. She sat and gestured to the chair in front of her desk.

Chad sank into the leather chair, a teasing gleam in his eyes. "Of course I recognize you. How could I forget those big hazel eyes?" His gaze did a slow, seductive scan of her face. "Or the taste of those lips." His voice thickened.

Bella held up a hand. "Stop right there. Friday night was strictly party time. It has nothing to do with my work. *Our* work. Whatever happened in that bar meant nothing. We won't mention it again. Understand?" Sheesh, when had she gotten so prim and proper? *Since the day you left Texas and invented a whole new life for yourself.*

Chad moved back in his chair. "Agreed. We're here to work. So let's get started."

A vague sense of disappointment settled in Bella's chest. Apparently he could easily forget *the kiss*. She wished she could.

◇◇◇

"We've covered a lot today." Bella closed her laptop and turned toward Chad. He sat next to her at the desk, so close that the heat of his body sent warmth curling through her. Their gazes locked. The wicked spark in his eyes told her he hadn't forgotten *the kiss* after all. She inhaled deeply, trying to slow down the wild beating of her heart.

They'd spent most of the day closeted in her office. She'd gone over their catalog files and explained their system. To her pleasant surprise, his insightful questions showed a good knowledge of art.

He rubbed the back of his neck and pushed away from the desk. Without his closeness, the room seemed chilled.

"I can understand why Hugo needs someone to organize these files." Chad stood and picked up the heavy chair to move it to the front of her desk. He'd rolled up his sleeves and the muscles of his forearms flexed with his movements.

Bella picked up a pen and rubbed it between her fingers, using the cool stainless steel as a shield for her mind. A shield from images of feeling Chad's strong hands on her naked body.

"You seem more than capable of getting all this into something coherent," she said.

His lopsided grin arrowed straight to her heart and lower. "Thanks for the compliment. Something tells me you're not one to give compliments lightly."

"I'm not." He'd figured her out so quickly. "The inventory isn't my job, but I've felt for a long time that something wasn't right with it. I swear we should have more inventory than these files indicate."

Chad stilled, then his shoulders relaxed and he smiled. "I'm sure everything's fine. It's a matter of organizing the files."

Bella glanced at the wall clock. "It's past five. Let's call it a day. See you tomorrow."

Chad gave her a little salute. "See you tomorrow,

Bella."

She watched his retreating back, enjoying the way his pants hugged his tight butt. She needed a drink, or several drinks, to cool her overheated libido.

◇◇◇

"How'd it go?" Hugo asked Chad a few minutes later when Chad stepped into his office.

Chad closed the door behind him and covered the short distance to Hugo's desk. It felt good to stretch his legs. Sitting all day, even next to the gorgeous Bella, tightened his muscles.

"You were right to be concerned, Hugo. Something seems very wrong with your inventory. The records were sloppily kept. You say the previous guy, Leon, up and quit?"

Hugo nodded. "That in itself is suspicious. I've discovered some photos missing, but without good records I can't be sure if there are more."

"Could the photos simply be misplaced?"

"I searched everywhere. They're gone."

"You think Leon may have stolen them?"

"If he did, he had to have help. He's not smart enough to do an operation like that on his own."

His mind whirling, Chad rubbed his forehead. "Have you heard from Leon since he quit?"

"No. I've left him messages, but nothing."

"Did he have any friends here?"

"I used to see him and Daria, our main sales person, talking at times. But he mostly kept to himself."

"I've got the dossiers on your employees, past and present. I'll check them all out." Chad strode toward the door, then turned back to Hugo. "What about Bella? Think she has anything to do with the thefts?" He didn't want to believe she could be involved, but he had to do a thorough investigation.

"I would be shocked if she had anything to do with it. Bella is honest and my right hand. She's been with me since the beginning, and a great manager. Someone I've come to rely on."

"Anything between you two?" The words spilled out. Although none of Chad's business, the thought of Bella and Hugo as a couple fired his competitive nature. He wanted Bella for himself. *Whoa, guy, slow down. You hardly know her.*

Hugo shrugged. "We go out together to functions where we have to make an appearance. She looks good on my arm."

"She'd look good on anyone's arm," Chad said.

"You got that right." Hugo chuckled. "There's nothing more than business between us. I like to play the field."

Chad and Hugo had attended boarding school together as high schoolers. Even then, despite his average looks, Hugo had a reputation as a player who liked to throw his money around. Chad could have been the same, but he didn't want to be like his father, Chadwick Prince, the *third.* Chad's whole life had been a rebellion against his father and his father's values.

"I remember our days at Winslow Academy. Guess you haven't changed much." Chad smiled to take the edge off his words. Hugo's playing around had never bothered him before, but he didn't want to think his old friend would use Bella.

CHAPTER FOUR

"Who is he?" Carlyn leaned over the table toward Bella.

Bella strained to hear her friend over the clink of glasses and the murmur of conversations in the busy restaurant. Feeling restless after spending the day with Chad, a man who stirred her with a strange longing, Bella had asked Carlyn to meet her for dinner. With the long hours she worked, she'd needed this rare night off. She wished Avery could have joined them, but Avery had gone to Vermont with Josh.

"Who is he?" Bella moved the stirrer around in her dirty martini. Not looking at Carlyn, she speared one of the green olives and popped it into her mouth.

"Don't play with me," Carlyn said. "You've had a dreamy look on your face all evening. It's got to be a man. Did Hugo finally ask you out on a real date?"

"No. He will someday."

"I can't understand why you want him. He has no sex appeal."

"He's cultured and stable and knows all the important people."

Carlyn reached across the table and placed her hand over Bella's. "You know Avery and I love you like a sister. We accuse you of being a snob, but you're not. What is this obsession you have with finding a husband who can give you security? That's so 1950's. You're smarter than that, and you know how to take care of yourself."

With a sly smile, Carlyn continued, "What did that orange-haired woman who gave you the snow globe tell you?"

"'Your true love will find you. So it is fated.'"

"Ah-ha! You remember every word."

Bella waved a hand in dismissal. "I don't believe that mumbo-jumbo crap. I'm not looking for love. Love hurts."

Carlyn's brows knitted in a frown. "Who hurt you?"

The waiter appeared with their food, saving Bella from answering. She concentrated on her meal. She'd already said too much. Avery and Carlyn were her best friends, but even they didn't know Bella's true background. They didn't know why security meant so much to her or why she refused to date good-looking men.

Chad was beyond handsome. Smart too. They worked well together.

No way would she get involved with him.

The next morning, Bella showed up for work juggling her usual vanilla latte, her briefcase, and her purse. She nodded to Hugo, on the phone, as she passed his office. A talented photographer well-established in the art world, Hugo embodied the kind of man she'd always wanted for a husband. So what if he didn't excite her? With Hugo, she'd have the safety she'd always craved. If she didn't love him, he couldn't hurt her.

Her thoughts went to Chad. Thinking about him heated her more than her coffee. He'd told her he'd worked for five different art galleries the last few years, and she wondered why. Sure, he knew a lot about art, which she admired, but it seemed like he couldn't hold down a job. So not what she needed in a man.

She entered her office and set her drink, briefcase and purse onto her desk. As she slipped off her coat, her gaze landed on the credenza behind her desk where the frog snow globe sat in the center surrounded by stacks of files. The frog stared back at her.

She narrowed her eyes for a better look. The globe seemed closer to the edge of the credenza. The cleaning crew must have moved it. She threw her coat onto a chair, then pushed the globe back to the center.

"Morning, Bella."

Chad's deep voice startled her. She turned around. He leaned against the doorframe, his arms folded across his chest. His white dress shirt with the sleeves rolled up exposed muscled forearms with a sprinkling of fine black hairs. Indigo jeans displayed long legs that went on forever. His overt sexuality made her knees wobbly. She backed up against the credenza. Damn, she could not allow her attraction to Chad to distract her from her work, and more importantly, from the life she'd carved out for herself. A life far removed from the dusty Texas towns where she'd grown up.

"Not a good morning?" he asked when she'd remained silent.

She blinked to dislodge the decidedly un-businesslike thoughts that had taken root in her mind. "Sorry. Good morning to you, too."

"You're looking especially nice," he said, moving closer. "But then you always look good."

"Thanks." She cleared her throat, fighting the pleasure his words provoked.

Bella sank down onto her chair and grabbed her latte,

taking a long sip. Thankfully, it had cooled enough not to burn. She glanced away, focusing on the snow globe, at the edge of the credenza. The edge? She jostled her cup, spilling some coffee over the side and onto her papers.

"Oh, my God. Look what I've done." Bella jumped up and pulled the box of tissues she kept on her desk closer. Chad rushed over and helped her mop up the liquid before it could do any damage.

"You seem distracted," he said.

"I have a busy day ahead." *You distract me. You and that strange little frog.*

"I'm meeting with Hugo in a half hour," Chad said. "You look like you need cheering up. Let's go next door to the coffee house. Breakfast on me."

"I never eat breakfast."

With a smile that showed even white teeth, he cupped her elbow. "Breakfast is important. It'll put you in a better mood."

She bristled. "Who says I'm in a bad mood?"

"Let's go." Still cupping her elbow, he led her out of the room.

They sat by a window overlooking Fifth Avenue. Outside, the sidewalks were filled with office workers and tourists, all vying for their own space. The shops along the street were already decorated for Christmas. Sheesh, Halloween had barely ended.

Bella scanned the moving crowd. She loved New York City. She'd moved here after college and had never looked back. With an art history degree, she'd pushed hard to establish herself in the cutthroat New York art world. She'd worked equally hard to rid herself of her Texas twang. Try as she might to forget her upbringing, it stayed with her, coloring everything she did.

She bit into her breakfast sandwich of egg, bacon, and cheese and tried not to watch the way Chad's large hands gripped his sandwich. She wondered what those hands would feel like on her body. She squirmed and reached for her mug of coffee.

Chad swallowed his bite of sandwich and set the rest onto his plate. His deep blue eyes studied her. "Tell me about Isabella Cassani. I find smart women extremely attractive."

"I hope you find one." She smiled to temper her words.

He laughed, then his gaze went to her lips. "You're a terrific kisser, too."

She clutched her mug so tightly, she feared the ceramic would shatter. Pushing the mug away, she said, "Can we please forget that kiss?"

"I'll never forget it." His husky voice covered her like rich, warm coffee. "I can see it makes you uncomfortable though, so I'll stop." He rested his elbows on the table. "Tell me about you. Where in Texas are you from?"

Widening her eyes, she said, "I'm from a small town in upstate New York." The lie rolled off her tongue too easily. She'd been telling it so long she almost believed it.

With a frown, he sat back. "New York? I could swear I hear a little Texas in your voice."

A flush crept up her neck to her face. "I can't imagine why you'd think that."

He shrugged. "I have an ear for accents. Hugo tells me your relationship with him is strictly business. True?"

At his abrupt change of topic, Bella dropped the sandwich in her hand back onto her plate. "Why do you ask that?"

"Just checking."

91

"It's really none of your business."

"You're right."

Bella turned her attention to the crowded sidewalk. She stiffened. Among the throngs of workers and tourists, bright orange hair stood out. As if she felt Bella watching, the woman with the orange hair turned. Bella stared into the eyes of the elderly woman who'd sold her the snow globe. The woman winked. A chill ran over Bella as the woman disappeared into the crowd. Her insides churning with a mixture of confusion and disbelief, Bella snatched up her purse from the table and stood. "We need to get back to work."

Chad followed Bella out of the coffee shop, enjoying the sight of her well-rounded backside in her close-fitting pants. Since that scorching kiss they'd shared at the Halloween party, he hadn't been able to get her out of his mind. Fate had a hand in bringing them together again. He believed things happened for a reason.

That unforgettable kiss had awakened the part of his heart that had been left to slumber. It had also awakened another part that hadn't had much action lately.

After the debacle in Philadelphia where he'd almost lost his job and where he definitely lost his heart, he never thought he'd be whole again. Amy had done a number on him, making him wary of trusting another woman.

He liked Bella and enjoyed their banter, but he wouldn't allow it to get too serious. He had to focus on his job. And protect his heart. Yet, he felt himself drawn to Bella in a way he'd never been drawn to another woman, not even Amy.

Despite his attraction to Bella, he couldn't rule her out as the person stealing the valuable photos from the gallery.

All employees were suspect. A good judge of character, he recognized Bella as a woman of integrity. But he'd thought the same of Amy too. And look where that had gotten him.

He and Bella didn't speak on the short walk back to the gallery. When they entered, Gwen gave them a little wave and a knowing grin. He gave Gwen a thumbs-up. He figured the receptionist for a natural-born matchmaker who'd set her sights on pairing him with Bella. He wouldn't fight her.

"Bella, I've been looking for you." A blonde bombshell, teetering on sky-high stilettos and wearing a body-hugging short purple dress, approached them.

When he and Bella stopped, the blonde skimmed her baby blues over Chad. "And who might you be?"

With an audible sigh, Bella said, "Daria, this is Hugo's new assistant, Chad Prince. Chad, this is Daria Younger, one of our sales force."

Daria held out her hand, the long fingernails painted deep green. "I'm Hugo's top sales person." Her full red lips curved in a seductive smile. "I heard some of the girls talking about you. You're hotter than they said."

Chad shook her hand and quickly released it. "Nice to meet you, Daria."

She hooked her arm through his. "I know you and I are going to get along wonderfully."

With a shrug, Chad looked back at Bella as Daria led him away.

CHAPTER FIVE

"You going to let that man-eater get away with that?" Gwen's words froze Bella on her way back to her office.

She whirled around and strode to Gwen. "What are you talking about?"

Gwen peeked up at her over her hot-pink-framed glasses. "You know what I mean." Her voice dropped. "Daria tries to get her hooks into every good-looking guy who walks into this place. I've seen you and Chad together. The sparks between you could set these exhibits on fire. Go for him. Don't let Daria latch onto him."

Bella shook her head. "You've been reading too many romance novels. Chad and I aren't interested in each other." Yet, her stomach had dropped at the sight of Chad and Daria together. She wasn't as immune to him or his charms as she wanted to be.

"I'm not wrong, Bella, and you know it."

"Later, Gwen. I have work to do." Bella started for her office again.

"It wouldn't hurt for you to read some of those romance novels. They'll put you in a better frame of mind," Gwen called after her.

Why did everyone think her in a foul mood today? She did read and enjoy romance novels, but wouldn't admit it. A practical woman, Bella had seen up close what obsessive love and passion did to a person. What happened to her mother would never happen to her. She was smarter. And too level-headed to believe she'd really seen the strange orange-haired woman who'd sold her the snow globe strolling Fifth Avenue. Bella had been working too hard lately. Stress and an overactive imagination played havoc with her mind.

When she reached her office, she closed the door with a bang, but she couldn't shut out the picture of Chad with Daria.

"Looks like Adolfo is having a successful show," Bella said to Hugo as their limo pulled up in front of the midtown gallery for a showing of photographs by the renowned Italian photo-journalist, Adolfo San Rocco.

"Too bad I couldn't snag him, but he wanted a bigger percentage than I could give," Hugo said.

"Everyone's buzzing about his amazing photos from Afghanistan," she said.

Hugo shrugged but didn't respond.

The limo driver exited the car and walked around to open Bella's door. She took the driver's proffered hand and got out, then smoothed her hand down the front of her short black cocktail dress and shivered. Although the crisp November air held hints of the coming winter, she wore no coat or stockings. For the sake of fashion, she'd endure the cold along with the strappy high-heeled sandals that made walking a challenge. Bella followed the trend. It gave her confidence. Having grown up with no permanent home and a mother who drifted from one Texas town to another after Bella's philandering father, Bella relished her façade of New York chic. Much as she tried though, she couldn't completely shake the insecure little girl who'd gone hungry, the little girl who now hid behind the stylish clothes and lifestyle.

Flashbulbs went off, pulling her from her trip down memory lane. Feeling like a fraud, she let Hugo take her arm. Famous in his own right, he'd garnered acclaim for his striking photographs of celebrities. Bella enjoyed the attention when they joined forces at these events. She widened her smile for the cameras as they entered the gallery. Going with Hugo to gallery openings and to select dinners with important clients had segued into a big part of her job. And she loved it.

Yet, alone in her bed at night, when silence and darkness enveloped her, she acknowledged the secret part of her that yearned for more, that craved love.

The Parisi gallery, sparsely furnished in gray, black and white, with ultra-modern black leather sofas and chairs spread throughout the rooms, always struck Bella as cold. She liked Hugo's smaller, more intimate gallery better.

Still, she felt the familiar buzz of excitement as the guests took in the photographs hung artfully along the walls. A few sculptures stood on pedestals, luring patrons close to relish the form and detail. This represented her world, one of beauty, a world she'd chosen.

Waiters eased through the crowd with trays of appetizers and flutes of champagne. Hugo lifted two glasses of champagne and handed one to Bella. Sipping the bubbly liquid, she smiled at the other guests as she and Hugo moved leisurely through the exhibit, stopping here and there to admire a photo that caught their attention.

"Adolfo is very talented," Hugo said, standing in front of a photo of a young Afghan girl with large, frightened eyes.

"He's captured the fear on that poor girl's face," Bella said.

"And the hope too," Hugo said. "Genius."

"Hey, you two." The deep male voice behind them made butterflies fly into a frenzy in Bella's stomach. Gripping her champagne flute, she turned slowly and raised her gaze to meet Chad's.

His eyes, gleaming with intensity, locked on hers. She couldn't look away.

"Chad, I didn't expect to see you here." Hugo's voice broke the spell.

Bella sipped her drink, hoping the cool slide of it down her throat would chill her libido. No such luck.

The men shook hands, then Hugo turned to speak to a well-dressed elderly couple Bella recognized as wealthy art collectors.

"What are you doing here?" she asked Chad when she found her voice. She winced at her accusatory tone.

Chad took a glass of champagne from a tray held by a passing waiter. "I get around. I know people here." With a teasing smile, he moved closer. "I actually know how to behave in polite company."

"That's—that's not what I meant." The heat that flared on her face told her she blushed.

He laughed. "That's exactly what you meant, but it's okay."

Unable to help herself, she scanned him. His tux fit him perfectly, looking custom made, the black fabric setting off his snowy white shirt, worn tieless. He stood inches from her. With his dark hair slicked back and the slight stubble of dark beard on his firm jaw, he looked like a macho hipster too cool even for the pages of *GQ*. The butterflies in her stomach fluttered furiously.

Be still, my heart.

Chad frowned. "Did you say something?"

"No." Crap. She'd spoken out loud. Thankfully, she'd whispered.

The next two hours passed in a blur for Bella. She smiled at people she knew, ate the savory appetizers, and studied the photos. But her attention stayed focused on Chad. He hadn't spent a lot of time with her and Hugo, but her whole body tingled with warmth, knowing he moved through the nearby rooms. Throughout the evening, she stole glances at him. Whenever he caught her staring, he gave her a sexy grin that swirled a mixture of anger and excitement within her. Anger that she couldn't control her attraction to him, and excitement that made her come alive every time their eyes met.

As Chad strolled around talking with the other invitees, seeming comfortable among the city's elite, Bella had the uneasy feeling she might be wrong about him. Chad Prince appeared more than a guy who drifted from job to job.

Finally, hours later, and boneless with exhaustion, Bella leaned against the wall near one of the exhibit rooms and blew out a breath, disturbing the tendrils of hair that had come loose from her expensive upsweep.

"Tired?" Chad's husky voice made her turn.

He stood so close, she inhaled his scent of soap and male.

"Yes. I worked all day and I have to work tomorrow."

"I get it." He bent toward her. "I haven't told you yet how amazing you look."

"Don't, Chad."

"You can't handle the truth?"

"I'm not interested in you. That's all."

"You're a bad liar." His eyes bored into hers, giving her the uneasy feeling he saw through the elaborate façade she'd constructed.

"Think what you will." Her voice sounded calm, but her insides quivered. She looked away to see Hugo heading toward them. Saved from her uncomfortable conversation with Chad. Her tight muscles relaxed.

When Hugo reached them, he gave Bella a contrite look. "Bella, I've been invited to the Walsh's for a late-night dinner. I have to accept. You know I've been trying to get them interested in some of my work. I'll call for the limo to drive you home. Will you be okay?"

Forcing a smile, she said, "Don't worry about me."

"I have an idea," Hugo said, shooting Chad a glance. "Why doesn't Chad share the limo with you? My driver can drop you off, then Chad. What do you say?"

"Chad probably has his own ride home." Bella crossed her fingers behind her back, willing that to be true. No way did she want to ride in the intimate confines of the limo with Chad Prince.

"I planned on a cab," Chad said. "Thanks for the offer of the ride. I'll take it."

Hugo patted Chad on the shoulder. "I'll call my driver now."

On the ride back to her Brooklyn Heights apartment, Bella stayed as far from Chad as the seat allowed. Despite the distance between them, her body felt overheated. She pressed against the door, fighting her desire to slide close and kiss Chad.

"Nice show," he said, breaking the quiet.

"Adolfo is very talented."

"And a nice guy. I spoke with him for a while tonight."

"He's always gracious to everyone he meets." Her insides screamed with her need to touch Chad, to press her lips to his. Instead, they were having this inane conversation.

When the limo pulled up to her building, the driver got out and walked around to her side to open the door. "Goodnight, Chad," she said as she prepared to get out of the car.

"Not goodnight yet. I'm walking you to your door."

Oh, boy. "You don't have to do that. I'm feet away from my building."

"What kind of gentleman would I be if I didn't make sure you got inside okay? No arguments."

With a sigh of resignation, she slid out of the car and Chad followed. She unlocked the outside double doors of the converted brownstone and entered the wide hallway. She lived in the apartment at the end of the first floor.

When they got to her door, she clutched her keys in her hand and faced Chad. "Thanks for walking me. I'm here now. I'll see you at work."

He stepped closer and reached out a hand to brush aside strands of her hair from her face. His thumb caressed her cheek. "I prefer your hair down."

Their gazes locked. Liquid heat rushed through her at a fevered pace. *Oh, hell.* He lowered his head to kiss her. She should kiss him, only to prove his first kiss had been an alcohol-fueled accident. Of course, she had to know.

She dropped her keys and purse and stood on tiptoe to wrap her arms around his neck. She returned his kiss, tentatively at first, then with the same hunger and urgency she'd felt the first time they kissed. He deepened the kiss, skimming his tongue along the seam of her lips until she opened for him. His lips and body seduced. She tightened her arms around his neck and reveled in his heat and masculinity. He tasted like champagne and chocolate. She wanted to devour him.

After several passion-filled minutes, he drew away and touched his forehead to hers. "Isabella, what am I going to do about you? You kiss like an angel, or maybe a devil. I can't get enough of you."

His harsh breathing and his tortured voice filled her with a surprising dose of feminine power. Her heart tripped wildly. She shouldn't have given in to temptation. This second kiss, hotter than the first, jumbled her already conflicted thoughts. She pushed away from him. "That shouldn't have happened. I need to go in."

He tipped her chin up with his fingers until their eyes met. "You want me as much as I want you. Why do you keep running away?"

"I'm not running. It's late." She grabbed her purse and keys from the floor, unlocked her door and slipped inside. Closing the door behind her, she pressed against it.

She wanted him.

No, she had a plan for her life that didn't include Chad Prince.

CHAPTER SIX

"Thanks. I'll send the contract by messenger today." Excitement made Bella grin even though the person on the phone couldn't see her. "I know we'll enjoy working with you. Once the contract is signed, we'll arrange for you to go through our gallery to decide how you want us to best show Mr. Syracuse's designs."

Bella hung up the phone and rubbed the back of her neck. The call with rising artist Titus Syracuse's agent had lasted almost an hour. But she'd gotten the contract to show Syracuse's work. She had to tell Hugo they'd finally scored the artist, a genuine coup for the gallery. The tightness in her neck disappeared. She'd done her job.

She yawned. The delight over snagging Syracuse had revved her adrenaline, but now her tiredness took over. After her scorching kiss with Chad last night, she'd barely slept. She hadn't seen him this morning, but she still felt the imprint of his lips on hers. She wanted him more than ever.

She glanced over at the snow globe. "Oh, shut up," she said to the grinning frog.

As she stood, her phone rang. A glance down told her Gwen called from the front desk. She connected the call. "Yes, Gwen. What is it?"

"There's a Mr. DiSabatino here for Daria, but she's at lunch with *Chad*."

The way Gwen emphasized Chad's name, Bella knew she disapproved of the other woman's pursuit of him. Truth be told, Bella felt the slide of disappointment at the news.

"Hugo took some collectors to lunch," Gwen said. "Could you help Mr. DiSabatino?"

"Sure, I'll be right out."

When Bella entered the reception area, a well-dressed middle-aged man stood chatting with Gwen.

"Mr. DiSabatino, I'm Bella Cassani. Can I help you?" She shook his hand.

"Thank you," he said. "I've been negotiating with Daria to buy the original of one of Hugo's photos. I've called her the last several days, but she hasn't returned my calls. I'm concerned. My client left for Hong Kong today but he'll be back in a week and he expects to have the photograph mounted and in his apartment when he returns."

"I'm so sorry, Mr. DiSabatino. What photo is it? I'll take care of it for you."

"The one of Emilie St. John."

"A great lady," Bella said. "That's one of Hugo's prized photos." Emilie St. John, *grande dame* of New York City, had died the year before at the age of one hundred. Hugo had sold prints of his iconic photo of her, but not the original, which had to be worth close to a quarter million dollars. Knowing Daria would have mentioned a pending sale to Hugo, Bella found it strange he had kept such good news to himself.

"Let me find it, Mr. DiSabatino, and have it mounted. I'll give you a call when it's ready. We'll be glad to deliver to wherever you want."

"Thank you, Bella." He reached into his pocket, pulled out a card, and handed it to her. "My contact information."

When he left, Bella and Gwen looked at each other. Gwen frowned. "That's odd. Daria is usually on top of things, especially something that involves a hefty commission for her."

As the gallery's top salesperson, Daria had good customer relation skills. Lately, her sales were off, and Daria had blamed it on the economy.

Bella looked down at DiSabatino's card and back to Gwen. "You'd think Daria would have closed this one as soon as possible."

"You'd think."

"I'd better go to the vault and look for the photo myself." All employees had keys to the vault which stored Hugo's extensive collection. The sales staff were in and out of the secure, temperature-controlled room, but Bella had very little reason to go there.

Bella opened the door to the vault and stepped inside. She switched on the light, then the computer which stored the location of each photo. Typing in the photo's description, she found its location. When she opened the cabinet drawer and searched through the photos, she couldn't find the one she sought.

Thinking it had been misfiled, she searched again. No photo. Dread pressed against her chest. Had someone stolen the valuable piece? Bella couldn't imagine any of Hugo's employees stealing from him. Perhaps Hugo knew what happened to the photo.

While Bella waited for Hugo to come back from lunch, she worked on the Syracuse contract.

"Got a minute?" At Chad's smoky voice, her heart stuttered. She looked up to find him in her doorway.

"What do you need?" As soon as the words were out,

she wanted to bite them back.

His eyes lit and his gaze fell on her mouth.

She cleared her throat and straightened her shoulders. "Do you need help with something?"

"I do. There are some files I can't figure out."

"Let me have Gwen print this contract and arrange for a messenger to deliver it, then I'll help you."

"Sure." He walked around her small office, finally stopping to look at the items on her credenza. "Nice snow globe. Where did you get it?"

She twisted around to see Chad holding the little globe.

"I got it at a craft fair on Long Island." The orange-haired woman's words popped into Bella's head. The snow globe had nothing to do with Chad, nothing at all.

Determined to ignore him and the funny things his closeness did to her insides, she emailed the contract to Gwen along with instructions.

Chad set the frog globe down, moved a chair next to Bella, and sat. She inhaled his fresh soap scent. The heat of his body warmed her. Uneasy around all that testosterone, she moved her chair a little bit away from his.

"Do I scare you, Bella?" he asked in a soft, sexy voice.

"Of course not." She punched keys on the computer, calling up the main catalog.

He put his hand over her fingers, stopping her from typing. When she looked at him, he said, "I think I scare you a lot. Why? We're two unattached people who are attracted to each other. I'd like to get to know you, to spend time with you. How about dinner tonight?"

She wished she had a fan to cool herself. "You move fast, don't you?"

"It's just dinner. I promise to be on my best behavior."

"I'm not interested in pursuing anything with you."

He moved his chair closer. "You've kissed me twice already. Don't say you didn't enjoy it. Give me one good reason why you won't go out with me."

"You're too good-looking." The words slipped out on a whisper.

He jerked his head up. "Too good-looking? That's a new one."

"I don't date good-looking men." God, she sounded so prissy.

"That's a little dismissive, isn't it? What if I said I don't date gorgeous brunettes with big hazel eyes? You'd say I'm a sexist."

"No, I wouldn't."

"What's really going on with you, Bella?"

She hadn't even confided her deepest fears to Avery and Carlyn. She couldn't reveal her old wounds to Chad. She barely knew him. Yet, a part of her felt he'd understand.

"Let's get to work." She turned her attention back to the computer screen.

An hour later, they'd gone over the catalog and Chad had a better understanding of their system. As they were finishing, Gwen rang Bella to tell her Hugo had returned.

"I need to see Hugo about some important issues," Bella said, standing.

Chad stood too. "Thanks for the help today."

Anxious to get away from Chad's disturbing presence that made her wish for things that could never be, Bella fled her office and headed toward Hugo's. When she got there, she closed the door behind her and walked to his desk.

He looked up from his computer and frowned. "You look serious. What's going on?"

"Good news and bad. We got the Syracuse contract. I had it messengered to his agent today."

Hugo's face broke out in a grin. "Terrific. Remind me to give you a huge bonus at Christmas."

She grinned back. "You'd better believe I'll remind you."

He folded his hands on the desk. "The bad news?"

Bella blew out a breath. "We have a customer who wants to buy the original of the shot you did of Emilie St. John."

Hugo's eyes widened. "How is that bad news?"

"At lunchtime, the customer's representative came here in person because he says he's been negotiating with Daria to buy the photo but she hasn't returned his calls. I went into the vault to get it to prepare for mounting." Bella gripped the sides of the desk. "The photo's gone."

Hugo froze, his face stark white under his tan. He shook himself as if escaping from a trance. "Daria's probably having it mounted and forgot to sign it out."

Bella chewed her lip and stepped away from the desk. His hesitation and his obvious shock told her he didn't believe Daria had sent the expensive piece to be mounted.

Hugo stood. "Thanks, Bella. Give me the client's number and I'll contact him. Don't worry. I'm sure it's all okay." He picked up his phone and punched in a number. "Gwen, tell Chad I want to see him in my office."

Feeling like a child who'd just been reprimanded, Bella handed him DiSabatino's card and left the office, passing Chad on his way in. Maybe Hugo wanted Chad to look through the computer files.

The thumping of her heart telegraphed her doubts about Hugo's behavior and increased her anxiety.

CHAPTER SEVEN

"What's up?" Chad closed the door to Hugo's office and took a seat in front of the desk.

His features tight, Hugo pushed aside papers. "Bella tells me that my most valuable piece is gone from the vault. I saw it there a week ago. "

"You said all your employees have keys to the vault."

At Hugo's nod, Chad scrubbed a hand over his face. Sometimes the gallery owners were clueless when it came to trusting their employees. "Damn it, Hugo, you should be more careful. Only give the keys to a few employees, the ones who need them."

"I trust all my employees."

"Apparently there's one or more you can't trust."

"Chad, I need to find out who's stealing from me. This is my work, my livelihood, and some scumbag—"

Chad stood. "I'll find the perps. I haven't failed anyone yet."

"You're the best the FBI has. I'm depending on you."

◇◇◇

"I think the dark green piece will stand out against that white wall." Bella pointed to a far side in the gallery's largest exhibit room. A few days after finding Hugo's famous photo missing, she toured the gallery with Titus Syracuse's agent, Jeffrey Hickok. A man known in the city's art community as

108

a barracuda who didn't follow rules when securing contracts for his clients, Hickok also came onto her every time they met.

As protection from the unwanted advances, she'd asked Chad to accompany them on the tour. She couldn't explain it, but she felt safe with Chad. Holding her tablet to input notes, he followed them.

"No, no, no. That simply won't do," Jeffrey said. "That green vase is Titus's most expensive piece. It has to be front and center in this room. We want to sell it."

Chad stepped closer. "If I might interrupt. Bella is right. I attended an exhibit for Franz Meyer last year in Frankford." He named one of Europe's top glassblowers. "The gallery showcased his most expensive piece in a corner near the back of the room. It forced those who'd come to see that one to walk through the room and look at his others. It also didn't seem as mercenary and obvious to have the most expensive piece upfront." Chad gave Jeffrey a slight smile. "Meyer sold that piece the same night."

Jeffrey pulled himself up to his full five foot seven inch height and flared his nostrils, as if ready to ask Chad how he dare interrupt.

"Chad has a good point, Jeffrey." Bella threw Chad a look of gratitude. "The dark green vase is one of the most exquisite ones Syracuse has done. People know of it. They would expect it to be in the front of the room. If we put it against the white wall, it will stand out and catch their eyes the minute they enter. They'll be forced to admire the other pieces on their way to the vase. It'll work. What do you think?"

A professional smile on her face, she waited.

Jeffrey pressed his lips together. With a sigh, he said,

"Okay, we'll do it your way."

"I'm sure you and Titus will be pleased with the show," Bella said.

Later, after seeing the agent out and locking the door, Bella strolled over to where Chad stood entering notes in the tablet.

"Thanks for helping out with the note taking and also for supporting me about the green vase."

"I aim to please."

His sexy grin pleased her all the way down to her toes. When he handed her the tablet, their fingers touched, igniting a spark within her that warmed her insides. She really needed to get control of her wayward libido whenever she found herself near Chad.

"Everyone's gone," he said. "It's time for us to go too. Let me take you to dinner."

"I don't think that's a good idea."

"Come on. Have dinner with me. As friends and co-workers only." He held up his hands. "I promise, only as friends. No kissing." His eyes gleamed with blue fire. "Not that I'd mind kissing you again."

They stood close. She could reach out her hand and skim her fingers over his lips. *Stop it, Bella.*

"What do you say?" he asked.

"I'm hungry so I guess we can go to dinner."

Chad put his hand over his heart. "You sound like I'm sending you to the gallows. I'm wounded."

She couldn't help laughing. "You'll survive. I'll get my coat." Grinning, her step light, she headed to her office and grabbed her coat and purse from the hook behind her door. As she reached for the light switch, her gaze landed on the frog snow globe. The strange orange-haired woman's words echoed in her mind. *Your true love will find you. So it is fated.* Bella hit the light switch hard, cloaking the room in darkness.

Chad was her co-worker. Nothing more. But no co-worker had ever made her insides turn to jelly with just a look, or made her dream of feeling those full lips all over her body.

Later, seated across from Chad at a small table in a homey Italian restaurant, contentment swirled with anticipation inside Bella. She'd eaten in this restaurant dozens of times, but she'd never noticed how bright the mismatched tablecloths were or paid much attention to the hokey pictures hung in crowded profusion on the walls. Chad brought a vibrancy into her life that made her feel alive and made her yearn for something unnamed that hovered beneath the surface of her mind.

"A penny for them," Chad said, raising his wine glass to her.

A slow burn started at her neck and spread to her face. She took a quick sip of her Chianti, letting the rich, warm slide of it down her throat relax her. "My thoughts aren't even worth a penny."

"I seriously doubt that." He set his glass onto the red tablecloth. "I want to know all there is about you, Isabella Cassani. You intrigue me."

She almost choked on the wine she'd just sipped. "I intrigue you? That's a line I've never heard."

His gaze searched hers. "It's not a line. You're one of the most interesting and smartest women I've met." His eyes strayed to her lips. "And your kisses are hot."

Determined to resist his appeal, she wrapped her fingers around the stem of her glass. "We're just co-workers.

111

Remember? No kisses or talking about kissing." She sounded so proper when she felt anything *but*.

His full lips tilted in one of his sexy grins that made warmth trace a line of heat through her.

"Agreed," he said. "No more talking about kissing you."

"Why do I not believe you?"

He threw back his head and laughed. "I guess you'll have to find out if I mean it."

True to his word, they didn't discuss kissing or lack thereof through dinner, and Bella settled into the cozy ambiance of their surroundings. She enjoyed herself more than she had in a long time. Dinner over, they walked along Fifth Avenue, admiring the Christmas decorations in the store windows. Bella drew her coat collar closer against the November chill. "I love Manhattan at this time of year with all the stores decorated for the holiday."

Chad cupped her elbow, pulling her closer, and wound her arm through his. Bella knew she should pull away. She didn't want to give him the idea she wanted anything other than a friendship with him. She liked walking arm-in-arm with Chad, liked it a little too much, and she kept her arm in his.

They stopped in front of Saks and she peered in the elaborately decorated window. Feeling like a little girl excited over the holidays, she wanted to press her face against the window. Something about being with Chad made her want to ditch the veneer of sophistication she'd cultivated all these years and be the half-wild, neglected little girl running through the dusty streets of Texas small towns, the little girl who had been free of the constraints of society.

When Chad put his arm around her shoulders, Bella leaned into him. His heat penetrated her heavy coat. When he put both arms around her waist and drew her to his chest, she sighed.

He rested his chin on the top of her head. "We make a good couple, in lots of ways," he whispered.

Bella stared at their reflection in the glass. He stood a foot taller than she, yet they looked like they belonged together, like a couple in love.

Fear knotted her chest. She wouldn't allow herself to fall in love. Love and passion made a person weak and vulnerable.

She freed herself from Chad. "I need to find a taxi and get home."

He frowned. "Okay. Is everything all right?"

"Everything's fine." She lied.

She was falling for Chad Prince.

CHAPTER EIGHT

Bella scooted her chair away from her desk and closed her tired eyes. Looking at a computer screen all day took its toll. The past days had been especially busy setting up shows for the coming year and putting the finishing touches on the Syracuse show scheduled to run after the holidays.

Through all the craziness her job could be at times, she couldn't stop thinking about Chad. They'd barely spoken since having dinner together a few nights ago. When they passed at work, he'd smile but keep walking. She guessed he'd decided not to pursue her.

She wanted him to pursue her.

Bella snapped her eyes open. Where had that come from? She couldn't be interested in a relationship with Chad Prince. No way. *Liar.*

"Bella." Hugo stood in her doorway, looking elegant as usual in a beautifully tailored suit.

She needed a husband like Hugo she told herself as she smiled at him. She didn't need passion in a relationship. Hugo would give her the comfort, stability, and security she craved. The little girl who still lived inside her would never again be hungry or unwanted.

As if pulled by an unseen hand, her gaze flew to the snow globe. She could swear the little frog's smile mocked her. *You're wrong, froggie. Chad's not for me. Hugo is what*

I need.

"Bella?"

She focused on Hugo again. "Sorry. What do you need?"

"It's almost closing time, and I know you've been working hard. I have a favor to ask. The Fischer's are in town, and they've invited us to dinner. This is last minute, but they're too important to turn down."

Diane and Bob Fischer were wealthy art patrons with their fingers on the pulse of the Manhattan art scene. They sponsored many up-and-coming artists, and Hugo liked to stay in their good graces.

"I always enjoy seeing the Fischer's," she lied. They were both, especially Diane, snobs who liked to through around their wealth and prestige. But for the sake of Hugo's gallery, Bella would sit through what promised to be an excruciating evening.

"Good," Hugo said. "We'll close up and head out to La Piano."

"I like that place." Another lie. The snooty restaurant served tiny portions and charged huge sums.

◇◇◇

"Where did you say your family is from?" Diane Fischer asked as they waited for their food at the restaurant, bustling with the cream of Manhattan society, people who went out to see and be seen.

Bella looked around, pretending not to hear Diane's question. The high society people Bella had desperately wanted to rub elbows with filled the room. Now she recognized the others as what they were—social piranhas.

"Bella?" Hugo said, a disapproving tone in his voice. "Diane asked you a question."

She turned back to Diane. "So sorry, Diane. What did you say?"

Annoyance on her face, the other woman said, "Where is your family from?"

"I've mentioned before that my family is from upstate New York." The lying, the effort it took to reach for that golden ring of belonging to the "right" social set, wore on Bella.

Diane studied her. Bella wondered if the woman suspected Bella's less than stellar social credentials. "I don't know anyone who lives *there*," Diane said, as if she found any place outside New York City distasteful as a painting on velvet.

Bella bristled. Her family might be dysfunctional, but they weren't snobs. She opened her mouth, ready to tell the snooty Mrs. Fischer that good people lived in many areas of the country. Bella sipped wine instead. For the sake of the gallery, and her job, she'd keep quiet.

After dinner, Hugo put Bella into a cab while the others waited inside the restaurant. Hugo and the Fischer's were heading to a small cocktail party near Midtown, but Bella begged off, claiming a headache. Not a complete lie. The beginnings of a wicked headache pulsed behind her right temple. She'd felt restless all evening. She never enjoyed the other couple's company, but she always liked being among the city's power brokers and society leaders. Not so much anymore. She'd think about why another time.

In her apartment later, Bella toed off her high heels as she strode to her bedroom to change. Dressed in yoga pants, a long-sleeved T-shirt, and barefoot, she headed to her kitchen for some comfort food. As she dug through her freezer looking for the ice cream, her cell phone rang. She grabbed it off the kitchen counter. When she saw Chad's name come up, her pulse leaped. "Chad," she said, surprised at the breathlessness in her voice.

"Hey, Bella. Hope it's not too late to call."

"Not at all. Is anything wrong?"

"I'm working on our catalog at my place and I have a question."

"Okay. What is it?"

They spoke for ten minutes until they cleared up the work issue.

"Thanks," he said. "I'll let you get back to whatever you were doing."

She laughed. "Digging in the dark recesses of my freezer for some ice cream."

"Hungry, huh?"

"Afraid so. I had dinner tonight at one of those Chi-Chi places that serves small portions."

"Do you like pizza?"

"Love it."

"What do you like on it?"

"The works."

"I'll order one and be right over."

"You're coming here?"

He'd already hung up.

Chad. At her place. With pizza. She looked down at her T-shirt and yoga pants. Hell. She didn't have much time. She wanted to look good for him. She shouldn't want to.

He's just a co-worker, she reminded herself again as she hurried to her bedroom to change. The pounding of her heart told her she wanted Chad to be so much more.

CHAPTER NINE

"I enjoyed this." Bella wiped her mouth with her napkin and picked up her glass of pinot noir. She and Chad sat at the breakfast bar in her kitchen finishing off the pizza he'd had delivered. "Thanks for the pizza."

He shrugged. "I'll take any excuse to see you."

Almost too charming, like a fairy-tale prince, Chad's closeness and his words thrilled her. But fear ate through her pleasure. She didn't believe in happy endings. Since sharing kisses with Chad, she didn't know if she'd be content with a passionless relationship any more. Damn Chad and his scorching kisses. He'd turned her world upside down.

He looked at the empty pizza box and chuckled. "We made quick work of that pizza." He held up the half-full wine bottle. When she nodded, he refilled her glass.

"I had dinner with Hugo and some important art patrons," she said. "We went to La Piano. They starved me."

Chad rolled his eyes. "I've eaten at that type of place." His features sobered and he set down his wine glass. "You and Hugo tonight. Strictly business?"

She blew out a breath and wondered if Chad was jealous of her and Hugo together. The thought pleased her more than it should. "I've told you before, Hugo is a close friend and a good boss. He's a nice guy—talented, responsible, stable. If he ever settles down, he'll make some woman a good husband."

Chad's gaze locked with hers. "A husband who's stable and responsible? What about passion and love?"

Damn Chad for making her face her deepest conflict. Like pails of paint thrown at a canvas, anger slammed into her. "Passion is overrated. A secure life is better than uncertainty, of not knowing where your next meal is coming from, of not knowing if you'll have a roof over your head." She'd said too much.

Bella tossed back the last of her wine and slammed the glass onto the granite counter. She knew her reactions were that of a spoiled child, but she couldn't help herself. She stalked into the living room and sank onto the sofa. Grabbing one of the decorator pillows, she held it against her stomach, as if it could protect her from the mixture of humiliation and uncertainty that spun through her like a never-ending kaleidoscope.

Chad followed and sat next to her. He gently took away the pillow and grasped her shoulders. "I didn't mean to upset you. I apparently struck a nerve. Talk to me, Bella. Tell me what's bothering you. I want to help."

Scowling, she looked away. "You don't know what I want."

"I think I do know what you want, and it's not Hugo or someone like him. Don't settle for less than you deserve."

Anger, her go-to defense mechanism growing up, flared again and she turned to him with narrowed eyes. "Aren't you settling? You're an educated, smart guy, but you float from job-to-job, with no real stability. Is that what you want from life?" She bit her lip. "I'm sorry. I had no right."

He slid away. "Is that what you think of me?" Hurt tinged his voice.

"No. Yes. I don't know."

His eyes softened. "You're an art expert. You know that sometimes you have to study a painting to get at its nuances and truth. People are the same way. Don't judge others by what you see on the surface."

"I don't mean to be so shallow."

His tender smile tugged at her heart. "You're not shallow. Whenever you want to talk, I'm here." He stood and looked down at her. "Goodnight, Bella."

Then he left, closing the door softly behind him.

She grabbed for the pillow again as a single tear slid down her face. She'd come off as selfish, self-absorbed, and spoiled. She didn't want to be that woman. She no longer knew the real Bella Cassani.

Chad had gone. She'd chased him away, maybe for good. In her mind, she heard the voice of the woman who'd given her the frog snow globe.

Your true love will find you. So it is fated.

CHAPTER TEN

The following Monday, Chad settled back in the chair in Hugo's office, stretching his legs in front of him. It had been a tiring but productive weekend. After leaving Bella's Friday night, he'd been unable to sleep. To keep his mind from images of kissing her, holding her, and much more, he dove into his work. Hugo had hired him to find the person or persons who stole his valuable photos. Chad had to keep his priorities straight. But damn, Bella had become a distraction, one he couldn't fight.

Forcing himself to focus on the job at hand, he tapped the folder he held and faced Hugo. "I've been through your employees' records, over and over until my eyes hurt. I searched the FBI files too."

"Did you find anything that might lead us to who is stealing my photos?"

"Nothing conclusive, but the FBI files unearthed some interesting facts about two of your employees." Chad slapped the folder onto the desk and pulled out some papers. "Did you know Leon Forte served time for theft and assault?"

Eyes wide, Hugo said, "No, I didn't. I had a background check done on him before I hired him. I recently started doing background checks on new hires."

Chad chuckled. "You might want to use another

121

company to do your checks. I found some fascinating information on Daria Younger too. She and Forte are from the same small Colorado town. She worked for an art gallery in Denver before heading east, around the same time as Forte, released from prison, headed east too."

His expression pensive, Hugo picked up a pen from the desk and rolled it between his fingers. "I knew Daria worked at a gallery in Denver and that she hailed from Colorado. The information I had on Forte said he grew up in Ohio."

Chad glanced down at one of the files. "He'd been born in Ohio but his family moved to Colorado when he was still a child."

"What's the plan now?" Hugo asked.

Chad gathered up his papers and stood. "We've got the full resources of the FBI on this. Next step would be to check the bank accounts of all your employees, and we've got people trying to find Forte. My hunch tells me he's the key."

Anger flitted across Hugo's face. "Someone stole almost one million dollars' worth of my prize photos. I want the scum punished."

"Don't worry. The art recovery department of the FBI is the best in the world."

"I'm counting on you, Chad."

Clutching the files, Chad left the office and headed to the small one he used. He wanted to do more searching through Bella's history. Using the FBI's resources, Chad had found that Bella grew up in Texas, in various small towns. Her family moved around a lot. He wouldn't share that information with Hugo unless needed, but Chad had to rule her out as a suspect.

He couldn't believe the woman he'd come to care for could be part of an elaborate scheme to steal the valuable art from Hugo. But then, he'd been fooled before.

◇◇◇

Bella hated Monday mornings, especially after a stressful, sleep-deprived weekend like the one she'd endured. She entered the gallery and waved to Gwen as she made her way to her office. Shutting the door behind her, she threw her purse and briefcase on a chair, set her coffee cup on the desk, and hung up her coat.

Easing into her chair, she closed her eyes. She needed sleep. She needed to quit thinking about Chad. The man invaded her waking thoughts and her dreams. Her body tightened, remembering the erotic dreams she'd had about him.

"Get a grip, Bella. You're a big girl. You can handle your feelings for Chad. It's lust, that's all. It's been a long, long time since you've been with a man."

At the soft knock on her door, her eyes flew open. "Come in."

Hugo stepped in and looked around. "I thought I heard you talking to someone."

"Nope. No one's here, just me." She glanced at the snow globe. The little frog trapped in the glass stared back. *No one here but me and froggie.* God, she'd lost it.

"Are you busy tonight?" Hugo asked.

"No." She just wanted to go home to bed.

"I know this is last minute, but I'm having a dinner party at my place. Twenty people. The Von Tropes are in town and I hope to entice them to show some of their extensive art collection at our gallery. It will bring in new customers for our other exhibits. As my office manager, I think it's important you be there."

"Of course."

123

"Great." He turned to leave, then looked back at her. "Daria is coming with Chad."

He left, closing the door behind him.

Daria and Chad?

Bella threw her pencil at the door.

CHAPTER ELEVEN

The maid opened the door to Hugo's lavishly decorated penthouse in one of New York's most expensive buildings. Smiling at the maid, Bella stepped into the apartment, slipped out of her coat, and handed it to the maid, then took a glass of white wine offered by Hugo's butler.

"Bella, welcome." Hands outstretched, a smiling Hugo strolled toward her.

He cupped her elbow and drew her into the sunken living room. "The Von Trope's brought the Gallagher's with them. I've been trying to get them to underwrite some of our shows. This will be a good night for the Lancashire Gallery. Come meet the others." He led her across the expansive living room.

Bella plastered on her best professional smile to meet the four elderly people who stood in a cluster by the floor-to-ceiling windows that afforded a view of the Manhattan skyline.

A half-hour later, most of the invitees had arrived. Bella counted eighteen, including her, spread around the elegant apartment. The majority of the guests were patrons and benefactors of the arts. She'd been to several of Hugo's dinner parties and knew the table conversation would center on the New York arts scene.

As she sipped her wine and snacked on tasty appetizers,

she kept glancing toward the door. Chad and Daria hadn't made an appearance yet. She dreaded seeing him with Daria, but couldn't help the surge of excitement at knowing Chad would be here. Somehow, he managed to make even the most routine events hum with life and vibrancy.

She glanced at the sunburst clock hanging on the wall. Dinner would be served soon. Still no Chad. He had to know it would be unconscionably rude to be late for dinner. If he didn't, Daria sure did.

As if she'd conjured them up, the maid opened the door, and Chad, with Daria clinging to his arm, were ushered in.

While Daria handed her coat to the maid, Chad glanced around the room. When his gaze met Bella's, he gave her a big smile. The couple moved into the room after taking wine from the butler. After Chad and Hugo shook hands, Chad said something to Daria, then headed toward Bella. Daria's enhanced lips formed a pout and she threw Bella a narrow-eyed look.

"Bella," he said in that smooth whiskey voice of his. "You look great."

"Thanks." When she looked into Chad's deep blue eyes, she forgot to be angry that he'd come with Daria.

"That color suits you. It makes your eyes greener." He scanned her with an appreciative gleam in his eyes.

She knew the tight, knee-skimming dark green dress looked good on her. One of her favorites, it had cost two weeks' pay. She could have worn something simpler tonight, but deep inside, she'd wanted Chad to eat his heart out that he'd been Daria's escort and not hers.

She let her gaze trail over him. Two could play this game. "You look good, Chad."

"Glad you noticed." His smile teased.

And he did look good, with a light stubble on his face, and wearing a dark blue suit with a white shirt worn tieless. A lot of men couldn't handle the hipster look, but on Chad it worked.

When the maid announced dinner, Daria ran to Chad as fast as her stilettos allowed. She threaded her arm through his, giving Bella a triumphant grin.

Hours later, Chad settled into the back of the taxi with Daria. He hated those overblown parties where everyone spent the night trying to impress the other guests. Growing up, he'd had to endure enough boring parties filled with self-absorbed people to last a lifetime.

Daria slid closer, and he moved away until he felt the door at his side. When Hugo had suggested Chad and Daria come together, Daria had jumped at it. Chad would have preferred to go to the party alone, but he needed to cultivate a friendship with Daria and gain her confidence. He felt in his gut she knew something about the thefts.

He'd rather have stayed in tonight, preferably with Bella, curled up on the sofa eating popcorn and watching old movies. He'd even watch a romantic comedy if it meant spending time with Bella.

She'd looked hot tonight in that green dress that hugged her lush curves. He wanted her. Badly.

"Chad?" Daria touched his face, forcing him to look at her. "You're so quiet." She pressed her full, red lips together.

"I'm tired."

"I know ways to make you come alive." She ran her fingers along his lapel.

"I'll bet you do." He suppressed a grimace.

The cab pulled up in front of her apartment building.

"Come in for some coffee?" she purred.

"Sure." He wanted to go back to his hotel, but the job demanded he investigate all possible leads and hunches.

Seated in front of the fire in Daria's modern apartment, obviously decorated by a professional, Chad thought of Bella's warm and homey place. His parents' houses had all been professionally decorated until nothing of the people who lived in them showed.

Bella's apartment reflected her innate charm. He'd delved into her past through his FBI resources and found nothing to hint she might be involved in the million dollar theft. Although he suspected she'd tried to forget her hardscrabble upbringing, he recognized the core of vulnerability in her. That vulnerability, and her sweetness, drew him to her. Among other assets.

He'd been raised with people like the ones he'd met tonight. Not the life he wanted, but he feared Bella yearned for it. He had to convince her she clung to the wrong dream.

"Here's your coffee. Cream only." Daria handed him a steaming mug and sat beside him on the sofa.

He sipped the coffee, tasting the Kahlua she'd slipped in. He'd had enough alcohol tonight. Maybe Daria planned to get him drunk. He put a hand over his mouth to cover his grin.

She snuggled closer. Her perfume, heavy with the scent of musk, stung his nostrils. Bella's light and flowery perfume suited her. Trying to get away from Daria's overpowering perfume, he put a little distance between them.

"Coffee's good," he said. "I didn't want any alcohol in it."

Her smile showed perfect teeth. "You're a big boy. You can handle it." She set her mug down on the coffee table and slithered toward him again. "I'm glad you came to work at the gallery. We don't get many hot guys there. We usually get the nerdy ones, like the last guy who had your job."

"What happened to him?"

Her eyes took on a calculating gleam before she shrugged and glanced away. "Who knows? Who cares?"

"Did you know him well?" Chad sipped coffee and studied her body language. Talking about Leon Forte made her uncomfortable, judging by the way she squirmed and wouldn't meet Chad's eyes.

"I barely knew Leon." She raised her gaze to Chad's and took his mug out of his hand, setting it next to hers. "Let's talk about you. Why's a smokin' guy like you doing grunt work for Hugo? With your looks and smartness, you could do more."

Smartness?

"Any suggestions?" he asked.

She frowned. "I know what Leon made and it wasn't much. The jerk didn't know how to stay out of debt."

"I thought you and he weren't friends."

"We talked sometimes. He liked to gripe about his piddling salary."

Chad looked around her apartment, at the expensive furnishings. "Hugo must pay you a lot."

She snorted. "Not enough to keep me in the style I deserve. I have to find other ways to make money."

He struggled to keep his voice calm. Now they were getting somewhere. "What other ways?"

She shrugged. "I know some people."

"What people?"

Her lips thinned and her features hardened. "Just people."

She'd shut down. When she moved closer until their thighs touched, he knew he needed to leave.

Chad stood. "Thanks for the coffee. Tomorrow's a work day. I'd better go."

"You could stay here."

"I never kiss on the first date." He winked, then made a beeline for the door.

While he waited for a taxi, his mind churned. Daria admitted she needed money to fund her lavish lifestyle. He wished the Agency would hurry with their examination of her bank accounts.

He just might finish this case before Thanksgiving.

Once the case wrapped up, would he see Bella again? He'd make sure he did. The more he got to know Bella, the more he wanted her in his life.

CHAPTER TWELVE

Swiveling in her chair, Bella looked out the window at the brick façade of the building behind the gallery. She'd had a hard time concentrating on work this morning.

Seeing Chad with Daria together at the party last night had affected her more than she would have believed. It shouldn't matter who Chad or Daria dated. Sure, Daria devoured men, then spit them out on a regular basis, but Chad could take care of himself.

As she turned away from the window, her gaze fell on the snow globe. The little frog sat as always atop his rock, wearing his golden crown. He might be the same, but she wasn't. Since the day the elderly woman had handed her the globe, Bella had felt different, as if waiting for something important. The life she'd carefully planned out—marriage to a successful man who would give her the security and stability she craved—no longer appealed.

Chad made her imagine another life, one filled with passion, love, laughter. Memories of her father's philandering intruded on her thoughts and tightened her chest. With her father, it had been all about the conquest of the women he chased. She didn't want to think Chad pursued her and Daria both. Bella wouldn't put up with a man like her father, wouldn't turn aside at her husband's infidelities, like her mother had. The man she married would always remain faithful to his marriage vows.

Guilt nudged her and she glanced back at the snow globe. Maybe she judged Chad too harshly.

Footsteps sounded outside in the hall, pulling her attention. Then Chad stepped into her office, holding a Styrofoam coffee cup. She couldn't stop the leap of joy her heart took when she saw him. He looked delicious, wearing faded jeans, his hair brushing the collar of his white shirt.

"Nice party last night," he said.

"Hugo's parties are always elegant."

Chad took a sip of his drink. "Hugo's got the money and the taste to pull it off." He strolled closer to her desk. "I prefer casual evenings watching TV and eating popcorn, with a gorgeous woman next to me."

His eyes darkened, and his gaze rested on her mouth.

"I can't picture Daria being happy sitting at home."

"Who said anything about Daria?"

"You were with her last night."

"A work thing. I would rather have been with you." With a wicked grin, he asked, "Jealous?"

Propelled by bad memories and anger at the jealousy she didn't want to admit, Bella stood. "I know all about guys like you, too good-looking to ever stay loyal to one woman. If you think you can play me and Daria, forget it. Those kinds of games aren't for me."

He flinched as if struck. "Whoa! Where'd that come from?"

Embarrassment coiled a knot in her stomach and heated her face. Bella sank slowly back onto her chair. "Forget it. I spoke out of line."

Chad set his cup on her desk and strode to the door. Closing it, he turned to her. "Let's talk. What's really going on?"

She slid her laptop closer. "Nothing's going on. Lots of work and stress."

In two strides, he'd rounded her desk and grasped her shoulders, gently pulling her up to face him. The smoldering intensity of his eyes held her, but the tenderness she glimpsed in their blue depths melted her resistance.

"Good-looking men like you can't be trusted." The words slipped out.

He slid his palms down her arms to hold both her hands. "Who hurt you?"

His words, spoken softly, tempted her to let go, to share her pain. She opened her mouth and closed it again. She couldn't. "No one hurt me."

"It's okay, sweetheart." Chad released her hands and pulled her against his chest. The steady beating of his heart soothed her.

He rubbed a hand up and down her back. For just a minute she'd allow herself to enjoy the comfort and security of his arms.

"Someday you'll trust me enough to tell me what's going on inside that beautiful head," he whispered. "Until then, remember I'm here for you."

Voices out in the hall made Bella pull free and jump back. Holding up her hands, she said, "I appreciate your concern, but we're at work. We can't do this. I barely know you."

"True, we haven't known each other long, and I'll take it slow if that's what you want. There's nothing between Daria and me. It's only you I'm interested in. Will you believe me?"

The sincerity in his voice burned away a little of her

fear. "I'll try."

"That's all I ask." A teasing glint came into his eyes. "Would it help if I made myself ugly? I could turn into a frog like that one in the snow globe."

She couldn't help laughing. "A prince into a frog."

"Whatever it takes."

She wanted to trust Chad, but she'd be cautious. Trust didn't come easy for her.

"I do need to get to work," she said.

"We're good now?"

"We're good."

After Chad left, Bella sat at her desk for long minutes, her mind whirling about the way Chad had torn apart everything she'd thought she wanted. It scared the crap out of her. She reached over and picked up the snow globe.

The frog stared back at her. "Okay, little froggie, should I trust Chad? Is he a prince, or is he a frog?"

The frog prince said nothing.

CHAPTER THIRTEEN

"You've been awfully busy the last few days. Anything going on?" An expectant look on her face, Daria waited for Chad to answer.

The tightness in Daria's voice set off alarms in Chad's head, and he wondered if she fished for information. They were having dinner at a small restaurant around the corner from the gallery. She'd suggested the dinner, and while he would rather have refused, he had a job to do.

He set down his wine glass and smiled. "The guy who had the job before me messed up big time. It's harder to fix mistakes than start over."

"That jerk Leon." Seeming unconcerned, she cut into her filet mignon.

Maybe he'd imagined tension in her voice a minute ago. As he enjoyed his steak, he studied her. Her perfectly highlighted blonde hair, her designer clothes and shoes screamed expensive, as did her ultra-chic apartment. Hugo paid her well, but not that well.

"You look good," he said, nodding toward her. "Nice clothes."

"Thanks." With a cunning light in her eyes, she set down her fork and focused her gaze on him like a laser. "You seem like a guy who appreciates the finer things in life. I know a man in Colorado who is always on the lookout for

135

good art. I send things his way when I find them." She grinned. "All honest, of course."

Chad frowned. "As Hugo's employee, shouldn't you give him first dibs on the art?"

Daria shrugged. "Hugo's got enough money. A girl's got to take care of herself." She pressed her palms on the white tablecloth. "You've been around the art world. Maybe you can get your hands on some stuff to send my guy in Colorado. He pays well."

"I have some contacts," Chad said slowly. "I might be able to get my hands on things he'd like."

"Perfect. You and I will make a good team."

He saluted her with his wine glass.

Later, Chad called his boss at the FBI and relayed the info he'd learned from Daria. Chad suspected the guy she used to work for now worked with her to steal from Hugo, and maybe others. Not very original of them. He'd run into these kinds of thieves many times in his work.

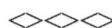

Saturday, exhausted, but with a sense of accomplishment, Bella held onto her mug of hot tea as she sank into the sofa in her living room. She sipped the tea, enjoying the sweetness of the mint. Setting down her cup, she glanced around her apartment. It felt as clean as it looked. Her only day off until next weekend, a long one for Thanksgiving, she'd spent today cleaning. Tomorrow, she would accompany Hugo to a gallery opening in the Village. She had a busy week scheduled at the gallery too.

As she reached for her tea, the cordless phone rang. When she saw the ID, she winced.

"Hello, Mom," she said as she answered.

"Why haven't you called?" her mom asked in the whiny

voice she'd perfected.

No "hello, how are you?" So like her mother.

"I called you a week ago, Mom. You know how busy I am."

"Always too busy for your mother."

Guilt and anxiety churned through Bella like clashing shades of paint. Talking to her mother always brought her down. Another round of guilt hit her for thinking that.

"Are you okay, Mom? Do you need anything?"

"I don't have enough for the rent this month. Can you lend me five hundred dollars?"

"I'll deposit the money into your account," Bella said on a sigh. "You don't have to pay it back." Calls from her mother asking for money were routine.

"Your father and that little bitch just had another baby," her mother spat out.

"Mom, it's been years since he left. Let it go. Make a life for yourself. You're an attractive woman. Surely, there are decent guys out there. Forget Dad. Move on."

"Move on," her mother shouted. "After what he did to me?"

Knowing the futility of arguing with her mother, Bella settled back in her chair and prepared for the rants.

When her mother took a breath from her tirade, the usual litany of her father's shortcomings, Bella said, "Mom, I've asked you before to move closer. Maybe to one of the boroughs. With your waitressing experience, you should have no trouble getting work."

"Texas is my home. I'll never leave."

Not so long as Dad is nearby.

Fifteen minutes later, her mother finally ended the call. Bella threw the phone onto the coffee table and grabbed her mug of tea, taking a sip. Cold. Her stomach roiled. She shouldn't let her mother affect her like that, but she couldn't seem to help it.

She rested her head on the back of the sofa and closed her eyes. Chad's image came to her, reassuring but disturbing. He'd gotten to her. His extraordinary looks made her wary of trusting him. She'd believed for so long that handsome men couldn't remain loyal to one woman. She'd had that lesson pumped into her by her mother from an early age. Maybe she needed to change that mantra, maybe she needed to allow that all men weren't created equal, and some men, maybe men like Chad, could behave with integrity and loyalty.

Anxiety had been keeping her from getting close enough to Chad to give him the chance to break her heart. She wouldn't be like her mother, pining after a man who couldn't stop his wandering eye along with other wandering body parts. But if Chad didn't wander...

Standing up, she grabbed her cup of cold tea and headed into the kitchen to boil more water. She couldn't shake the uncertainty that wound through her. Her instincts told her Chad Prince had a decent core, that she'd unfairly brushed him with the broad stroke she used for all good-looking men.

CHAPTER FOURTEEN

The following Wednesday afternoon, the tomb-like quiet of the empty gallery grated on Bella's nerves. With Thanksgiving tomorrow, most people had last-minute chores to complete or had started the holiday early. It had been a productive three days for Bella. She'd contracted with the agent of an up-and-coming artist to show the artist's work and made contact with the agent of another artist getting a lot of buzz on the art circuit.

Restless, she left her office to stroll out to the main gallery to talk to Gwen. "Slow today, huh?" she said when she reached Gwen's desk.

"It always is right before Thanksgiving. Same as Christmas Eve. My invitation to dinner tomorrow stands. We always have room for one more."

"I appreciate the invitation, Gwen. You have a wonderful family. Enjoy them. I don't mind being alone."

Gwen nodded toward the door. "You don't have to be alone."

Bella followed her gaze to see Chad striding into the gallery. The sight of him made her pulse ratchet up a few notches.

"I asked Chad if he had plans for tomorrow," Gwen said. "He told me no, but he turned down my invitation too. I bet he wouldn't turn down yours."

Bella gave Gwen what she hoped was a withering stare. "Stop playing matchmaker."

Gwen shrugged. "Just sayin'. You'd better get him before Daria does."

Smiling, Chad walked up to them. "How are the two most beautiful women in the gallery?"

"You're full of it," Gwen said with a laugh. "But keep the compliments coming."

Chad put a hand over his heart. "You wound me, Gwen. I don't throw out empty compliments."

Gwen snorted. "Right!"

Chad turned to Bella. "Got plans for tomorrow? If not, maybe we can find a restaurant that's open and have dinner together. Holidays are no time to be alone."

"I don't mind being alone on a holiday. I love to cook and I plan to cook a Thanksgiving meal for myself." She felt Gwen's stare boring into her. "Would you like to come to my place for dinner?" Bella heard herself ask.

"I'd like that. Thanks. I'll bring the wine."

Fighting the excitement and uncertainty that made her insides tremble, Bella said, "Okay. Two o'clock?"

He frowned. "I know my way around a kitchen. How about I come at noon and help you, then we can watch some football."

"Noon it is."

"Great! I need to see Hugo about something now. See you tomorrow at noon." With nods to her and Gwen, he marched away.

"Way to go, Bella." Gwen held up her fist. "Fist bump."

"Seriously?" Shaking her head, Bella bumped fists with Gwen. "I don't know why I let you talk me into that."

"Me? I remained silent. You invited him. Admit you

wanted to."

"I admit nothing. I'm going to close out for the day. Have a great Thanksgiving. I'll see you Monday."

Bella smiled as she headed back to her office. She'd be with Chad all day tomorrow. Her smile faded as the full force of what she'd done hit her. All day alone with Chad. Anxiety kicked up the butterflies in her stomach.

CHAPTER FIFTEEN

Humming, Bella set the dining room table. The savory scent of the turkey roasting took her back in time to the few Thanksgivings when her family seemed happy, when her parents smiled and her father acted glad to be home. She shook off the melancholy. Today she would focus on the here and now. Music and sounds from the Macy's Thanksgiving parade played on the TV. Almost noon. Chad would be here soon. Damn her pulse. It jumped every time she thought of spending the day with him.

Rubbing her hands together, she surveyed the table with a critical eye. Growing up, Thanksgiving meals were usually overcooked turkey, boxed stuffing, sweet potatoes with marshmallows, and frozen boxed vegetables. Her mother had no matching dishes or silverware, and their tablecloths were plastic. None of that had mattered the few times they'd sat down together as a family and enjoyed each other's company.

Since her college days, Bella read all she could on the art of entertaining. She knew the proper way to set a table, and with her generous salary, she'd been able to buy good china, silverware, and glassware. She'd bought her tablecloth, white linen, hand-embroidered with Brussels lace edging, at a high-end antiques store. She straightened one of the knives and rearranged the wine glasses. Satisfied with the placement, she stepped back.

A twinge of guilt hit her when she thought of her mother alone today in her small mobile home. If her mother weren't so hell bent on staying close to Bella's father and harassing him every chance she got, she could be here now enjoying the holiday with her only child. Bella put a hand over her mouth as if she could somehow stop her unkind thoughts.

The doorbell rang. "Settle down," she muttered to her skyrocketing pulse as she strode to the callbox. "Yes?" she said into the speaker. It had to be Chad, yet she knew to be careful.

"It's Chad."

"Come in." Bella pressed the button to unlock the main door, then opened the door to her apartment and waited for him.

He sauntered toward her hefting two overflowing grocery bags. A large bouquet of fall blooms peeked from the top of one. "Happy Thanksgiving," he said when he reached her. To her surprise, he bent and kissed her on the cheek.

Happiness flowed through Bella as she took the bag with the flowers and stepped into her apartment, Chad close behind. "What's in these, besides the beautiful flowers?"

"Lots of good stuff," he said.

He followed Bella to the kitchen where they deposited the bags onto the counter. Reaching into one, he lifted out two bottles of red wine. "Libations for milady."

Laughing, she took the bottles and set them down. "Thank you, kind sir."

While he emptied the bags and spread the contents onto the center island, Bella pulled a crystal vase from a cabinet, filled it halfway with water, and arranged the bouquet in the vase. She set the flowers on the dining table and went back into the kitchen.

"Thanks for the flowers. They're beautiful."

With a frown, she studied the items Chad had brought— sweet potatoes, marshmallows, and a large bag of frozen green beans, along with the other ingredients for green bean casserole.

She picked up the bag of marshmallows. "What's all this? Please don't tell me you're going to make sweet potatoes with marshmallows."

He grinned and pushed up the sleeves to his navy blue sweater, exposing muscular arms sprinkled with fine dark hairs.

Crap. Why did he have to look so good? Did the man never have a bad day?

"Sure am going to make sweet potatoes with marshmallows," he said. "And green bean casserole. They're my favorites. It's not Thanksgiving without them."

"That's so clichéd."

"That's why I like them. Very classic Thanksgiving fare. Reminds me of the childhood I wish I'd had."

With a wry smile, she said, "Reminds me of the childhood I wish I hadn't had."

He studied her. "There's a story in there somewhere. Maybe you'll tell me later."

No way.

"I have things I planned to make," she said.

"I figured you would want to cook gourmet stuff, but it's Thanksgiving and we have to go traditional. It's the law."

Shaking her head, she grabbed two wine glasses from the cupboard and pulled out the bottle of white wine from the refrigerator. When she'd filled the glasses, she handed him one and pressed her hip against the counter while she sipped her drink. "I didn't take you for a traditionalist."

He shrugged. "My family's Thanksgiving dinners were events rather than family affairs. I've learned a new appreciation of all things traditional."

"Where did you grow up?"

A mask seemed to come over his features and he stilled. "Florida."

Bella frowned. Chad had his secrets too.

As he sipped some wine, the closed look disappeared from his face. Setting down his glass, he grabbed a baker's box and handed it to her. "Cannoli. They need to be refrigerated. Let's prepare this stuff now so all we have to do later is put it in the oven. Then we can relax and watch the game."

"The parade's over," she said glancing at the TV.

"Turn on the radio. We'll listen to Christmas music while we work."

"Seriously? Christmas music?"

"Sure. They're playing it on some stations now. Don't tell me you don't like Christmas songs, too. I'll have to teach you to respect the traditional." He moved closer and skimmed a finger along her bottom lip. "I'd like to teach you a lot of things."

"Back off, mister. We're here to cook." Chuckling, she stepped away. Despite the lighthearted banter between them, his words provoked excitement in her.

Chad laughed. "Christmas music and we cook. Agreed?"

"Agreed."

They worked side-by-side while classic Christmas tunes wafted through the room. Bella enjoyed cooking, but with

Chad next to her, the routine tasks took on a new exhilaration that made her want to sing along with the radio. Since the day she left Texas for college on the East Coast, thanks to a full scholarship, she'd tried to reshape herself into a sophisticated woman of the world, shaking the dirt of small-town Texas from her shoes. *You can take the girl out of Texas, but you can't take Texas out of the girl.* The refrain, which she tried to ignore, ran through her head often.

Now, preparing the "traditional" foods with Chad, nostalgia gripped her with the force of a Texas wind storm. Much as she'd tried to forget her past, she missed her mother, even missed the terrible Thanksgiving food her mother had served. Tears burned Bella's eyes.

Hours later, filled with food and contentment, Chad pushed his chair back from the table where the remnants of their meal were spread out. "Best Thanksgiving meal I've ever had." He patted his stomach. Having grown up eating the elaborate dinners his parents' cook prepared, he relished simple foods now.

Bella's large hazel eyes gleamed and she smiled. He'd never seen her so relaxed. He hoped he had something to do with that.

"You cooked most of the meal," she said.

He lifted his wine glass in salute. "We did it together. We make a good team."

Her face pinked. Gorgeous, sweet, and smart. His determination to protect his heart, his fear of falling in love again, dissipated with each minute he spent with Bella. He wanted her. In every way.

"We should clean up," she said. "Then have dessert."

When she started to stand, he waved her back down.

"Sit. We've got plenty of time. We'll do the dishes together so it won't take so long." He lifted the bottle of wine. "There's enough here for two more glasses. Hand yours over."

Their glasses full again, he settled back into his chair. "Where in Texas are you from?" He knew, but some perverse part of him needed her to tell him, to show she trusted him enough to confide in him.

"I told you I'm from upstate New York."

"I hear a little bit of Texas in your voice."

She stilled and he feared she wouldn't answer. When her features relaxed, he knew he'd won.

"You guessed my secret," she said. "I grew up in different small Texas towns."

Elation made him smile. *Yes!* He'd breached the shell she'd erected around herself. She trusted him, if only a little. A start. "Parents still living?"

"Both. My dad has a new family." Bella ran a finger over the rim of her glass. He'd heard the hurt in her voice.

"Your mom?" he asked.

"She's a waitress at a small café. She doesn't have much of a life."

"I'm sorry for her."

"I am too." Bella locked gazes with him. "Let's not talk about my family. Tell me about yours."

His turn to be evasive. Because of his undercover work, he didn't reveal much about his family to anyone. He'd also tried to distance himself from his parents, people to whom money and social standing meant everything. He would give Bella the watered-down version of his life, the one he almost believed.

"Raised in southern Florida," he said. "My parents own

147

a business." *A small lie.*

"Siblings?" Bella asked.

"Brother and sister. I don't see my family much." He'd been *persona non grata* since he chose the Agency over the family business. He didn't share that with anyone. He told himself he didn't care what his family thought of his life choice, but truth be told, it hurt. The last few years, his sister had reached out to him and invited him home for the holidays, but, motivated by pride, stubbornness, and hurt, he always refused.

Chad finished his wine and stood, stretching his arms above his head. "Time to clean up." Keeping busy would get his mind off his family.

Bella frowned and he got the impression she wasn't satisfied with his description of his upbringing. Then she stood too. "The sooner we clean up, the sooner we can get to the dessert."

"Now you're talking."

Thirty minutes later, the kitchen sparkled, the dishwasher hummed, and Bella and Chad sat in the living room with mugs of steaming coffee and a selection of cannoli in front of them on the coffee table. Like sweet, warm chocolate, satisfaction flowed through Bella. The day had been perfect, and it hadn't ended yet. She sighed.

"What should we watch?" Chad asked.

I want to watch you, Bella wanted to say. Her hungry gaze devoured him. Faded jeans hugged his long legs, and his dark blue sweater stretched across his broad chest. His tousled hair made him look younger, and somehow vulnerable. He'd held something back when he talked about his family earlier and she wondered what. She'd seen a glimmer of hurt in his eyes too when he said he didn't see much of his family. She wanted to know everything about Chad Prince, even the mundane, ordinary things. Desiring his closeness and his heat, she slid toward him.

He turned to her with darkened blue eyes. "What do you want to watch?" he asked again, his voice thick.

"Let's channel surf. You pick." Bathed in the afterglow of a good meal and Chad's exhilarating company, Bella didn't care if he wanted to watch monster trucks cutting through icy roads.

"Channel surfing it is." As he went through the stations, she sipped her coffee and nibbled on a chocolate cannoli.

"Perfect," he said after a few minutes.

"What?" She looked at the screen. "*Miracle on 34th Street*? I haven't seen that in years."

"Any objection to watching it, or is it too *traditional* for you?" His eyes and voice teased.

"You've had me doing *traditional* stuff all day. Why stop now?"

In companionable silence, they watched the movie while they drank their coffee and ate the luscious desserts. Despite the excitement Chad brought to her life, a part of her relaxed in a way she hadn't for a very long time. She felt safe with him. Secure. The thought froze her with her mug partway to her mouth. Safe and secure with Chad? He wasn't a stable kind of guy, not with his constant job changes. He'd told her he rented a small apartment on the West Side, with a month-to-month lease. Not the kind of place to set down roots. Yet, Chad possessed something reassuring, something that made her trust him.

Almost as if he could read her thoughts, he turned to her. "You okay?"

"Sure." She finished her coffee and set the empty mug down.

"You remind me of the Maureen O'Hara character in this movie," he said.

"I do?"

He nodded. "You're very no-nonsense. I suspect you don't believe in anything you can't see, including love."

He'd figured that out too. "I believe in love, for others. Just not me."

Chad cupped her shoulders and drew her closer. His warm breath, sweet with the scent of chocolate, fanned her face. "Why not for you?"

"I don't need it."

"Everyone needs love." His deep blue gaze studied her. "Do I frighten you, Isabella Cassani?"

"Of course not." She pulled away and put distance between them.

"You're a terrible liar," he said softly. "You know how attracted I am to you, but you're afraid."

She glanced away, not wanting to look into his knowing eyes.

He touched her chin until she faced him again. "Tell me who hurt you, sweetheart. Let me help."

She stared at him for long minutes. The understanding in his eyes and the tenderness in his voice pulled the words from her, almost as if a gentle hand rested on her shoulder, urging her on. "My father has always been movie-star handsome," she said. "Women were constantly all over him. They didn't care about his marital status. He rarely turned any of them down. He never held a job for long, and my mother and I followed him around Texas as he went from one job to another."

The caring on Chad's face reached out to her heart, folding her into a cocoon of warmth. She swallowed around the lump in her throat and continued. "My mother knew about my father's infidelities but she turned a blind eye. She told me when a woman loves a man as passionately as she loved my father, she stands by that man regardless of how he treats her. She said his other women meant nothing. I never believed any of it. She also said my dad might take lovers but he always came back to her."

Bella released a bitter laugh. "Until he didn't. When I was seventeen, he got some young woman, only a few years older than me, pregnant. He told Mom he'd never loved anyone the way he loved this woman. Then he was gone from our lives. I loved him." Bella fought tears. Damn, she hated to cry.

Chad cradled her face between his large hands. "Sweetheart, because your father couldn't be faithful, it doesn't mean all handsome men are like that."

She touched Chad's arm, wanting to feel his smooth, hot flesh, then pulled back. Clasping her hands on her lap, she looked down. "You're right about me. I am afraid of you and what you make me feel. I had no stability growing up. I want, no need, security in my life. There's no room for love or passion. They weaken a person." She met his gaze again. "I'm not weak."

He took both her hands between his and held them firmly. "I get why you feel that way. You're not your mother and I'm not your father. If you trade love and passion for security, how long before you're dead inside, before you realize your mistake? Trust your feelings. Take a chance on me. On us. Let's see where this goes." His tender gaze held her. "I've been hurt in the past, yet I'm willing to trust again.

That's how much you're coming to mean to me."

She wanted to ask who had hurt him, but now wasn't the time. "I don't know, Chad. I had my life all planned out, then you came along. I can't love you."

He caressed her cheek with his thumb. "Bella, what am I going to do with you?"

With a low moan, his mouth descended on hers. His lips were soft, cautious at first. He pressed harder, tempting her to give in to her desires, to forget her plans and let him take her where she wanted to go. Unable and unwilling to resist what he offered, Bella deepened the kiss, opening to him. A slow ache began to build in her, a yearning to break free of the constraints she'd put on herself, to let wildness consume her.

Their tongues danced and mated. Pierced by longing and need, she uttered small cries. They slid down onto the sofa together. His large body covered hers. His lips, his tongue, and his hands explored, inflaming her. She wrapped her arms around his neck, emboldened to demand more.

When he slipped his hand under her sweater, she bucked, arching her hips against his hard erection. She filled her lungs with the masculine scent of him. She needed no other dessert, only Chad.

He left her mouth to trail kisses down her throat to her collarbone. Bella rolled back her head, giving herself completely. On fire, she couldn't think, could only feel. Her body craved him, her soul needed him.

He massaged one of her breasts, eliciting low moans from her. He lifted her sweater, exposing her silk-clad breasts to his passion-filled eyes. Then he stopped abruptly and sat up, a tortured look on his face. She slipped her sweater down and scrambled up.

"What is it?" she asked, her voice unsteady.

Gripping her shoulders, he pulled her closer. "I want you. Badly. Please believe that. But I can't. Not now. Not yet."

Embarrassment punched her in the gut. "I understand."

He gently shook her. "No, you don't, and I can't explain. But I will. Later. Forgive me, Bella."

"There's nothing to forgive." Pride made her stand, putting distance between them.

He stood too. "I think I'd better go."

"You should."

When he bent to kiss her, she stepped away. "You're not married, are you?" She flattened her palm on her trembling stomach.

He jerked back. "Of course not. Do you have that low an opinion of me?"

She shook her head. "No, but I had to ask."

His eyes softened. "See you at work Monday. Thanks for dinner."

Like a thief who'd stolen her heart, Chad strode out of her apartment. Maybe out of her life.

Bella sank against the closed door. The room felt cold without Chad. He could be playing her. But why would he when she'd offered everything she had?

Chad may have stolen her heart, but damn if she'd allow him to break it.

CHAPTER SIXTEEN

The following Monday after the long holiday weekend, Bella's throat felt scratchy and her eyes burned. Lack of sleep left her tired and irritable. Thanksgiving night, she'd been ready to throw away all caution and make love with Chad. Good thing he'd stopped because she wouldn't have been able to.

Clutching her cup of vanilla latte, she shouldered through the crowded Manhattan sidewalks heading for work. Chad hadn't called all weekend. She hoped he wasn't playing a game—get a reluctant woman all hot and bothered, then walk away. Leave her wanting more and she'd come begging. One of her father's young girlfriends had shown up at their house once and told Bella how her father had manipulated her in the same way until she'd agreed to an affair with him.

Bella's instincts told her Chad wasn't a player like her father. If he were, he would have called by now, ready to go in for the conquest. The thought consoled her more than it should have.

As she approached the gallery, a shiver ran over her. Police cars lined up along the curb, and uniformed patrolmen swarmed out front. Heart thumping, she pushed open the glass doors. A cop held out a hand stopping her.

"Gallery is closed, Miss," he said.

"I work here. What's going on?"

"The other employees are in the break room." He nodded toward another cop. "He'll take you there."

Frowning, her heart rate still accelerated, Bella followed him. She stopped, staring, as cops led a handcuffed Daria out. Chad, dressed in a suit and tie, walked behind them. Hugo, his face stricken, brought up the rear.

Chad glanced at her. He nodded but kept walking.

When Bella got to the break room, she found the other employees huddled together by the window. Gwen ran over when she saw Bella.

"What's going on?" Bella asked.

Gwen grabbed her arm and led her to an empty table. "You won't believe what happened."

Bella set her purse and briefcase on the floor and plunked her coffee onto the table. "I saw them lead Daria out in handcuffs."

Gwen's eyes were wide behind her tiger-striped frames. "She stole almost one million dollars' worth of Hugo's best photos. She and Leon were working together. They sold the photos to a gallery owner in Colorado. The federal authorities picked up Leon over the weekend and he sang like a canary."

"Oh. My. God." Feeling overheated, Bella unbuttoned her jacket and slipped it off. "I noticed some photos missing, but I never, I just never…" She let her voice trail off.

"Can you believe Daria could be smart enough to pull off something like this?"

"Wow! Just wow!" Bella swallowed a big gulp of coffee. Her heart rate had slowed to some semblance of normality. "Why did Chad leave with Daria and the cops? Was he involved?" It couldn't be. Her trust in him couldn't have been that misplaced.

Gwen rested her arms on the table, a glint in her eyes. "Here's the best part. Chad is FBI, assigned to an art recovery unit. He's been investigating the thefts." Grinning like the proverbial Cheshire cat, Gwen settled into her chair.

"Chad? FBI?" Anger punched Bella in the pit of her stomach. "All this time, he let me believe he was something else. The rat."

"You can't be serious," Gwen said. "The man had an undercover job. Get a grip."

Bella sipped coffee, fighting to control her emotions. "You're right. It's just—"

"You fell for him," Gwen interrupted. "And now you wonder if he amused himself with you while on assignment."

"How did you know that?"

Gwen shrugged. "Classic romance trope."

"For God's sake, Gwen. This isn't a romance novel."

"Hey, don't shoot the messenger."

"I'm sorry. What happens now? With Daria, I mean."

"Chad said for us to stay here and they'd let us know when things settle down. I doubt Hugo will open the gallery today so we'll probably all go home."

Anger and regret knotted a tight ball in Bella's chest. Romance novels had happy endings. If Chad had amused himself at her expense, she wouldn't have her happy ending. The thought struck her like a blow to the face. Deep down, she wanted a happily-ever-after. And she wanted it with Chad.

She wondered if she'd ever see him again.

The little frog inside the snow globe stared at Bella. She grabbed it from the kitchen counter and strode into the living room to set it on the coffee table. Heading back to the kitchen, she made up her mind to throw away the silly thing. That frog and the eccentric woman's words were responsible for making her go off-track, for making her believe things that could never be. She didn't know what had prompted her take the globe home from the office. When the police told the employees they could leave because the gallery wouldn't open that day, she'd had a strange and overwhelming compulsion to take the damn frog home with her. She could swear the thing mocked her about her not-so-happy ending with Chad.

She'd been home for hours but had been too wound up to do more than pace from room to room, with the living room TV turned to a local news station. When the front of Hugo's gallery came on the screen, Bella stopped pacing to watch. The camera captured a defiant-looking Daria herded out in handcuffs, surrounded by several men in suits that Bella assumed were FBI, Chad included, behind her. Then came Hugo, his expression shocked. Bella's heart tugged at his dismay. He didn't deserve this.

She grabbed the remote and turned off the TV, then threw the remote onto the sofa. The familiar ache of betrayal twisted in her stomach. Chad! She'd been right. He'd kept his true identity from her. "But he couldn't tell you the truth, Bella," she said, needing the reassurance of her own voice.

She couldn't shake the worry she'd been no more than a pleasant diversion. "Stop it right now. Quit obsessing. If he used you, why didn't he take you to bed Thursday night? You were sure ready and willing." She carried on a conversation with herself, the first clue she'd lost her mind.

Her stomach rumbled, reminding her she hadn't eaten since breakfast, and it was now two in the afternoon. "For

God's sake, eat something." She had to quit talking to herself.

Determined to stop thinking about Chad, she stomped back into the kitchen, opened the refrigerator, and pulled out the ingredients for a sandwich using leftover turkey, stuffing, and cranberry sauce. She turned on the radio. Christmas songs filled the room. She quickly switched to a station playing rock tunes. The traditional Christmas songs reminded her of making Thanksgiving dinner here with Chad, and of the happiness and sense of belonging she'd felt with him.

The sound of her doorbell stopped her in the process of spreading mayo on the sourdough bread. Her heart thumped. She wiped her hands on a towel and turned off the radio, then went to the call box. "Yes?" she said into the speaker.

"Bella, I need to see you. May I come in?"

At the sound of Chad's voice, her heartbeat drummed harder. She pressed the button that would open the outside door. His footsteps sounded along the tiled hallway, then a knock at her door.

She opened to a tired-looking Chad. Chewing her lip to keep from flinging herself into his arms, she stepped aside to let him in. They stared at each other. "Do you want a turkey sandwich?" she blurted. "And something to drink?"

He scrubbed a hand over his face. "That would be great."

As she prepared the sandwiches, Chad sat at the center island, nursing a glass of iced tea, and watched her. "It's been a hell of a weekend," he said. "I've had very little sleep. It took a lot of work to coordinate the arrests."

"You should have gone back to your place to rest, wherever your place is." She winced at the edge of bitterness in her voice.

"Hugo put me up at a hotel in midtown. I live in Connecticut, but I'm seldom there."

"I see." She concentrated on the sandwiches, but couldn't stop the bud of anger that popped inside her. Something else Chad had lied about.

"I needed to see you," he said quietly. "We have to talk."

"After we eat." Her appetite seemed to have disappeared with Chad's appearance, but she wanted to delay whatever bad news he had to tell her.

They ate in silence with only the ticking wall clock for company. Bella surprised herself by finishing all of her large sandwich.

"I needed that." Chad pushed away his empty plate and swigged the last of his tea.

"More tea?" she asked. Bella's mother may have had her faults, but she'd trained Bella to be polite.

"No, thanks. We've put this off long enough. Let's go into the living room."

He pushed back his stool and stood, holding his hand out to her. Ignoring his hand, she stood and headed to the living room, trying to disregard the hurt that flashed in his eyes at her snub.

"I'm still shocked about Daria," Bella said when they were seated on opposite ends of the sofa. She placed her hand on one of the pillows, prepared to throw it at him if he admitted he'd used her, or worse, was married.

He shook his head. "I wasn't surprised. Sadly, I've seen it all. You'd be amazed what people will do for money."

"What happens now, to Daria and her co-conspirators?"

"They'll be charged and bail set, probably a high one considering the value of what they stole. The FBI will offer the Colorado gallery owner a plea deal in exchange for information as to who bought Hugo's photos. Hugo's understandably upset, but hopefully he'll recover all he's lost."

"I hope so. Hugo is a good friend."

"I've known him a long time. He's a decent guy." Chad smiled. "When I first started this assignment, I thought there might have been something between you two."

"We've always been just friends." At one time, she'd wanted more than friendship with her boss, but Chad changed all that. She wouldn't admit to him that he'd made her realize she couldn't settle for less than a full, loving and passionate relationship with a man.

Drawing a breath, she asked, "How did you come to suspect Daria?"

"We investigated everyone who worked at the gallery."

Bella widened her eyes. "Even me?"

"We had to. You can understand that. By process of elimination and good detective work, we narrowed it to Daria and Leon. The FBI's been looking for Leon since we took this case. Finding him this weekend gave us the break we needed."

Chad's gaze captured hers. "I can't discuss details with you because of legalities. But I don't want to talk about the case. I want to talk about us."

Bella clasped her hands tightly on her lap. "Is there an *us*?"

"I hope so."

"I get you were working undercover, but a part of me feels betrayed. I can't help wondering if you used me as a nice distraction."

He winced. "No, Bella, never. My feelings for you are

real."

What feelings? She wanted to ask, but she had to know something else first. "You asked me about my background, but you already knew, didn't you? You investigated me."

"I'm not proud I grilled you on what I already knew, but I figured if you told me the truth, it would mean you trusted me. I may be selfish, but I needed your trust." His gaze softened. "Please forgive me."

With his words, some of her hurt filtered away, but she wouldn't let him off the hook yet. "Why did you suddenly walk out on me Thanksgiving night?"

"I wanted you. More than I've ever wanted anyone. Guilt that I couldn't be honest with you yet forced me to leave."

"What else have you kept from me? Is Chad even your name?"

He slid closer. "Chad Prince is my real name. I hated lying to you and giving you half-truths, but it was necessary."

He took her hands in his. "I was hurt once before, on an assignment in Philadelphia eighteen months ago. A woman involved with the crime played me. I fell for her and lost sight of the mission. Damn near lost my job. I didn't plan to fall in love again, especially with a woman I met while on a case." His lips tilted in a gentle smile. "But there you were, my Mad Witch of Manhattan. I've been under your spell ever since."

"Love?" she whispered, scarcely able to breathe.

"I've fallen in love with you. You're smart and talented. As much as you try to hide it, you're sweet and loving too. You've still got a little of small town Texas in you, and that makes you all the more loveable. And adorable."

Bella lowered her head, trying to digest all he'd said. She'd fooled most everyone with her veneer of sophistication. Deep down, she'd always felt like a fake, had always been ashamed of her background. None of that seemed to matter to Chad.

He released her hands and skimmed a finger along her jaw line until she met his gaze. "Bella, is there a chance for me? I can't imagine a life without you in it."

Tears clogged her throat. "I'm having a hard time with this. It's too much to take in."

"From that first kiss on Halloween, I knew you were special. I would never hurt you. I won't give up on you unless you tell me you have no feelings for me."

She couldn't speak, couldn't say the words that would send him away, not when she'd fallen in love with him too.

He pulled her toward him. His mouth claimed hers in a deep, drugging kiss that told her the truth of his words. Old fears made her hold herself rigid at first, but every cell in her body wanted him, wanted his love. She pressed against him, tunneling her hands through the thickness of his hair, and deepened the kiss, pouring out her love, never wanting to let him go.

His breathing labored, he ended the kiss and stared down at her with an expression of wonder. "Love isn't neat and packaged. Sometimes it just happens. Could you learn—?"

She put her finger over his lips, stopping him. "I do love you, Chad."

The brightness of his smile touched her all the way to her heart.

He gathered her to him and held her tenderly. Stroking her hair, he said, "My Bella."

Finally, he pulled away, but still held onto her hands. "I know how much stability means to you, that you wanted someone like Hugo. I'm not like him. I'm as stable as I can be with a job that takes me all over the world. I don't want to lose you. We'll make it work."

Bella glanced over at the snow globe sitting on the coffee table. Turning back to Chad, she said, "Someone knew what I wanted more than I did."

Your true love will find you. So it is fated, the eccentric old woman had said. Chad had found her. Bella sure hadn't expected to love a man with the consuming passion she felt for Chad.

He frowned and raked fingers through his hair, messing it up in a way that made him look younger and boyish. Bella's heart swelled with love for this man who, although not what she had once wanted, was everything she needed.

"Who knew what you wanted more than you did?" he asked.

"I'll tell you all about it someday."

He slid away from her. "I have something more to tell you. I want everything out in the open between us."

At his serious tone, dread settled in her chest. "What is it?"

"My full name is Chadwick Prince the Fourth."

"Ookay."

"You haven't heard of my family?"

Bella shook her head.

"My family owns Prince Enterprises, the largest import-export company in the country and one of the largest in the world."

She stared at him as the full significance of his words penetrated her brain. She couldn't speak.

"My family has money," he said. "Lots of it."

"They do?" *Way to sound like an idiot, Bella.*

"They're very influential, too. In fact, I met Hugo at boarding school. If I chose, I wouldn't have to work another day in my life. I declined to work at the family business and joined the FBI to do some good in this world." With a wry smile, he continued, "My family hasn't forgiven me yet."

Confusion splashed in her mind like varying colors of paint thrown at a wall. "Let me get this straight. Not only are you an FBI agent, but your family is wealthy and influential?"

"Afraid so. Don't hold it against me."

"Are you estranged from your family because you chose the FBI over working for them?"

"That's part of it. My family shunned me when I decided to join the Bureau. I was bitter at the way they treated me. I've also spent most of my life trying not to be as obsessed with money and social standing as my parents. When I was growing up, my father had a string of mistresses. My mother knew, but she stayed with him. She loved the money and being a socialite more than she cared what my father did. I never want to be like my father."

"Oh, Chad." He'd experienced firsthand what infidelity did to a marriage. Bella knew with certainty she could trust him.

"The last few years, my sister has invited me back home, to Florida, to spend the Christmas holidays with them," he continued. "She reached out, but I would have none of it. Loving you made me see where my hurt and stubbornness closed my heart to my family. I opened my heart to you, and I don't want to shut it again. I want to make amends with my family and accept my sister's invitation this year." Chad pulled Bella closer. "And I want you to come to Florida with me."

Chewing her lip, her mind jumbled, her gaze went to the globe. The little frog sat smiling atop his rock, as if encouraging her to take the leap of faith Chad offered. He loved her, and she loved him. That was all that mattered. Her old doubts had almost kept her from fully embracing her love for Chad.

With a smile, she turned back to him. "You made me see I want a full, loving, and passionate relationship with a man. With you. I won't settle."

Happiness glowed from his eyes. "I promise to give you all my love, all my devotion, and all my passion."

She cradled his face between her hands, his beautiful face, the face of the man she'd love forever. "I love that you accept me for who I am. I won't feel shame anymore because of my upbringing. My parents had problems, but they're still my parents. I'd love to go to Florida with you to meet your family. Then maybe later, we could go to Texas together."

"It's a deal."

Bella laughed with the joy and happiness that bubbled up in her. She wound her arms around Chad's neck and met his exultant blue gaze. "I wanted a frog and I got a prince. But I would love you as much even if you were a frog."

"What?"

"You talk too much. Shut up and kiss me."

He did just that.

As they kissed, Bella opened one eye to find the little frog staring at her. She could swear it winked. Could there be magic in that snow globe, or could it be the magic of love?

Chad was her magic, one that would last forever.

***

165

Her Red Riding Hood Valentine

By

Cara Marsi

A magical snow globe sets the stage for romance between a drama teacher who no longer believes in love and an enticing photographer picturing a different life. Manhattan drama teacher Carlyn Cameron used to be a firm believer in happy-ever-after, but since the last smooth-talking charmer devoured her heart, she's sworn off men, especially those of the arrogant, too-good-looking variety. And the "wolf in an Armani suit" hired as photographer for the school play she's written and is directing definitely falls into that category. Like the Big Bad Wolf, she fears he's hiding his true self.

Photojournalist Wolf Martinez has seen more than his share of ugliness through the lens of his camera. The nomadic life he leads doesn't allow much time for serious relationships, especially now, but the feisty red-headed drama teacher looks good enough to gobble up. Once he finds his way out of his current forest of troubles, he'll be back on the prowl to his next adventure.

Carlyn can't seem to escape this particularly scrumptious wolf, especially after he moves into the apartment next door and charms her grandmother. He may be smokin' hot, but can she trust him not to steal her heart? And Wolf finds himself irresistibly drawn to Carlyn, but can he picture a new life for himself, with room for two?

PROLOGUE

Ten days before Christmas, Long Island, New York

"Love this snow globe with the little elf." Carlyn Cameron reached for one of the globes set on the festively decorated table at the Christmas craft fair. Before she could touch the globe, the elderly woman selling them put out a hand, stopping Carlyn.

Sparkling brown eyes behind cats-eye glasses met Carlyn's. The seller's bright orange hair, in a shade not found in nature, and piled high in a sixties beehive, shone in the overhead lights.

"Dearie, this one is for you." The woman picked up a different snow globe and handed it to Carlyn. When their hands touched, a chill ran up Carlyn's arm. A buzzing in her head drowned out the cheerful voices in the high school gym. Her friends, Avery and Bella, each clutching the snow globes the eccentric woman had chosen for them, seemed to disappear.

Carlyn studied the globe in her hand. Little Red Riding Hood, holding a covered basket, stood in the center of the glass orb. Glittering flakes fell on her, making her blood-red cape shimmer with silver. Behind Red Riding Hood stood a large black wolf, looking as if he wanted to devour her.

Carlyn met the old woman's eyes again. The buzzing in

her head cleared. "Red Riding Hood?"

"Trust the healing power of love to find you," the woman said in a sing-song voice. She'd said equally enigmatic words to Carlyn's friends. Like a character in a scary movie, the eccentric woman sure knew how to create atmosphere.

Avery cradled her own snow globe and stared at Carlyn's. "I got Santa and a tree. Whatever that means."

Bella held out her globe with the little frog wearing a crown. "Guess I'm going to kiss a lot of frogs."

"The future holds many surprises," the lady with the orange hair said.

Carlyn shivered. Things were getting stranger and stranger.

Bella snapped her fingers. "I get it. Little Red Riding Hood because you've got bright red hair."

"Watch out for the wolf," Avery said, laughing.

Carlyn glanced from Avery to Bella. "I'm not afraid of the big, bad wolf."

CHAPTER ONE

Christmas Eve, the following year, Vermont

"That's the woman I'm going to marry."

Carlyn Cameron stopped in the middle of smoothing her emerald green satin gown over her hips and jerked her attention toward the deep masculine voice a few feet away. Her gaze collided with dark brown eyes that glittered with amusement. The owner of the eyes smiled at her and winked.

She scanned the tiny church vestibule. The only people there were her, Brown Eyes, and Avery's brother-in-law, a happily married man, who laughed and walked outside. Left alone with Brown Eyes, who held a large camera, they traded stares.

With an expression Carlyn hoped made it clear his lame come-on didn't work, she gave him a quick once-over. Good-looking, in a rough-hewn, motorcycle-rider kind of way, with long, thick black hair tied back from a high-cheekboned face, his tall, muscular body did his tuxedo proud. Bad-boy types born to ride usually didn't do it for her, but she couldn't turn away from Brown Eyes. His bronzed skin, the slight slant to his eyes, and his chiseled features spoke of American Indian or Hispanic heritage.

Carlyn knew Brown Eyes' type – hot and sure of themselves with women. But she had to admit he did have a unique pickup line.

He raised an eyebrow. He knew she checked him out, and by the amused expression on his face, he enjoyed it. Heat crept up her neck. With a lift of her chin, she held his gaze for moments before she forced herself to turn away.

Once she'd dreamed of love, romance, and happy-ever-after. But that dream had died. Some men couldn't be trusted. At least not the hot ones. And Brown Eyes, no doubt, fell into that group—good-looking and too confident in that knowledge. She had no use for a man like that. She'd been involved with someone too handsome for his own good, her dream lover come to life, a man like the heroes in the romance novels she devoured.

He'd been no hero.

Bella, Avery's other bridesmaid, approached, drawing Carlyn's attention from Brown Eyes. "Avery is asking for you. She thinks her hair needs touching up and you're the only one who can do it." Bella rolled her eyes. "A typical nervous bride. Avery looks perfect, but she doesn't believe it."

"With all those women in that small room, and all that perfume, I came out here to get some fresh air." Carlyn scowled at Brown Eyes. "It's too fresh out here for my taste."

He threw back his head and laughed.

Bella glanced from Carlyn to Brown Eyes, then shrugged.

The two women headed back to the dressing room.

"Hold on a minute, Red. Let me get your picture." Brown Eyes' voice stopped them.

Carlyn whirled around and faced him. "My name is not Red."

He grinned, his perfect teeth white against the bronze of his skin, and lifted his camera, clicking away. He focused on Bella and took a few shots. "Two of the most beautiful bridesmaids I've ever seen."

Carlyn put a hand on her hip. "You're full of it."

He stepped a little closer. "If I can't call you Red, what can I call you?"

"Bridesmaid number two."

Chuckling, he held out a hand. "I think we got off on the wrong foot. I'm Wolf Martinez, wedding photographer."

Wolf. Of course. She could be rude and ignore his outstretched hand, but Carlyn wouldn't spoil Avery's big day. "Carlyn Cameron." When they shook hands, shivers, like tiny points of pleasure, skittered up her spine. Carlyn yanked her hand free.

"Hello, Carlyn Cameron." Wolf's gaze made a leisurely sweep down her body, then back to her face. His full lips tilted in a cocky grin, letting her know he liked what he saw.

"We'd better get back to Avery." Bella threaded her arm through Carlyn's. When they'd moved away, she leaned down to whisper in Carlyn's ear. "Wow! That man is smokin'."

"He's an arrogant jerk with a silly come-on. He says he's going to marry me."

Bella stopped in front of the dressing room door. "Really? How romantic!"

"It's not romantic. His name suits him. He's a wolf in Armani."

Bella chuckled. "Wolf in Armani. I know you're a drama teacher, but aren't you being a bit theatrical?" Her features sobered and she studied Carlyn. "You were always the romantic one. What happened to you?"

"Tyler happened. The cheat. After that experience, all my romantic dreams vaporized like stage smoke."

"He lied to you and took advantage. You shouldn't allow what that scum did turn you off all men."

"Let it go, Bella. I'm no longer the naïve romantic, and that's a good thing."

As the two women entered the dressing room, Carlyn turned to find Wolf Martinez watching her. He smiled.

Arrogant jerk!

CHAPTER TWO

Exhausted, Carlyn sank onto her chair at the bridal party table, sighing as she toed off her high-heeled shoes to wiggle her toes. Avery and Josh's lively wedding reception showed signs of finally slowing down. Carlyn couldn't remember the last time she'd danced so much.

The band played Paul McCartney's "Yesterday" as couples swayed together on the polished wooden floor. The jewel tones of the women's dresses complemented the tasteful red, green, and gold Christmas decorations. Avery and Josh stood together at the edge of the dance floor, talking quietly, seeming lost in each other. Near them, Bella and Chad, arm-in-arm, observed the dancers.

Happiness for her friends brewed sadness with a splash of self-pity in Carlyn. Of the three of them, she'd been the one to dream about a knight in shining armor who would take her away to an enchanted place where happy-ever-after reigned. Avery and Bella had been cynical about love but they'd found happiness, while she, the romantic, now bore the mantle of cynic.

She felt someone staring and twisted around to see Wolf Martinez watching her from across the room. No knight on

174

a white horse but a wolf in a tuxedo. Smokin' or not, she'd sworn off men. She had to admit Wolf worked hard taking shots of the wedding and the reception. He had a way of making people feel at ease, of coaxing the best smiles and poses from them. She could picture him, with his glamorous looks, jetting around the world shooting photos of exotic places. That certainly suited him better than taking wedding photographs.

As she studied him, he slipped his camera strap over his head, freeing his hands, then plucked two flutes of champagne from the tray of a passing waiter and strolled over to her. She braced herself for more flirting. Bella and Avery had urged her to flirt back with Wolf, to let loose, at least for today. The wounds Tyler inflicted were still so raw, Carlyn couldn't, wouldn't, even think about getting involved with another man. And the next man would be someone so unexciting he couldn't help but be trustworthy.

"So, Red, what are you doing sitting here all by yourself?" Wolf handed her one of the glasses of champagne and settled into the chair next to her.

"Do. Not. Call. Me. Red," she said through clenched teeth.

"With that amazing hair of yours, I can't be the only one to call you Red."

"The last guy to call me that was Billy Johnson, and he got a black eye."

Wolf laughed. "How old were you and Billy Johnson?"

She couldn't help the chuckle that escaped her. "Ten."

"Are you going to give me a black eye too?" he asked.

"No, because I'll never see you again after tonight."

He grinned. "Don't be so sure."

"Oh, I'm sure."

He tilted his head, studying her, a teasing glint in his eyes. "Your hair looks good up like that, but I think I would prefer it down over your shoulders."

His words and the smoldering intensity of his deep brown eyes ratcheted her pulse up a few notches.

She met his gaze with what she hoped was a stern demeanor. "How you like my hair doesn't matter at all."

"I think maybe it does a little."

She took a sip of her drink, hiding her smile. Truth be told, she enjoyed sparring with him.

The image of the small snow globe with Red Riding Hood and the wolf flashed into her mind. Absolutely not. He had nothing to do with the globe. After tonight, she would never see Wolf Martinez again.

Someone called his name, and they both looked over to see Josh signaling Wolf that he needed him.

"Duty calls," Wolf said, as he stood. "I'll be seeing you."

"No, you won't."

She couldn't help admiring his long-legged gait as he strode away, and the way his tuxedo enhanced his muscular frame. Needing to cool herself, she took a long swallow of champagne.

CHAPTER THREE

New Year's Day, Brooklyn, New York

"Here it is, Grandmom. What do you think?" Carlyn opened the door to her apartment in the Cobble Hill section of Brooklyn and ushered her grandmother through. She set the elderly woman's suitcases on the floor and closed the door.

Her eighty-year-old grandmother, Eva Cameron, swung her gaze around the room and smiled. "It's lovely, dear. So eclectic and creative with all the bright colors and mismatched furniture."

Carlyn moved to this apartment less than a year ago, and her family had yet to see it. Her parents, in a hurry to get from their home in Maine to North Carolina to visit Carlyn's brother, his wife, and their new baby, had driven Grandmom to Carlyn's and promised to see her apartment on their way back.

Carlyn grimaced as her grandmother continued to scrutinize the room. "You don't like it, do you?"

"Why do you say that? Your place is lovely and different."

177

Feeling like a schoolgirl craving approval from her teacher, Carlyn gathered her unruly curls into a ponytail, then released her hair to let it float around her shoulders. Her grandmother's approval meant more than any teacher's. "I know it's different from what you and Mom like. You like neutral colors and things that match."

"You're your own person, Carlyn. And that's as it should be."

With a smile, Carlyn hugged her grandmother. "I'm so happy to have you here. I'll show you to your room."

A drama and English teacher at a prestigious private high school in Manhattan, Carlyn had always had a creative bent, unlike the rest of her family. She'd painted each room in her small apartment a different bright color. She liked to mix modern furniture with flea market finds, especially anything Art Deco.

"Here's your home for the next six weeks, Grandmom." Carlyn switched on the Tiffany-like lamp in the tiny bedroom, the walls painted turquoise, where her grandmother would sleep.

Eva had her own suite in Carlyn's parents' house in Maine, but hadn't felt up to a trip to North Carolina. Carlyn had gladly agreed that her grandmother could stay with her. She and Grandmom shared a special bond, and it would be good to have company for a change, especially after her boring New Year's Eve. With Avery on her honeymoon and Bella in Florida with Chad, Carlyn had gone to a party at a co-worker's last night. One of the few there without a date, she left soon after midnight.

"What a charming room. I'm sure I'll be very comfortable here, Carlyn." Eva slipped off her coat and laid it on the antique four-poster bed.

"Rest, Grandmom. I'll unpack for you, then we'll have dinner. How about Chinese or a pizza?"

"Pizza sounds divine."

"Pizza it is." Carlyn met her grandmother's green eyes, so like her own. Eva's fading short red hair had once been bright and curly like Carlyn's. "School starts the day after tomorrow. I hate to leave you alone."

"Don't worry about me. I have a stack of magazines and my Kindle, and there's always TV."

Briefcase bulging with papers to grade for the pop quiz she'd given her students today, Carlyn stepped into the elevator and hit the button for her third floor apartment. She sank back against the wall. The first day of school after the Christmas holiday always drained her.

As the elevator doors began to close, a male voice shouted, "Hold the elevator!"

Carlyn quickly hit the button that opened the doors.

"Thanks." The guy who'd shouted got in and smiled. Surprise replaced his smile.

Carlyn froze. "You! The wolf in Armani. What are you doing here?" The doors slid closed. The elevator, always slow, lurched upward while her heart seemed to drop to the floor. In the confined space, Wolf's scent of soap and the outdoors teased her senses, arousing a hot curl of awareness within her.

"Wolf in Armani? Is that what you call me?" He chuckled. "I don't know whether to be flattered or insulted."

"It's not a compliment."

"Do I detect a little sarcasm, Red?"

"Don't call me Red." She put a hand on her hip. "Are you stalking me?"

179

His features tightened. "I'm as shocked as you are that we're meeting again. Do I seem like the kind of guy who would stalk a woman?"

"No, but I don't really know you."

Wolf scrubbed a hand over his face. "Can we start over? Be friends?"

"I doubt we'll see each other again."

His eyes teased. "You said that at the wedding."

Shrugging, Carlyn remained silent as the elevator made its sluggish ascent. She couldn't help but check him out, though. With his indigo jeans that showcased legs that went on forever, black boots, and a tan sheepskin jacket, she could picture him riding the range, snow whirling around him, as he searched for calves that had gotten lost from the herd. *Sheesh!* At Avery's wedding, she thought Wolf looked like a biker bad boy. Now, he looked like a rugged cowboy. She'd read too many romance novels. And she found Wolf too darned attractive.

When the elevator bell dinged for her floor, Carlyn exhaled in relief. At least she would be done with Wolf. "Goodbye," she said. He stepped back to let her exit, then followed her.

She turned and almost collided with his broad chest. She clenched her free hand at her side, fighting the urge to run her fingers over the smooth sheepskin, and under, to feel his muscles beneath. She lifted her gaze to his. "Where are you going?"

"My new apartment." He nodded toward the door next to hers. "3C."

She gripped her briefcase handle tighter. "No! You're playing with me. Gigi lives there."

He grinned, showing those even white teeth. "She's a

friend. She got a call for a photo shoot in Paris for the next six weeks. She's letting me use her apartment."

"What?" Carlyn swallowed around the lump in her suddenly dry throat. "You *are* playing me. Gigi would have told me if she had a shoot in Paris."

He held up his hands. "Don't kill the messenger. She probably didn't have time to tell you. Apparently the model hired for the shoot broke her arm in a freak accident and Gigi got the call to replace her."

Although happy that Gigi, an up-and-coming model, had gotten this big break in Paris, Carlyn wanted to shake her fist at Fate. Of all the places to live in the New York City area, what cruel joke did Fate play to bring Wolf to her doorstep for the next six weeks?

Could her day get any worse?

Her apartment door opened and her grandmother peeked out. "I thought I heard voices." Eva gave Wolf a friendly smile and stepped into the hall. "I'm Eva Cameron, Carlyn's grandmother. Are you a friend of hers?"

"Nice to meet you, Mrs. Cameron." Wolf stepped toward Eva and held out his hand to shake hers. "I'm Wolf Martinez. Carlyn and I met at Avery and Josh's wedding. I'm going to be her neighbor for a while."

Her grandmother's grin got wider. "How lovely. Please call me Eva. You must come to dinner sometime. I make a great beef stew. How about tomorrow evening?"

Noooo! Carlyn resisted the urge to push her dear grandmother back into the apartment. "Grandmom, I'm sure he has other plans."

He turned to Carlyn with a wolfish grin. "I have no plans tomorrow. I'd love to have dinner with you and your grandmother."

"Wonderful," Eva said. "How about six?"

"Great. See you then." Whistling softly, he pulled a key out of his jacket pocket and unlocked his apartment.

His temporary apartment, Carlyn reminded herself.

"Let's get inside, Grandmom."

When they'd stepped into her apartment, Carlyn shut the door and faced her grandmother. "Grandmom, I love you, but why did you invite Wolf? I don't like him."

"Why ever not, dear? He seems like a nice young man." With a teasing grin, she added, "And so handsome. Or hot, as you young people say."

"He's an arrogant jerk, too handsome for his own good. I know his type."

Her grandmother put a hand on her hip and glared at her. "Carlyn Mary Cameron, since when did you get so mean-spirited?"

Carlyn sighed, releasing some of her frustration. "I'm sorry, Grandmom. It's been a rough day. I'm putting together a new play for our school's Valentine's Day festivities, and things aren't going well. Let me change and we'll get dinner. We'll cook together. It'll relax me. That and a glass of wine." Carlyn started toward her bedroom, but her grandmother put a hand on her arm, stopping her.

"Not until you tell me the real reason you dislike that nice Wolf. You're almost thirty-four. I understand you young women value your independence, but it's good to have a man to share your life with. I'm sure there are many women who would be thrilled for Wolf to take an interest in them. I saw the way he looked at you. He likes you."

"I've never given him reason to think I'm interested. He and I got off on the wrong foot when he photographed Avery's wedding. I don't want a relationship with any man now." She wagged an index finger at her grandmother. "If you have notions of fixing me up with Wolf, get them out of your head."

"Okay, dear. I promise not to interfere in your love life."

"Why do I not believe you?"

Her grandmother laughed. "Take off your coat and have that glass of wine. You need it."

CHAPTER FOUR

When Carlyn got home the next afternoon, her grandmother had the small dining room table set with Carlyn's best white damask tablecloth. Candles in green Depression glass candlesticks were arranged around the mismatched vintage Fiesta Ware dishes. Carlyn inhaled the calming, homey scent of beef, potatoes, and carrots simmered in Grandmom's special gravy that filled the apartment. Her grandmother had gone all out to impress Wolf.

Wolf at dinner with them. Despite her mistrust of him, a spark of excitement ignited in Carlyn. She would acknowledge her attraction to him and move on. After her experience with Tyler, she no longer trusted gorgeous guys who made her knees wobble.

"Table is nice, Grandmom." She slipped off her coat and hung it in the closet.

"Thank you, dear. I love entertaining."

"I wish you'd entertain anyone but Wolf." Carlyn clamped a hand over her mouth. She'd vowed to herself she'd be cordial to him.

"What did you say, dear?"

"Nothing."

Eva stepped out of the small kitchen area, wiping her hands on a towel. Her smile faded as she scanned Carlyn.

"What?" Carlyn said. "You don't like my outfit?" She waved a hand over her black pencil skirt, black tights, green ankle boots and silk blouse in varying shades of bright green.

"I'm sure what you're wearing is all the style now. Why don't you change into that nice yellow cashmere sweater I got you for Christmas? It brings out the color of your hair."

"If it will make you happy."

"Wear it because Wolf will like it."

With a low growl that made her grandmother laugh, Carlyn stalked into her bedroom.

At six o'clock sharp the doorbell rang. "Would you answer that, dear?" Eva called from the kitchen. She'd refused Carlyn's help with the dinner, insisting Carlyn relax. Like she could relax with the *wolf* at the door.

Carlyn had changed into the yellow sweater and her favorite black skinny jeans. To keep her outfit from being too conservative, she'd added a large Art Deco rhinestone brooch she'd bought at a flea market, and red heels. Carlyn told herself she wanted to look nice to please her grandmother.

Yeah, sure, said a small voice inside her.

Heart thumping, she fluffed her hair, then opened the door to Wolf. His sexy smile branded her with heat and left her as speechless as the real Riding Hood confronting the big, bad wolf.

They stood staring at each other. He held a bouquet of deep red roses and a basket with a blue-checkered cloth covering. "May I come in?" he finally asked.

"Sure. Sorry." She stepped back to let him through, then shut the door.

Turning to face her, he studied her so intently, she shifted from one foot to the other.

185

"I knew your hair would look great loose like that, Red," he said.

"Stop calling me Red." His nearness tightened a delicious knot in her stomach, making her harsh words come out on a breathless whisper.

A wicked glint lit his eyes and he leaned closer. "Maybe we can figure out how you can make me stop calling you that."

"What?"

"Wolf, how nice to see you." Eva came over to them, her face wreathed in a smile. She glanced at Carlyn. "Where are you manners, keeping this poor man standing by the door?" With a sweep of her hand, she ushered Wolf into the living area.

"These are for you and Carlyn." He held out the flowers and the basket to Eva. He nodded toward the basket. "Dessert. Cornmeal cookies."

"Thank you," Eva said. "How sweet." She took the basket, lifted the cover, and sniffed. "Heavenly. I've never heard of cornmeal cookies. I can't wait to try them." She turned to Carlyn. "Please put the lovely flowers into a vase, dear. They'll make a nice centerpiece on our table."

Carlyn gingerly accepted the bouquet from him, afraid the heat swirling through her would ignite and set the flowers on fire if she touched Wolf.

"Please have a seat," Grandmom said to Wolf. "Would you like some wine?"

"Sure, thanks. I hope you like the cookies. They're an old Native American recipe, passed to me by my mother and grandmother."

"You bake?" Eva asked.

"It helps me relax."

Carlyn listened to their conversation and stole furtive glances at Wolf as she arranged the flowers in a white milk-glass vase. Strange a man like Wolf who seemed as if he breezed through life without a care would need something to relax him. And baking, of all things. Wolf Martinez had hidden talents, ones she'd like to discover. She shook aside the thought. She had no interest in him. *Liar.*

Later, as they prepared to sit at the table, Wolf pulled out their chairs, then his own. Before he sat, he stopped, his attention drawn to the nearby server. "That's an interesting snow globe." He moved closer and picked up the globe, studying it. "Red Riding Hood and the wolf. Don't think I've ever seen one like this before."

A chill passed over Carlyn as she watched him holding the globe. "I got that at a craft fair the Christmas before last. Let's eat before the stew gets cold." She didn't understand why, but she needed to get Wolf's attention off the snow globe.

They ate in silence for several minutes, Wolf seated next to Carlyn, and Grandmom at the other end. Wolf raised his glass of red wine toward Grandmom. "Eva, this is the best beef stew I've ever had."

Eva beamed like an actress accepting an award. "I bet you say that to all the girls."

Carlyn expected her grandmother to start giggling. *Sheesh.* Wolf possessed a lethal charm. Just like Red Riding Hood's wolf.

He shook his head. "Never said that before about beef stew."

Eva laughed. "I suspect you're not from around here, young man. Where were you raised?"

"Born and raised in Las Vegas."

187

Carlyn dropped her spoon into her bowl. It clattered against the ceramic. "Nevada?" *Way to sound like an intelligent woman, Carlyn.*

Grinning, Wolf said, "Yes, that Las Vegas."

Carlyn took a sip of wine to hide her embarrassment. "I meant I didn't think anyone actually came from Vegas." She had to stop before she embarrassed herself further.

"Not everyone in Vegas is a tourist," he said.

"Of course not," Eva said, with a sharp look at Carlyn. Eva turned back to Wolf. "Were your parents from Vegas too?"

"My dad. My mom is from Arizona. They met when they were in the military together."

"How romantic," Eva said. "Isn't it, Carlyn? I know you love romance."

"I don't love it anymore." Carlyn took a spoonful of the thick stew and tried to ignore Wolf, but his overt sexuality reached out to her, warming her more than the comforting food.

A draft, so light she thought she might have imagined it, whispered over her. Something compelled her to glance toward the server and her Red Riding Hood globe. Snow swirled through the globe, coating Red and the wolf in silver. Wolf had shaken the globe when he handled it, but the flakes should have settled by now.

Carlyn almost choked on her stew. She grabbed her wine glass and washed down the food. Her grandmother and Wolf stared at her.

"You okay?" he asked.

"I'm fine," she croaked. She shifted her focus back to the snow globe. No flakes fell inside the glass. She must have imagined it.

"How long have you been a photographer?" Eva asked Wolf with a smile. "Indulge an old lady with all these questions."

Grateful for the distraction, Carlyn concentrated on her dinner, but every cell in her body felt attuned to Wolf's sensuously disturbing presence.

Wolf returned Grandmom's smile. "For this delicious stew, I don't mind a few questions. I started in high school with my first camera. I worked my way through college taking photos, and over the past fifteen years since college, I've made a living at it."

Eva nodded her head, as if approving his career choice. "How wonderful. What do you do besides weddings?"

"I've only done Josh and Avery's."

He'd been so professional at the wedding, Carlyn had assumed he'd worked many of them. He made his living at photography. But what kind and where?

Grandmom wiped the corner of her mouth with her napkin before settling her gaze on Wolf again. "If you're not a wedding photographer, what kind of pictures do you take?"

Carlyn suppressed a smile. Her grandmother could show the FBI a thing or two about interrogations.

Wolf stilled for a minute, as if he considered not answering. "I work freelance for various news organizations," he finally said.

A photojournalist. Of course. She should have known. Carlyn wondered if he had the proverbial girl in every port, like a sailor. Another reason to fight her attraction to him.

"A globe-trotting journalist," Grandmom said. "How exciting. What brings you to New York?"

"I'm between assignments and I have some business to take care of." Wolf turned to Carlyn. "What type work do you do?"

At his abrupt change of subject, Carlyn had a niggling suspicion he wanted to divert attention from himself.

"I teach English and drama at Wilbur Academy, a private high school in Manhattan."

He raised an eyebrow and set down his spoon. "Drama? I'm impressed."

"Carlyn is a wonderful actress too," Eva said, pride evident in her voice. "She's an even better playwright."

"Now I'm intrigued. Have you had any of your plays produced?" he asked.

Carlyn rubbed her fingers over the tablecloth, using the cool, smooth damask as a talisman to vanish the coil of anxiety that knotted her chest. She loved writing plays but her fear of rejection kept her from submitting to an agent. "My school is putting on one of my plays Valentine's Day. I'm directing."

"I'd love to see it." Wolf sat back, waiting for her to go on.

She glanced at her grandmother, who remained frustratingly silent. "It's just high school," she finally said. "Nothing like you're used to, I'm sure."

He studied her with those knowing brown eyes. "You don't know what I'm used to," he said softly.

"I plan on going to the play with some of Carlyn's friends," Eva said. "Wolf, you can join us."

Carlyn shot her grandmother a look from narrowed eyes. Putting on a play in front of her family and friends had already given her stage fright. Adding Wolf to the mix upped her nervousness a few notches.

"Thanks for the invitation, Eva," Wolf said. "It's a date. We'll go to the play together."

The big smile Grandmom gave Wolf made her look ten years younger. Seeing Grandmom so happy evaporated some of the anxiety Carlyn felt about Wolf having dinner with them now, and at the prospect of him seeing her play. For Grandmom's sake, she would tolerate him.

"You remind me of my grandmother, Eva," Wolf said a few minutes later.

Eva stopped buttering her roll. "How sweet of you to say. How am I like her?"

He set down his spoon. "My mother's mother lived with us. My parents worked and my grandmother took care of me. I'm an only child. Grandma was the greatest—loving, kind, and fun to be with. Like you. She taught me to bake and taught me the language of her people, the Navajo, and some of their ways."

Carlyn could see the love for his grandmother reflected on Wolf's softened features. The wall she'd erected around her heart crumbled a little. Now she understood why Wolf treated Grandmom with such respect.

"Is your grandmother still alive?" Grandmom asked gently.

Wolf stared down at the table, then back to Grandmom. "She died several years ago," he said in a flat voice. "Stuck on the other side of the world, I couldn't get back for the funeral. I'll always regret that."

Carlyn lifted her hand, wanting to comfort Wolf, to touch him in empathy. She quickly withdrew her hand. "I'm sorry, Wolf. That must have been painful." She caught his gaze and shared a sympathetic smile.

"I'm sure your grandmother would understand why you couldn't get back for her funeral," Grandmom said. "You need to stop feeling bad about that. She must have known how much you loved her."

He raised his wine glass and saluted them both. "Thanks. I appreciate the kind thoughts. I don't know many people in New York, and you both have made me feel welcome."

"There's a lot of stew left," Grandmom said. "Eat up."

"Yes, ma'am." Wolf picked up his spoon and dug into his stew.

Through the rest of dinner, Wolf made them laugh with his stories of growing up in Las Vegas. Carlyn wondered about the real Wolf, and suspected the charming man who entertained them with witty stories wore a disguise much like the wolf in the Red Riding Hood fable. Something about him made her want to peel back his layers to reveal the man behind the mask.

Dinner finished, Grandmom stood and began clearing away the dishes. Wolf stood too and took the dishes from her. "You rest, Eva. You cooked a great dinner for us. We'll clean up."

"Wolf is right," Carlyn said. "Relax. Watch TV. Later we'll have coffee and dessert."

After a quick cleanup, Carlyn made coffee, and the three of them sat in the living room to watch a movie and enjoy the delicious cookies Wolf had brought.

The movie, a comedy, over, Grandmom pushed up from her chair. "It felt good to laugh like that. I'm a bit tired now. I think I'll go to my room."

Wolf stood and took one of her hands in his. "Thanks for the delicious dinner, Eva. The food was great, but the company even better."

"Thank you for the wonderful cookies and beautiful flowers. Feel free to stop in anytime," Eva said. "After all, we're neighbors."

"I'll be sure to do that."

At the thought of seeing Wolf more often, anxiety and excitement coalesced into a ball of warmth in Carlyn's stomach. *Down, girl. He's so not for you.*

After Grandmom went to her room, Carlyn and Wolf cleared the dessert dishes, then Carlyn started the dishwasher. She turned to Wolf. "Thanks for helping."

He moved closer until they were a whisper apart. His intense eyes locked with hers. "It's always a pleasure to work beside a beautiful woman, Red."

She backed up until she felt the counter edge against her spine. "You have got to stop calling me that."

"What will you give me if I stop?"

"Seriously? Why should I give you anything?"

"I don't know what I did to turn you off."

"You don't know? How about that pickup line of yours?"

He frowned, then grinned. "You mean the 'That's the woman I'm going to marry' line?"

"That would be the one."

"Will you believe me if I tell you I've never said that before?"

Too damn attractive, the awareness that darkened his eyes spiked her pulse. But Carlyn had learned her lesson well. Attractive men couldn't be trusted. "No, I don't believe you've never said that before."

Frustration flashed over his face. "Let me make it up to you, Red."

"Stop calling me that."

"I'll make a deal with you. You kiss me and I won't shove any more stupid lines at you, and I'll stop calling you

Red."

"You're crazy." Her gaze wandered to his full lips, and she finally acknowledged to herself what she'd wanted since the first time she saw Wolf Martinez. She wanted to kiss him, wanted to run her fingers through his hair, wanted to feel his muscular body against hers. If they kissed and she felt nothing, she could move on and quit obsessing over him. That would work.

She pulled herself up to her full five-foot-two. "One kiss, that's it. Then you don't call me Red again. Or throw me any come-ons."

"It's a deal."

He pulled her to him and bent to brush a butterfly-soft kiss on her lips. His hand cupped the curve of her jaw. He tasted like coffee and sugar. Carlyn held herself rigid at first, but his lips pressed harder on hers, hot and passionate, teasing a response from her. Her entire body began to tingle and tremble, and her eyes drifted shut.

With a murmur, she wound her arms around his neck and kissed him back. His touch seared her flesh. When he sucked her bottom lip, she opened to him, welcoming him.

She reached up and tugged at the leather cord holding back his hair, freeing it to her eager touch. She tunneled her hands through the thickness of his hair as tiny cries escaped her. His deep, drugging kiss possessed her. She didn't want it to end.

He cradled the back of her head and molded her body to his. An ache built between her legs. Her breasts tightened, pushing against her sweater.

With a groan, he pulled free and rested his forehead against hers. "Carlyn."

The way he said her name, raw, filled with yearning,

built a twisting, needy fire in her, threatening to consume her. She didn't know what to say. Like a villain in a fairy tale, reality reared up, pounding fear into her. She slid away from Wolf, drew in a breath, held it, then exhaled. "You won't ever call me Red again, right?"

His skin stretched taut over his high cheekbones, and his ebony hair fanned out over his massive shoulders. He was magnificent. Her hungry gaze devoured him.

He gripped her shoulders and looked down at her with an expression of wonder. "If I call you Red, will you kiss me like that again?"

I'll kiss you even if you don't call me Red. She shook her head. "One kiss. That's the deal."

He took strands of her hair and twisted them around his finger. "One kiss from you will never be enough."

CHAPTER FIVE

After he left Carlyn's apartment, Wolf sat alone in his darkened living room. Carlyn's lips seemed imprinted on his. He'd had no right to kiss her, to lead her on. Once he healed, he'd be back to chasing stories in the most dangerous parts of the world. His lifestyle didn't leave room for lasting relationships. He didn't even have a permanent home.

Unfortunately, knowing he wasn't good for her didn't stop him from wanting her. From the first moment he'd seen the petite redhead with the twinkling green eyes, he'd felt an attraction that blindsided him. He didn't know what had compelled him to utter the line about her being the woman he planned to marry. He'd never said that to any woman before and he'd never given any thought to marriage, until he saw her and then those fateful words left his mouth. He didn't regret the words. Carlyn, her flaming hair like a beacon, lured him to dream the impossible. The intelligence in her eyes and her sweet smile spoke to the deepest part of his heart.

At the wedding, he'd wanted to get her phone number, but he knew instinctively Carlyn was a forever kind of woman. He couldn't be the man she needed, at least not now. He'd seen too many failed marriages among his colleagues.

When, and if, he married, his commitment would be for a lifetime.

He didn't believe in fate, yet he and Carlyn had been brought together again. A crazy, nearly impossible, circumstance. Soon after Josh and Avery's wedding, he'd run into Gigi, whom he knew through mutual friends, on the subway. Frantic to have someone watch her apartment for the time she'd be away, she'd pleaded with him to stay there. Figuring her place would be more comfortable than the hotel where he'd been staying, he'd accepted. Never in a million years would he have expected to move next door to the sweetly seductive Carlyn.

He'd turned her off with his brashness, but that boldness had saved his ass more times than he cared to count as he'd traveled the globe to different war zones. In embattled parts of the world where emotions ran high, where everyone grabbed at whatever joy they could find, he'd had his share of desperate affairs, but he'd never known the hunger and need he'd felt when he kissed Carlyn tonight. The way she'd given herself so freely told him she felt the same.

He wanted her.

He needed to leave her alone.

She deserved a stable guy, one who'd always be around for her. One who wasn't damaged. He wasn't that guy.

Sweat formed on his brow. He gripped the chair arms to control the trembling in his hands. Images slammed through his mind like a never-ending horror film. Death and destruction with bullets flying and blood gushing from wounds. Wolf rubbed his forehead, but he couldn't dislodge the little girl's gray eyes, her pleading eyes. He'd failed her.

At Josh's urging, he'd come to New York to heal from his PTSD. He needed time. He'd met Josh when he'd been embedded with Josh's Army unit in Iraq. They'd kept in touch, and Josh tried to help him now. He'd hired Wolf to take the pictures at his wedding. The jubilant atmosphere of the wedding only served to remind Wolf of the life he'd never have. He'd chosen a different path.

Josh pressed Wolf to get help for his PTSD, but Wolf refused. He'd deal with this himself. He'd always been strong. He could do it. But Carlyn shouldn't have to deal with his problems. From now on, he'd leave her alone. The thought slammed him with another round of sadness.

Carlyn's taxi slowed for traffic and she stared out the window at the pedestrians scurrying along the Manhattan sidewalks, bundled against the January cold. What a forty-eight hours! She'd had trouble concentrating at work and her students had begun to notice. At last night's rehearsal, her assistant had discovered a mistake Carlyn had missed in the script. Two days after her Earth-shattering kiss with Wolf, he dominated her waking hours and her dreams. She absolutely needed to quit thinking about Wolf.

She'd been the same way with Tyler at the beginning, unable to get him out of her mind. They'd met soon after the eccentric elderly woman had sold her the Red Riding Hood snow globe. Seeing Avery so happy with Josh, Carlyn had been sure the snow globe had worked its magic on her, too, and sent her Tyler. Wrong!

After two fairytale months with him, she'd convinced herself that her teenage fantasies of a big wedding and a handsome groom who would love her forever had come true. Not!

The taxi sprang forward, jerking her back to the present. Carlyn rubbed a finger over her lips as the memory of Wolf's kiss dissolved her memories of Tyler. She wanted more of Wolf's kisses. Her mind said *no*, but her body said *yes*.

She exhaled in relief when the cab pulled up in front of the restaurant where Bella and Avery waited.

She found her two friends seated and enjoying wine. The women hugged, and Carlyn ordered a glass of wine. Her friends glowed with the happiness love had brought them.

Through dinner, Avery told them about her short honeymoon in San Francisco. She and Josh planned a longer trip to Italy in September. Bella, her face more animated than Carlyn had ever seen, talked about spending Christmas in Florida with Chad's family and their upcoming trip to Texas to visit her parents. Both women promised to attend Carlyn's school play on Valentine's Day.

Later, Carlyn lay in bed unable to sleep. Like a video on a loop, her mind kept replaying the evening with her friends. Although happy they'd both found love with wonderful men, their happiness sharpened Carlyn's loneliness.

She fluffed up her pillow and sank back down again. Of the three of them, she'd been the one who'd believed in love, in forever-after with the perfect man. Avery had wanted a man as ambitious as she. Yet, she fell in love with Josh who wasn't what she'd thought she wanted, but now, she and Josh were madly in love. The same with Bella. She'd wanted a passionless marriage to shield her from hurt. She threw all that aside when she met Chad. The passion between them shone from their faces when they were together.

Wolf's image intruded on Carlyn's thoughts. A smooth charmer, exotic and sexy, his nearness made everything surrounding her more vivid. Colors were sharper, sounds clearer, as if her whole body danced to a tune only she could hear. His sincerity and caring toward her grandmother showed a depth to his character. She shouldn't assume Wolf and Tyler were cut from the same cloth.

She punched her pillow again. She'd be a fool to trust Wolf. And she was no fool, not any more.

CHAPTER SIX

Carlyn held up her script, jabbed a finger onto the paper, and took a calming breath. The scent of pine oil used in cleaning the school auditorium teased her nostrils. Suppressing a cough, she faced her student, the lead in her play. "Stacy, you're supposed to be super excited that the hottest guy in school asked you to the dance. Please show us your excitement." Her voice resonated through the mostly empty theatre.

Sixteen-year-old Stacy let out a bored sigh and studied her fingernails, then looked at Carlyn. "Miss Cameron, I wouldn't get worked up about a guy asking me to a dance. Guys ask me out all the time." The teen pouted and stamped her foot. "Why do I have to have a scar on my face? My skin is perfect. I don't even have acne."

Carlyn massaged her temple. *God help me.* Directing teenage actors took more patience than herding cats. "Stacy, this is why it's called *acting.* Maybe *you* get asked to a lot of dances in real life, but your character, Amy, is a nerd, very shy, and she has a disfiguring scar. The cool kids mock her. Now, the school's wickedly sexy bad boy has asked her to the most important dance of the year. Put yourself in her place. How would you feel if no boy ever asked you out, and now one has, and the cutest guy in school at that?"

Carlyn waved the script. "Listen up, everyone." When she had the attention of the others in the cast, she continued. "Remember, Amy is a trusting, sweet girl, and Dylan is the school bad boy. All he really wants is love and understanding, but he hides that. The mean girls have crushes on Dylan, but he scares them a little. Dylan senses he doesn't scare Amy and that she sees through his defenses to the real him, and this is why he likes her. The lesson learned is that Amy sees the good in people. She sees Dylan's swagger as a disguise, to hide his deep hurt."

Carlyn turned her attention back to Stacy. "Stacy, dig deep into yourself and become Amy. You can do it. I wouldn't have chosen you for the lead if I didn't know you're a good actor."

Stacy raised her shoulder in a half-hearted shrug. "Okay. I'll try."

"Places, everyone," Carlyn said. "Let's take it from when Amy meets her friends after school and tells them Dylan has asked her to the dance."

Carlyn sank onto her director's chair at one corner of the small stage. The thick canvas cradled her butt, tempting her to relax and take a nap. Lack of sleep last night after dinner with her friends, then dealing with teens who didn't seem to understand the concept of acting, made the beginnings of a headache pulse behind her right temple. If she couldn't get her students to buy into her play, to live the parts, they'd never be ready for the Valentine's Day premiere.

"Carlyn, there you are." At Mr. Henninger's booming voice, Carlyn signaled to the kids to take a five minute break. Just what she needed, an interruption from the school's headmaster. Plastering a smile on her face, she stood and turned toward him. And froze.

Crap. Her lack of sleep had brought on hallucinations. That couldn't be Wolf, camera in hand, standing next to Mr. Henninger. She walked carefully down the steps leading from the stage, expecting to wake any second from this new nightmare.

Mr. Henninger rubbed his hands together. "Carlyn, Wolf tells me he knows you. This works out wonderfully."

"Hey, Carlyn." Wolf's wicked smile reminded her of the Big Bad Wolf meeting Red Riding Hood in the forest.

No fairytale, but Wolf in the flesh. She cleared her throat and nodded to him, then turned to her boss. "Mr. Henninger, what works out wonderfully?" Afraid of the answer, she stiffened, bracing herself.

"We want to give your show as much publicity as we can," Mr. Henninger said. "Our plays have always been good fund raisers. Wolf has agreed to photograph every aspect of the production, starting now. We'll post the pictures in the newspapers and put them in a booklet that we'll sell. I think it's a great idea, don't you?"

"Uh, sure." She'd be working with Wolf? She must have done something very bad to annoy the Fates, because they definitely had it in for her. First, Wolf moved in next door, and now he would be her play's official photographer.

Unbidden, her Red Riding Hood and wolf snow globe popped into her mind. *I don't believe in magic,* she repeated to herself like a mantra.

"Carlyn?" Mr. Henninger's voice brought her back to Earth.

"Good idea to have an official photographer," she lied. Considering Mr. Henninger had given the okay for her to put on her original work, she'd have to go along with anything he wanted.

"It's the weirdest thing," Mr. Henninger said. "I'd never thought of a professional photographer until the waitress at the coffee shop next door suggested it the other day. She even gave me Wolf's website where I could contact him."

"Waitress?" Carlyn asked. "Which one? I know them all."

He tapped his chin and squinted as if thinking too much hurt him. "Never saw her before that day, or after. Elderly. Strange orange-colored hair in a style straight out of the sixties. Very friendly. After I contacted Wolf, and he agreed, I went back to thank her. The other employees said no one with her description worked there." He shrugged. "Maybe she'd been switched to a different shift and that's why they didn't know her."

Chills, like cold fingers scraping over her skin, gave Carlyn goosebumps. "Of course, they didn't know the new employee on another shift. That's it." Her voice sounded far away. The elderly woman who'd sold her the snow globe had had orange hair. Cue *The Twilight Zone* music. Her imagination had run amok.

Henninger nodded at Wolf. "I need to get back to my office. I'm sure you two have details to discuss."

After the headmaster walked away, Wolf turned to Carlyn. "Guess we'll be working together."

With effort, she pulled herself out of *The Twilight Zone* and back to the real world. She frowned up at Wolf. "I sure didn't expect to see you here. New York is a big city, yet we keep running into each other."

He leaned closer "This is what happens when you mess with Fate. You end up with me."

Despite his teasing voice and words, the flash of

vulnerability that sparked in his eyes provoked curiosity and a smidgen of regret in Carlyn. Sure, Wolf seemed full of himself, but that didn't give her the right to treat him rudely.

"I don't believe in Fate," she said in a softer tone.

"How about coincidence?"

She chewed her lip. "Maybe."

"Now that we've gotten that settled, tell me about your play and introduce me to your cast."

His gaze drifted to her mouth. She knew he remembered the kiss they'd shared. Her fingers itched to loosen his hair and run her hands through its thickness, to touch his lips, to kiss him again.

"Here." She thrust the script at him, as if it could protect her from her traitorous musings.

He took the paper and scanned it, then raised his gaze to hers. "'Amy's Choice.' What's it about?"

"Trust and finding the good in people. In my play, the school bad boy is a good guy deep down, but he has dark secrets. He's healed by the love of a sweet girl."

"I like it. How did you come up with that idea?"

"It popped into my head one day when I looked at my Red Riding Hood snow globe. I wondered what if the wolf hadn't wanted blood but love and understanding."

He smiled. "Interesting. That's your creative mind at work. When I think of the fairytale, I think of the wolf devouring Red and her grandmother."

Carlyn frowned. "I'm surprised a photojournalist would take a job doing pictures for a high school play."

With a wry smile, he said, "Me, too. I started to refuse Henninger when his email came through my website, but something made me call him and agree." He shrugged. "I'm between jobs and I'm free. I don't need the money and it's for a good cause so I'm donating my time."

"That's really good of you." Warmth at his generosity settled in her chest and she began to relax a little.

"It's not a big deal."

"It is a big deal."

Hearing giggles from the stage, Carlyn turned to find her entire cast staring. The girls were in a cluster, watching Wolf, excited expressions on their faces. If only she could elicit that much enthusiasm from them during rehearsals. The boys stood to the side looking sullen. *Crap.* More trouble. She needed her cast to work as a unit.

"Come meet the actors," she said, heading toward the stage. "We still have a lot of rehearsing to do."

"My camera's ready," he said. "And I'm ready for whatever you throw at me."

The heck with the kids. She wanted to throw herself into his arms and kiss him senseless.

CHAPTER SEVEN

The next day, Carlyn found it hard to concentrate during her classes. After school, she'd see Wolf again. He'd gone home with her on the subway last evening, but to Carlyn's relief, declined Grandmom's invitation to dinner. Too much of Wolf Martinez could be dangerous to Carlyn's mental health.

Last period over, she gathered up her papers and stuffed them into her briefcase.

"Ms. Cameron." At Stacy's voice, Carlyn looked up from her desk.

Stacy and some of the other girls in the play crowded together in the doorway of her classroom. They'd hiked up their uniform skirts to above their knees, against school regulations. They each wore more makeup than usual.

"Girls, you'd better drop the hems on those skirts. You know you're not supposed to hike them up."

"It's after school hours," Mandy whined.

"As long as you're on school property, you follow the rules," Carlyn said.

Rolling their eyes and shrugging, the girls lowered their skirts to regulation length.

"Is Wolf coming today to take pictures?" Stacy asked.

"Yes. Now get to the theater so we can get started."

Whispering and giggling, the girls left.

Now the shorter skirts and extra makeup made sense. Dealing with teenage hormones had been hard enough without Wolf's presence stirring up the girls' libidos. Carlyn snapped her briefcase shut. She preferred to herd cats.

God, help me get through this and put on this play without anything else happening. She hit the light switch hard as she exited her office.

When Carlyn got to the school's theater, she found Wolf there taking pictures. The girls posed for him while the boys threw daggers at Wolf with their eyes.

Give me strength, Carlyn prayed.

"Hey, Carlyn." Wolf strode toward her. "Great crew you've got there." His features softened as he studied her. "You look nice. That orange scarf brings out your hair."

"Hi, Wolf. And thanks." At his compliment, her face heated, and she knew she blushed. Fighting her attraction to him, she stroked the soft cashmere scarf, a vintage one she'd bought at a flea market in London.

Unable to help herself, her gaze trailed over him. Wearing black jeans and a black sweater, and with a hipster stubble on his square jaw, he looked like the macho hero in a biker movie. A movie she'd see over and over just to watch him.

Stop it. She acted as googly-eyed as the teen girls. Carlyn threw her coat, purse, and briefcase onto a chair and marched toward the stage. "Places, everyone! We have a lot of work to do."

The rehearsal went better than usual. Carlyn suspected the girls wanted to impress Wolf with their acting ability and the boys wanted to impress the girls and get their attention off Wolf. Whatever the reason, it gave Carlyn hope for the success of her play.

After rehearsal, Wolf insisted on paying for a taxi to take Carlyn and him back to Brooklyn. Sitting so close in the intimate confines of the backseat, a slow, warm ache began to build in Carlyn. She pulled her jacket collar closer as if she could fight the strange yearning that pulsed through her.

"The play's coming along well," Wolf said into the charged silence.

"It is. The kids are working hard."

"You should be proud of them."

"I am."

He reached out and touched her hand where it lay on the seat. "You okay?"

"I'm fine. Just tired." *Tired of fighting my attraction to you.* Carlyn stared out the window, silent, for the remainder of the ride.

As they exited the elevator onto their floor, Carlyn's grandmother came into the hall. Carlyn suspected she'd been watching for them.

"You both look like you've had a long day," Grandmom said. "I've got dinner ready. Wolf, we've plenty. Please join us."

Carlyn had given up trying to fight Grandmom's obvious matchmaking. If Wolf noticed, he hid it. She'd gotten to know him a bit during the last two days working together. He might be a charmer, but he wasn't a slacker. He worked hard taking the pictures, lining the kids up for their shots, making them feel comfortable. She admired his skill and dedication. But she wouldn't allow herself to let down her guard around him. She didn't need any man in her life right now.

"Thanks for the dinner invitation, Eva. Some other time," he said. "I've got plans for tonight."

An unexpected surge of jealousy spiked in Carlyn. She wondered if his plans included a woman. What Wolf Martinez did in his private life didn't concern her, she reminded herself.

An hour later, Wolf trudged into the basement room of the small church. When he looked at the men and women crowding around the table where a coffee maker and donuts invited everyone to eat, he turned, ready to flee. He'd finally taken Josh's advice to seek help for his PTSD, but now he wanted nothing more than to bolt.

A hand clamped on his shoulder, stopping him. He gazed into the kind blue eyes of a middle-aged man. "Welcome, soldier," the stranger said. "I'm Bill Hayes. Come in. Stay. We can help."

"I'm not a soldier."

Hayes frowned. "Weren't you referred here by the military?"

Wolf nodded. "I'm a photojournalist. I've been embedded with units in Afghanistan and Iraq."

"Ah. We've had a few journalists here." The other man gestured with his hand. "Come. Meet everyone."

Wolf darted his eyes toward the door. The opening beckoned, and for a moment, he yearned to escape. No, he'd never run away from anything in his life, and he wouldn't start now. He caught a quick, calming breath. "Okay."

As a photographer, Wolf knew how to make small talk, to carry on conversations with strangers, to put them at ease. All that failed him now as he held a cup of coffee and bit into a donut. Despite the friendliness of the others in the PTSD support group, he felt like the awkward teen he'd been, before photography gave him a purpose in life.

After the coffee and donut break, Wolf sat in a circle with the ten others as they related their stories. He listened with half an ear, shoring up his courage.

"We played soccer with the kids in the morning," one of the men was saying. "By the afternoon, the village had been destroyed." The gruff ex-Marine swiped at his eyes. The others offered murmurs of understanding. The people on either side of the guy patted his arms.

After giving advice and encouragement to the ex-Marine, the group turned their attention to Wolf. He could avoid it no longer. He wiped his palms down the sides of his jeans. He could do this. He must do this. He couldn't go on the way he'd been, couldn't tolerate the nightmares and the sweats. His career, his life, depended on it too. Taking wedding pictures and pictures of high schoolers putting on a play wasn't him, wasn't what he wanted, what he'd worked so hard for.

Wolf straightened and swung his gaze around to the others. "My name is Wolf Martinez. I'm a photojournalist. Over the years, I've had multiple assignments with various Army units in Afghanistan and Iraq. The things I witnessed…" He scrubbed a hand over his face and stared at a spot on the far wall. "I thought I'd handled all that, but I know now my PTSD started a long time ago, but I didn't recognize it." His voice broke and he leaned forward with his hands clasped between his knees. "The little Iraqi girl who begged me to save her family finally broke me. I still see her image in my mind. I couldn't save them."

The people sitting around the circle faded, the room faded. Wolf was in Iraq again staring down at the face of the sweet child who'd seen too much death and ugliness in her short life.

Someone took his hand, pulling him from his torturous memories. The former Army nurse who'd told the story of an infant dying in her arms knelt before Wolf.

"It wasn't your fault, Wolf. You must believe that."

"I don't know if I can." Like the insurgents in Iraq overtaking a village, doubts rushed at Wolf. He squeezed the nurse's hand.

"You can and you must," she said softly. "We're here to help. Tell us your story."

CHAPTER EIGHT

"That Wolf is a nice young man," Carlyn's grandmother said. The two had finished dinner and were watching a sitcom.

"He's okay." A part of Carlyn wished Wolf had joined them for dinner. He'd admitted he didn't know many people in New York, and she wondered where he'd gone tonight.

"Carlyn Mary Cameron."

At her grandmother's sharp tone and use of her full name, Carlyn swiveled to face her. "What?"

"Wolf Martinez is more than okay. The sparks between you two could light this room. Why are you denying the obvious?"

Bristling, Carlyn hit the mute button on the TV remote. "I'm not denying anything. He's arrogant. Thinks because he's so good-looking, he can swagger around like some...some wolf in Armani. I'm off men for now. Maybe for good."

Her grandmother laughed. "Wolf in Armani. I like that. I don't find him arrogant and I like his swagger. He's a confident man. I find that very sexy."

"Grandmom!"

Her grandmother waved a hand. "Just because I'm old

doesn't mean I can't enjoy looking at a handsome man."

Carlyn turned the sound back up on the TV, stopping the conversation. She tried to watch the show, not really seeing the screen. She agreed with her grandmother. Wolf's confidence was sexy as hell. She'd come to know him as a talented photographer, a man who treated her grandmother and her students with kindness and respect, and a man who had depths she suspected he tried to hide. The vulnerability and sadness she glimpsed in his eyes at times arrowed straight to her soul.

For the sake of her still-broken heart, she vowed again to resist him.

After another week's worth of rehearsals, Carlyn felt confident she could put on a successful play. The kids finally gelled as a unit. She wondered if Wolf's presence had helped them feel like "real" actors. Whatever the reason, she felt grateful.

Rehearsal over, she said goodnight to the kids as they tramped out. She guessed they were as ready for the weekend as she was. She rolled her shoulders to relieve the tension from her muscles and grabbed her coat from a chair. As she struggled to get her arm into one of the coat sleeves, someone came up behind her and helped. She felt Wolf's heat and inhaled his unique scent of soap and male. He smoothed her coat over her shoulders, then turned her around to face him.

"It's Friday," he said. "Let's grab a bite to eat."

"A date?" *Crap*. Where had that come from?

"A date? Sure. You make it sound like a trip down death row."

She shook her head. "I don't know."

"Then we'll have a non-date."

Carlyn snatched her purse from one of the seats and held it close, using it as protection from Wolf's charm, from her insane desire for him. "I know better than to get involved with a man like you." The words slipped out. She wanted to bite them back.

"A man like me," he said softly. "You've never been with a man like me." Then before she could react, he pulled her to him. He dipped his head and took her lips in a kiss, tempting and luscious. She dropped her purse. His lips softened over hers, and her control shattered.

Flames seemed to lick over her skin, burning away her anxieties. With a small groan, she wrapped her arms around his neck, molding her body to his taut frame. His tongue, soft and hot, probed her mouth. He slid his hands along her spine, burning her to her core. Her body felt weightless and languid.

His kiss deepened and became more demanding. All her will and resistance vaporized into the air. She craved this man. The thought re-ignited her qualms. To give herself to him completely would mean giving him her trust. She wasn't ready to do that.

With a gasp, she pushed away, wiping her lips as if she could wipe away the memory of Wolf's kiss.

His breathing labored, he gripped her shoulders. "Will you go to dinner with me?" A challenge lit his eyes. "Or are you too afraid?"

"I'm not afraid of you." *Only what you do to me.*

He stepped back and held up his hands. "I know I come on too strong at times. I'm really attracted to you, and I like you, I like being with you. If I promise not to kiss you again tonight, will you go out with me? No strings attached. Just

215

two friends enjoying each other's company."

When he looked like he did now, sincere and vulnerable, a little bit of her heart melted along with her worries, but still—spending another second in his company?

When she hesitated, he said, "I have some ideas for the photos that I think will get more people to come to your play. Let's have dinner as two co-workers discussing a project. Will that work for you?"

The more tickets they sold to the play meant more money for the school. She and Wolf should discuss his ideas. She ignored the inner voice that told her she wanted to have dinner with Wolf for no reason other than to be with him.

"Okay, I'll have dinner with you. As co-workers."

He leaned closer. "Does that mean I don't have to promise not to kiss you?"

"Oh, that promise still holds. No kissing again. Ever."

"I promised not to kiss you tonight. I never said anything about ever again."

CHAPTER NINE

"Thanks for dinner," Carlyn said when she and Wolf stood in the hallway outside their apartments. "I loved that funky little Mexican place. Such fun, and great food. All the time I've lived here, I didn't know that place existed. Grandmom is right. I need to get out more." She'd had a good time with Wolf. She'd pegged him for a haughty, brash guy, but he knew how to tell humorous stories that denigrated himself. Maybe she needed an attitude adjustment about him. She could like him, but not lose her heart to him. Sure she could.

"Glad you liked the place," he said. "I discovered it a few years ago on one of my trips to Manhattan." He stepped closer. "Having you with me made everything more enjoyable tonight." His voice had thickened. He caressed her cheek with his thumb. "Your grandmother is right. You need to get out more. With me."

His touch electrified every part of her body. She backed away until she pressed against her apartment door. "Don't do that."

A wicked spark shone in his eyes. "Do what?"

"You promised no kissing."

"I didn't promise not to touch you."

"Stop teasing."

"Who's teasing? You must know I want you."

Shivering at the sudden rush of pleasure his words provoked, she lowered her gaze. She needed to protect herself against the yearning for him that ignited a fire in her, a fire she might never extinguish.

She met his eyes again. "Wolf, I can't do this. I have no interest in any kind of relationship with you or any man right now. I'm focusing on my career." *Oh, but I want you to kiss me.*

His eyes softened. "Who hurt you?"

She frowned and shook her head. "I need to go in or Grandmom will worry about me."

With a resigned expression, he moved away. "I won't press you, but maybe someday you'll tell me who made you so wary of men, and why."

"Good night, Wolf." She slid her key into the lock and opened the door, slipping inside. She shut the door, shutting him out of her heart. The quiet told her Grandmom had retired early. Carlyn padded softly to her own room. She wasn't so sure anymore that she wanted to push Wolf away. Frissons of anxiety and excitement raced up her spine.

Wolf walked slowly back to his apartment. He closed the door behind him and threw his keys on the small table nearby, knocking over a statue of a brass monkey that rested on the table. "Damn it!" He picked up the statue and put it back. A tall lamp illuminated the living room, crowded with overstuffed furniture and knickknacks. The place reflected Gigi's over-the-top tastes. He preferred a sparse décor, but he lived a nomad's life, staying in hotels, some five-star, some little more than hovels, around the world.

Rubbing his hand over his face, he sank onto a velvet chair with tufted cushions. He played with fire, coming on to Carlyn so strongly. No matter how hard she tried to project the persona of a sophisticated woman of the world, he sensed the sweet vulnerability in her, the insecurity she tried to hide. She'd told him she'd been raised in a small town in Maine. She carried that small-town girl with her. He grinned. If he told her that, she'd probably haul off and hit him. He needed someone like Carlyn in his life, someone who could soothe away his demons, a woman who would stand by his side. He shook aside the thought. He would never subject a woman to the kind of life he led.

He massaged the back of his neck, fighting the ever-present angst that had become a part of him. He needed to get back out into the world, to take the photos that might save a life, the photos that would call people to a cause. If he didn't beat this PTSD, he'd be lost.

And if he successfully fought it, he'd soon leave the country on another assignment. He'd possibly never see Carlyn again. He pinched the bridge of his nose and leaned his head back. He'd allowed himself to get close to her. For her sake, he'd pull away. He didn't want to hurt her.

After the weekend, the next two days at school passed quickly for Carlyn. Rehearsals had gone well. Optimism that she could pull this play together in time for Valentine's Day put a spring in her step as she hurried down the hall and out the school's front doors. Snow had been forecast for tomorrow. Her students had been restless today, sensing a snow day coming.

Carlyn could use a lazy snow day, but she worried about

losing rehearsal time. Every day until the play's opening was critical. As she strode toward the subway, she looked over her shoulder, half hoping she'd see Wolf sprinting behind her. He hadn't shown up at rehearsal yesterday or today, and when she'd seen him at her apartment building the day after their dinner together, he'd been cool to her. Maybe he'd finally gotten the hint she wasn't interested. Regret knotted her stomach. A part of her wanted him to fight for her.

CHAPTER TEN

By the time Carlyn arrived home, snow had started falling. The next morning, eight inches of the stuff crippled New York City. Schools were closed. She and her grandmother sat in the kitchen having a leisurely breakfast, a rarity during the week.

"I can't believe these New Yorkers," Grandmom said, setting down her coffee mug. "Eight inches of snow and the city closes down. That would be nothing in Maine."

"I know, Grandmom." Carlyn shrugged. "Since I've been living here, I freak out too with just a few inches."

Grandmom laughed. "Wuss." She finished her scrambled eggs and pushed the empty plate away. "I wonder what Wolf is doing today." She turned toward Carlyn with a sly grin. "Maybe we should invite him over. There must be a movie or two we can stream and all enjoy. We can make popcorn."

Shaking her head, Carlyn set her mug onto the granite countertop. "Grandmom, we don't need Wolf. We can have a great time by ourselves. I'm sure he has better things to do than hang out with us." A snow day with Wolf would be heavenly, but she already liked him more than was safe to her heart.

"Chill," Grandmom said. "Sometimes you think too much."

"Chill? Who are you and what have you done with my grandmother?"

Grandmom chuckled. "I got that from the kids I mentor." She leaned her elbows on the counter and met Carlyn's eyes. "My dear, I think you doth protest too much about Wolf. I know you like him, and I know he likes you. And I think he'd hang around here with this old lady if it meant being close to you."

"You don't know what you're talking about." Carlyn averted her gaze, hoping her grandmother wouldn't see the lie in her eyes.

A knock at the door made them jump.

"Who could that be?" The excitement that swirled through Carlyn like furious snowflakes told her Wolf stood outside.

She brushed a hand over her hair, messed up from sleep, and looked down at the yoga top and pants she wore. She was so not ready to see Wolf.

"You're fine, dear," Grandmom said. "I don't think Wolf will mind at all."

The doorbell rang again, propelling Carlyn from her stool. With a glare at her grandmother, she strode to the door and looked through the peephole. Just as she thought, Wolf stood there, looking better than any man had a right to this early in the morning. She opened the door to him.

Wearing a dark green sweater and faded jeans, and holding a basket covered with a red-checkered cloth, he looked good enough to devour. Frozen to the spot, Carlyn drank in his hotness. Her heart tripped wildly.

"'Morning," he said.

"Carlyn, where are your manners? Let the poor man in," Grandmom called out.

"Oh, sure. Come in." Carlyn stepped aside for Wolf, then shut the door, leaning against it. The sight of all that falling snow must have addled her brain because she couldn't stop looking at him, at the way his jeans hugged his muscular thighs, and the way his sweater stretched across his broad back.

"Hi, Eva." With long-legged strides he walked to the kitchen area and deposited his basket onto the counter in front of Grandmom.

"What have you got there, young man?" Grandmom asked.

"Chocolate chip cookies."

Carlyn mentally pulled herself together and headed back to the kitchen. "I love chocolate chip cookies. Did you bake these yourself?"

"Sure did. This morning." Wolf opened the checkered cover to reveal golden cookies bursting with melted chocolate chips. "Have one." He held the basket out to Grandmom, who took a cookie, then to Carlyn.

Carlyn bit into the cookie and groaned. "This is wonderful."

Wolf's eyes met hers. Something hot and pulsing passed between them.

"We're very glad you like to bake, Wolf." Grandmom's words thawed some of the sexual tension that hung over the room heavy as the snow falling outside. "You're spoiling us, isn't he, Carlyn?"

"Uh, yes. We love your baking." She grabbed her mug off the counter and took a long swallow of the cooling coffee.

"Thanks, neighbors. I'm always glad to share." He glanced at Carlyn. "I heard the Manhattan schools are closed today."

She nodded. "I love snow days, but not when it means losing a day or two of rehearsal."

"Have some coffee, Wolf, and sit," Grandmom said.

"Thanks." He sat at the counter and took the mug of coffee Grandmom poured.

"I wouldn't worry much about rehearsal, Carlyn," he said. "The kids are doing great and the play is coming along. A few days off might make your actors fresh and ready to go."

"I hope you're right."

"Carlyn and I are planning to stream some movies today," Grandmom said. "Will you join us? We'll have popcorn and wine, and dinner later."

"Sounds great. There's something I want to do first though."

"What's that?" Grandmom asked.

He shifted to face Carlyn. "I hear Central Park is beautiful when it snows. The subway is running. I want to go into the city, but I hate to go alone. Will you go with me, Carlyn?" Nodding toward Grandmom, he said, "You're invited too, Eva."

Grandmom held up a hand. "You young people go along. I couldn't handle all that walking."

A rush of adrenaline shot through Carlyn's veins. Wolf Martinez spelled danger in every way. She opened her mouth to say no. Her gaze fell on the Red Riding Hood snow globe. Central Park. Snow. Maybe she could learn to trust herself with him, for a little while.

HER RED RIDING HOOD VALENTINE

Turning to Wolf, she said, "I'd love to go to Central Park with you."

CHAPTER ELEVEN

It had stopped snowing by the time they got to Manhattan. Wolf breathed in the crisp, snow-laden air, enjoying the sights of a city coming to life. Pedestrians scurried by, faces red from the cold. Shopkeepers called out to each other as they shoveled snow from the sidewalks in front of their stores. Cars moved slowly in the wake of the large snowplows that rumbled by clearing the roads.

As Wolf and Carlyn walked, he took her hand in his. When she didn't pull away, he felt a tug on his heart. As many times as he told himself he should not get involved with her, her sweetness and her trust were a balm to his weary soul, a soul that had seen too much of the underside of life. The thought of spending the day alone at his apartment had propelled him to seek Carlyn out, to use her goodness to help him forget, for a while.

"It's a glistening fairytale place," she said, her eyes meeting his as they entered the park. Her green eyes sparkled like the sun shining on snow, and her flaming red curls spilled from the black knitted cap she wore. Wolf wanted to gather her into his arms and never let her go. She reminded him of a Christmas angel ornament come to life. If only he could stop time and make this moment last forever.

Inhaling the cold air, he scanned the park. Teenaged boys and girls, heads bent over their phones, walked along, seeming oblivious to nature's splendor spread before them. Couples strolled hand-in-hand, and young children broke free of their parents to run laughing through the snow. Joggers sprinted by, and even a few intrepid bicyclists carefully negotiated the snow-covered trails. Wolf saw a man on cross-country skis a little farther away. He shook his head. Nothing could deter some New Yorkers from their exercise rituals.

Carlyn dropped his hand and grinned at him with a teasing glint in her eyes. "The park may look like a fairytale, but I'm no princess." She ran to a small pile of snow and quickly grabbed a handful to press into a ball.

"Oh, no, you don't." Laughing, Wolf checked around for snow he could shape into a ball. He wasn't quick enough. Carlyn threw a snowball that hit him squarely in the back.

Wolf gathered some new-fallen snow in his hands and formed a ball. The light snow wasn't as good as the heavier stuff for making first-class snowballs, but it would do.

He threw his snowball and hit Carlyn in the arm. Her delighted laugh rang out in the clear air and raced straight to Wolf's heart. He wished he could make her laugh like that all the time.

"My aim's better than yours," she taunted as she pressed more snow between her hands. Aiming, she prepared to throw, but Wolf ducked and she missed. "I'll get you." She started to chase him.

Wolf let her get close, then turned and tackled her, sending them both to the soft snow-blanketed ground. He braced himself over her.

Her laugh died and her eyes darkened. He stared down at her, at her cheeks pink from the cold, and at her full mouth, inviting him to taste. With a groan, he bent to capture her lips with his. She wound her arms around his neck and kissed him with enough heat to melt the snow around them.

He ran his tongue along the seam of her lips until she opened to him. They tasted each other for several passion-filled minutes. The excited screams of kids running through the park finally tore Wolf from his sensual trance. He ended the kiss and leaned over her, his weight on his forearms on either side of her head.

Carlyn opened her eyes, still smoky with passion. Her delectable lips were red from his kiss. She reached up and skimmed a gloved finger over his mouth. "I feel like I'm in a Hallmark movie."

He chuckled. "Our Hallmark movie would be hotter than anything you'd see on TV."

She flushed and glanced away.

He stood and reached down to grab her hand and help her up. She wouldn't look at him.

Wolf touched her chin with his fingers until their eyes met. "Hey, it's okay. I'd never do anything you wouldn't want."

She exhaled, sending wisps of her breath into the icy air. "I know that. I can't get involved with you. I can't get involved with any man. It's too soon."

He put a finger over her lips. "We won't talk about that now. Let's walk."

When Wolf took her hand again, Carlyn didn't resist. His big hand engulfing her much smaller one made him feel protective. Not that Carlyn needed protection. A smart, independent woman, she could take care of herself. Yet, a part of him wanted to cherish her and shield her from harm. When a blast of freezing air hit them, Carlyn shivered. Wolf put his arm around her shoulders and pulled her against him. "You're cold. Let's get something hot to drink, then head back to Brooklyn."

"Sounds good."

Later, they sat at a small café overlooking the ice skaters at Rockefeller Center and drank rich hot chocolate. Seeming as contented as a kitten on a sunny windowsill, Carlyn wrapped her hands around her mug. "This is the best hot chocolate ever."

"It is good, but I suspect anything hot would be good right now."

Her eyes danced. "You're right." She gazed out over the skaters. "I haven't ice skated in years, but I've always loved it. Everyone out there looks so cheerful and colorful."

He chuckled. "And probably freezing their butts off. I've never ice skated in my life. Not much ice in Las Vegas."

"I'll have to teach you."

He held up a hand. "Seeing how ruthless you are in a snowball fight, I'm not sure I trust you on the ice."

Her joyous laugh sent a jolt of pleasure through him. He sipped more of his drink and met her gaze over the rim of his mug. Setting down his drink, he reached across the table to place his hand over hers. "I've had a great time today."

"Me, too."

Carlyn had found a way into his heart and made him begin to imagine a life with her by his side. A kernel of anxiety opened in him. He didn't know if he could change, if he could give up the life he'd known for fifteen years.

"Wolf, will you be leaving soon on an assignment?" Her gently spoken words drew him from his jumbled thoughts.

He didn't want to think about leaving her, not yet. "Probably."

"Tell me about your work."

When she looked at him like that, her clear green gaze studying him, he wanted to hand her his heart. "I'd rather not talk about me," he said.

She tilted her head and watched him, as if trying to see through him. "You're nothing like I thought in the beginning," she said, her tone soft.

Relieved she didn't ask any more questions about his work, he released her hand and grinned. "I'm not so arrogant after all?"

"You're arrogant all right."

"You smiled when you said that. It's a start."

"You're a tad over-confident, but you're a hard worker and talented. I admire what you've done with my kids." Her smile grew wider. "Grandmom likes you."

He laughed. "That was my plan all along. Get the grandmother to like me, and you'd fall into place."

Her lips twitched. "Watch it, mister. You're getting too sure of yourself."

Grinning, he picked up his mug and finished his drink. Despite her teasing, she still held part of herself back. Someone had hurt her. Wolf wanted to punch the guy's lights out. A perverse part of him needed to know who put the hurt he saw in her eyes. He leaned closer. "Who hurt you?"

She turned away.

Damn! He'd gone too far and ruined their day together.

Carlyn ran a finger down the side of her mug, then turned to lock gazes with him. "I always believed in love, a fairytale type love," she said, her voice whisper-soft. "My parents have been married over forty years, and they still hold hands and stare at each other with stars in their eyes. That's what I wanted."

"Wanted?"

"I no longer believe in happy-ever-after. And that's okay. I see things more realistically now. I have to find my own happiness. I can't depend on anyone else."

He frowned. "That's a little cynical for someone as warm as you. True you have to make your own happiness, but it's good to share your life with someone. What's his name?"

"Whose name?"

"The man who hurt you." The thought of Carlyn with another man slammed Wolf with an unwelcome hit of jealousy.

Her shoulders sagged and she lifted her mug to her mouth and drank. He thought she wouldn't answer. Pushing aside her mug, she folded her hands on the table and stared out the window. "I met Tyler a little over a year ago. He was everything I'd always wanted in a man. Talented, ambitious, hard-working, affectionate. He treated me like a princess— showered me with gifts, sent me flowers, and cooked dinner for me. He took me to the trendiest spots in the city and made me feel like the only woman in the world."

When Carlyn met Wolf's gaze again, sadness reflected in the depths of her green eyes. "Through it all, he told me he loved me, that he'd do anything for me. I thought I'd found my very own fairytale prince." She let out a bitter laugh. "He was no prince."

"What happened?"

"He cheated on me. With his wife."

Wolf jerked his head back. "What?"

"Seems good old Tyler, the prince, was a serial cheater. He lied to me. Told me he was single. He had a luxury apartment in SoHo, a real bachelor pad, and a wife and kids in the 'burbs." Carlyn's voice had taken on a hard edge. "I wasn't his first conquest. He had a pattern of seducing gullible women, then dumping them when they got too close. A few days after I told him I loved him, he confessed he had a wife."

Carlyn's eyes filled with tears. The urge to protect and soothe her drove Wolf from his seat, ready to fold her into his arms. When Carlyn gave him a confused look, he sat back down. He didn't want to spook her after she'd bared her heart to him. "I'm sorry, Carlyn. That must have torn you apart. You're better off without that scumbag."

She looked down at the table and traced a finger over the scarred wood. "I know, but I feel like a character in a bad soap opera. I wanted so badly to have my prince on a white horse and my happy-ever-after that I let down my guard."

"Hey, look at me," he said softly.

When her eyes slid to his, he smiled. "Don't blame yourself for being a kind, loving, and trusting woman. And don't ever change."

A tear rolled down her cheek. Wolf reached across the table and wiped it away with his finger.

"I don't know why I told you all that," she whispered. "Thanks for understanding."

"What are friends for?" He stood and dug into his pocket to pull out his wallet. Drawing some bills from it, he threw them on the table, shoved his wallet back into his pocket, then held out his hand to Carlyn. "Let's go. Grandmom will get worried."

Carlyn smiled and put her hand in his, allowing him to

help her stand. "Oh, she's your grandmother now?"

Wolf put his arm around Carlyn and kissed the top of her head. "Grandmom likes me and I like her."

"So you're not the big bad wolf coming to devour the helpless old grandmother?"

He pulled Carlyn against his chest. "No, but I'd like to devour her granddaughter."

CHAPTER TWELVE

As they walked to the subway station, hand-in-hand, the quiet beauty of the snow-filled city enveloped Carlyn in a sense of peace she hadn't known for a long time. Her healing after the wounds inflicted by Tyler had begun. Talking to Wolf, being with him, released some of the pain she'd been holding. She slid a glance at him. Strands of his long midnight hair had loosened from the leather thong and brushed his rough-hewn face. Despite the modern style of his black leather jacket, jeans, and biker boots, she pictured him dressed in the garb of the Plains Indians, riding his horse with the speed of the wind whipping over the grasslands.

When she shivered, Wolf pulled her closer. Comfortable and easy to talk to, he made her feel alive again. She snuggled against him. She was falling for him. A part of her had begun to dream again. The thought scared the crap out of her. She'd held the ache from Tyler's betrayal close as a protection against hurt.

Carlyn drew in a deep breath and held it for long seconds. She couldn't risk another broken heart. She would not allow herself to love Wolf Martinez.

◇◇◇

At school the next day, the grumpy expressions on the

faces of the students and faculty reflected the sluggishness Carlyn felt throughout her body. It seemed no one wanted to be there after the unexpected day off.

Carlyn had spent another near sleepless night, tossing and turning, filled with images of Wolf. From the first time she'd seen him, she'd been attracted to him. Even with his lame come-on line about marrying her, she'd felt his allure. If she allowed herself to love him, what then? She barely knew him. He could truly be a predatory wolf, luring her into trusting him, then striking, consuming her heart. Maybe she wasn't being fair to him. One thing she knew for sure—he'd leave soon for some distant part of the world. She'd be alone, possibly nursing another broken heart. The worries and doubts—and the longing for him—muddled in her mind until she woke with a headache.

She'd see him this afternoon at rehearsal. It would be better for her self-preservation if she never saw him again. The thought of never seeing Wolf again ripped a hole in her heart.

At rehearsal, the kids were cranky, and Carlyn couldn't blame them. With Valentine's Day less than two weeks away, the stress of pulling the play together wore on her already stretched nerves. It didn't help that Wolf showed up, said a few words to her, then proceeded to take his photos, ignoring her. He left after a gruff goodbye that made Carlyn want to throw her director's chair at him.

Nursing a beer, Wolf sat in his apartment and picked up the TV remote, idly clicking through the stations until he found a cop show. He'd been attending the PTSD meetings twice a week for several weeks, yet the nightmares persisted. After spending yesterday with Carlyn, a day that made him realize all he'd given up by his globe-trotting lifestyle, he'd tossed and turned in his bed most of the night.

He'd wanted to talk to her today at rehearsal, but he needed to keep some distance until he worked out his feelings toward her. In the short time he'd known her, she'd turned him around, made him long for a different life. He needed time to figure out what he wanted. First, he had to heal.

Barely noticing the show playing on the screen, he sipped his beer as his mind whirled with images of Iraq. The military had called him a hero for saving that little girl's life. By the time he'd gotten her out of the burning hovel, the flames were too thick to save the rest of her family. He'd promised her, and he'd failed her. Regret, like a fist, grabbed his heart and squeezed.

At the soft knock on his door, he jerked his head up. "Come in. It's open." He muted the TV.

Carlyn slipped inside, a hesitant expression on her face. She blinked, adjusting to the dimness, then raised her eyes to him. "I brought back your basket." She held out the basket with the checkered napkin tucked inside.

"Thanks. You can put it on the table. Do you want a beer?"

"No, I'm good." She put the basket down and strode over to him. "What's wrong, Wolf?" She knelt in front of him and put a hand on his knee. "We had a great time yesterday, and today at school, you hardly spoke to me. Now, you're sitting here all alone in the dark."

He clenched his free hand, resisting the urge to touch her, to run his fingers through her soft curls. "It's not dark. There's light from the TV."

With a wry grin, she said, "Very little light. Tell me

what's wrong. Maybe I can help. I'm a good listener."

"I don't need your help." He hadn't meant to sound so harsh.

At the hurt in her eyes, he wanted to take her into his arms and kiss away the pain, hers and his. He didn't know if he could stay here, if he could change his life. If they got close and he left, he might break her heart. Wolf would do whatever he could to safeguard her from hurt, even if it meant losing her.

"Thanks for bringing the basket," he said.

She stood slowly, disappointment etched on her smooth features. "Okay. See you tomorrow at school."

"I won't be there. I have an appointment." His support group had decided to meet earlier than normal tomorrow. Wolf couldn't miss any of the meetings. He had to heal and get back to his work.

He chugged his beer as Carlyn walked slowly out of his apartment. Maybe out of his life. He threw the empty beer bottle across the room, and fittingly, it shattered on the hardwood floor.

CHAPTER THIRTEEN

Wolf didn't show up at rehearsal the rest of the week. "No big deal," Carlyn said to her reflection in her mirror. She sat at her vanity table in her bedroom Friday evening putting the finishing touches on her makeup. With him acting so distant, he made it hard to fall in love with him. She pressed a hand to her stomach. Too late.

"You've got it bad, girl. You tell yourself you don't want a relationship, especially with a guy who's too handsome. Not to mention that he's leaving the country soon. Then, you go right ahead and fall in love with him." She had to quit talking to herself.

She threw her makeup brushes into the drawer and slammed it shut. She'd had a great time with him in Central Park a few days ago, then bared her soul to him. When she reached out to him the other night, as a friend who wanted to help, he almost threw her out of his place. The jerk.

Willing steel into her spine, she stood up from the vanity stool. She needed to get going. Avery and Josh had invited her, along with Bella and Chad, to their Manhattan apartment to view the photos from the wedding. Spending time with her friends would put her in better spirits.

Although seeing the happiness between the other couples might dampen her mood.

When she came out of her bedroom, she found Grandmom sitting on the sofa sipping tea and watching her favorite soap that she'd recorded earlier. Grandmom put down her cup and smiled at Carlyn.

"You look nice, dear. That red sweater becomes you. Not many redheads can carry off that color."

"Thanks, Grandmom." To cheer herself up, Carlyn wore her favorite sweater with her indigo skinny jeans and her bright red stiletto booties. She'd pulled her unruly hair into a ponytail, the better to showcase the vintage pearl drop earrings. She wondered why she'd taken such care when she'd be the proverbial fifth wheel tonight. "Are you sure you don't want to come with me, Grandmom? Avery and Josh included you in the invitation."

Grandmom waved a hand. "I'm fine settled here with my tea and my soaps. You young people have a good time."

"I won't be late." Carlyn hauled her dark green leather jacket from the closet and slipped it on. She wrapped her favorite wool scarf, in a rainbow of bright colors, around her neck, and pulled on green leather gloves. After kissing her grandmother on the cheek, she slung her small cross-body red purse over her and exited her apartment.

And came face-to-face with Wolf leaving his place.

Feeling awkward as the nerdy teen character in her school play, Carlyn shifted uncomfortably.

"Hey, Carlyn. How have the rehearsals been going? I have more pictures than I need and I had some things to do so I figured I'd skip the last few days."

She'd been worrying about him and wondering if he'd gotten over his funk, and he acted as if he hadn't given her a thought. Hurt tightened her throat. Like any good actor, she'd play her part and pretend she didn't care. "The rehearsals have gone better than I could have hoped." She smiled. "We may bring this thing in on time after all."

"Of course you will. You're a talented playwright and director."

"Uh, thanks."

"Heading out?" he asked.

She nodded. "Manhattan."

"Me too." He studied her. "You wouldn't happen to be going to Avery and Josh's?"

Uh-oh. The tightening in her throat spread to her chest. "I am."

"So am I. We can share a cab."

She could refuse but that would be silly. They'd end up at the same place anyway. "Okay." Strange Avery hadn't mentioned Wolf when she'd invited Carlyn. Or maybe not so strange. She suspected what her friends were up to and she'd have none of it.

The photos Wolf had taken at the wedding were extraordinary. The colors popped off the paper, vivid and real. He'd captured the happiness on the faces of the wedding party and guests, in real poses, and nothing that came off contrived. The love between Avery and Josh reflected in their eyes and smiles. Carlyn's respect for Wolf's talent grew.

Embarrassment warmed her face as she perused all the pictures he'd taken of her. If the others noticed, they mercifully kept silent. When Wolf offered to give her several of the photos of herself and have them framed, her friends could hardly hide their glee.

Matchmakers!

Later, her stomach filled with Josh's five-alarm chili, and sipping red wine in front of a crackling fire, Carlyn's contentment mingled with the excitement Wolf's nearness always provoked in her.

As she watched her friends, sadness and a spark of unwanted envy surged in Carlyn. Newlyweds Avery and Josh snuggled close on the leather sectional. Bella and Chad, seated at the other end, touched each other's hands as if they couldn't get enough of the other person. Carlyn sat in the center of the large sectional, with Wolf perched on the chair facing them.

Barely listening to the conversations of the others, she looked across to Wolf. He seemed to sense her stare because his gaze met hers. The fire in his eyes lit a flame of want deep inside her. She shifted.

"How's the play coming along?" Avery asked, breaking the spell between Carlyn and Wolf.

"Really well." Carlyn directed her attention at Avery. "For a while I doubted we'd be ready by opening night on Valentine's Day, but we'll make it."

"It's a great play," Wolf said. "Carlyn's a terrific writer and director. I hope you're all coming to the play. You won't be sorry."

"We wouldn't miss it," Bella said. "Carlyn tells us you've taken some amazing pictures."

"They're wonderful." Carlyn couldn't keep the enthusiasm out of her voice. "We're using them to publicize the show. This will be our best fund raiser ever."

"Your school should bring in a lot of money considering Wolf Martinez is the photographer," Bella said. She leaned forward to focus on Wolf. "I've seen your amazing photos from Afghanistan and Iraq. My gallery would love to show them. What do you say? I'll talk to my boss about it."

Wolf's features tightened. "Thanks for the offer, but I'm not interested." He looked down at his watch. "It's getting late. We'd better be going."

Confusion flitted across Bella's face. "Okay. If you change your mind, let me know."

"I wish you didn't have to leave," Avery said.

Anxious to diffuse the sudden tension in the room, Carlyn stood too. "Wolf is right. We've got a long cab ride."

Avery shook her head. "I still can't believe you two live next door to each other. Talk about coincidence. I'll get your coats." She jumped up and headed to the small coat closet.

"Wolf, can we talk a minute?" Josh asked.

"Sure." Wolf followed Josh into the kitchen.

"What just happened?" Bella asked Carlyn. "Wolf acted so strange when I mentioned having a showing at the gallery."

Carlyn held out her hands and shook her head.

"Let it go, sweetheart." Chad pulled Bella back to sit close to him. "Wolf has some things he needs to work through."

Carlyn looked toward the open kitchen. Josh and Wolf appeared to be in a serious conversation. Josh put his hand on Wolf's upper arm as they talked. Wolf's rigid posture and closed features communicated his discomfort.

Tension rode in the silent cab with Carlyn and Wolf on the trip back to Cobble Hill.

Finally, they were at their building and Wolf paid the fare, refusing to allow Carlyn to pay any of it. When they exited the elevator on their floor, Carlyn turned to Wolf.

"Good night," she said.

"Carlyn." He stepped closer.

She put her hands on his chest, stopping him.

"What's wrong?" he asked.

"I thought we were friends, but when I reached out to you the other day, you sent me away."

Sadness flashed in his dark eyes. "I'm sorry, Carlyn. I didn't mean to hurt you. There are things going on I have to work out. Will you trust me a little longer?"

At the sincerity and hope in his voice, warmth settled in the center of her chest. She would trust him, but be cautious.

When she nodded, his eyes softened and he gathered her to him. He bent to take her lips in a fervid kiss that quickened her blood. She melted into him. He backed her up until she pressed against the wall. Consumed in his heat, in her own fiery need for him, she softened against him, winding her arms around his neck.

He trailed hot kisses down her throat. With quick movements, he pushed aside her scarf, unbuttoned her jacket and spread the coat apart. When his lips brushed the tops of her breasts exposed by the vee of her sweater, she groaned. He kissed her mouth again, his lips hot and demanding, while he gently massaged her breasts with his large hands. Her knees had the consistency of jelly. She wrapped her arms around his waist and gave herself over to his skilled mouth and hands.

Body on fire and her insides liquefied, she wanted the kiss to go on forever. Too soon, he drew away.

Still holding her against the wall, Wolf raised her arms above her head and grasped her wrists with one of his hands.

"We're good together," he whispered.

"Sex isn't enough to keep a relationship going." Her voice shook. "I'm not ready for this, Wolf. You're not what

I want." The lie rolled off her tongue. He was everything she wanted but didn't need.

"What do you want?" His intense brown eyes searched hers, the heat in them warming her as much as his touch had.

"I want a stable, ordinary guy who will always remain loyal and always be there for me."

"And I'm not that guy?"

"You're exciting and sexy. That's not enough. I don't know much about you. When your sublet is up, you'll go away. I don't even know if you have a permanent address, or if Wolf is your given name or a nickname."

Regret flickered in Wolf's eyes and he stepped back. "You're right. I live a gypsy life and go where my work takes me. I don't have a permanent address. Some of my stuff is stored at my parents' place in Vegas, but I don't live there. Wolf is my given name. My mother's father was a Cherokee from the Wolf clan. My mother's mother is Navajo, and my dad's family came from Spain in the 1700's and settled originally in California. Now you know."

He skimmed a finger over her bottom lip. "I've fought my feelings for you from the beginning. It's been a losing battle. You deserve that guy who's steady and who will always be here for you. I don't know if I can be that guy. Goodnight, Carlyn."

She felt him watch as she unlocked her door and slipped into her apartment.

She leaned against the closed door as a tear burned a trail down her cheek.

CHAPTER FOURTEEN

Grateful Grandmom had gone to bed, Carlyn fixed herself a cup of tea and sat at her desk with her laptop. Knowing she wouldn't sleep, she pulled up her latest work-in-progress, a play darker than what she usually wrote. Writing always took her mind from her troubles, but tonight she had her doubts.

Wolf's kiss intruded on her thoughts, marring her concentration. She glanced toward the window, the curtains drawn tight against the February night, and rubbed her lips. His kiss had provoked a craving in her for something wild and untamed, a need no other man had ever incited. She knew very little about Wolf, and despite her first reaction to him, she'd seen his different sides, compelling her to think better of him.

Carlyn rubbed a hand over her tired eyes. She liked the way Wolf interacted with her students. He'd gained their trust. He knew how to bring out the best in people. She'd become ashamed of her initial assessment of him. He'd even brought out her better angels, helping her heal, teaching her not to assume a man who looked like him couldn't be trusted. So afraid of being hurt again, she'd closed her mind to

Wolf's good qualities.

The evening played back in her mind. When Bella mentioned Iraq and Afghanistan, Wolf had closed up. Why? Carlyn stared at her computer screen and slapped her forehead with her hand. *Duh.* She'd been so caught up in trying to resist him that she'd never done an Internet search for him.

She opened the browser on her computer and typed in "Wolf Martinez." Up popped a full page bearing his name. She clicked on a heading marked, "Photos of an American Hero." Pictures of Wolf, dressed in fatigues, surrounded by soldiers, came up. The landscape looked forbidding, desolate, like a dead planet.

The pictures were accompanied by an article titled, "Photojournalist Wolf Martinez Saves Iraqi Girl's Life." Insides shaking, Carlyn clicked on the link.

Goosebumps rose on her arms, despite the hot tea she sipped, as she quickly perused the article. Wolf had been embedded with a division of American soldiers. They'd been searching an Iraqi village for insurgents when the village had come under attack. When one of the houses caught fire, they heard a little girl's screams. Against orders from the commanding officer, Wolf had rushed into the house. He came out minutes later carrying the five-year-old girl. When he handed the girl to one of the medics, she'd begged him to rescue the rest of her family. Promising he would, Wolf ran to the house again. Flames kept him from entering. Soldiers pulled him back seconds before the house blew up.

According to the article, Wolf hadn't wanted any attention for what he'd done, but the Army lieutenant had told the media, and Wolf the journalist had become the story. Carlyn's tea sat cooling as she read on, mesmerized by this different view of Wolf. She learned that he, together with a group of journalists, had set up a fund to bring wounded Afghan and Iraqi children to the United States for medical treatment not available to them at home.

When she finished the article, she sat back, her mind a whirl of emotions. Wolf had risked his life for that child and had helped other children. Guilt formed a vise around her heart. She'd given him the role of villain, when in reality he played the hero.

The weekend passed in a blur for Carlyn. Although kept busy with household chores, grading papers, and spending time with her grandmother, Wolf dominated her thoughts. She'd knocked on his apartment door a few times, but he never answered. She heard no noises coming from inside and assumed he'd gone out. When she called his cell phone, she got his voicemail. After leaving two messages with no response, she feared he was avoiding her. Beginning to feel like a stalker, she backed off, hoping he'd come to her.

The weekend over, her days were frantic with final rehearsals. Thankfully, they ran as smoothly as a well-choreographed Broadway musical. She should have been delighted. Instead, anxiety, confusion, and regret resided in her. She could not put Wolf out of her mind. Her own hurt and selfishness had led her to misjudge him. True, she'd come to see him for a kind person, but she hadn't always treated him fairly.

He'd shown up at rehearsals early in the week and took additional photos, but barely spoke to her. Valentine's Day, the opening night of her play, rapidly approached. She focused all her energies into her play. She'd deal with Wolf and her feelings later.

After another long day when Wolf came to the rehearsal and left quickly, Carlyn helped her grandmother clean up from dinner. She loaded the dishwasher and turned it on, then looked at Grandmom. Maybe she should ask her grandmother's advice about Wolf. The older woman liked Wolf from the beginning. Maybe she could tell Carlyn how to handle her feelings for him. Not able to figure out how to broach the subject, she said instead, "I'm so glad you'll be here to see my play."

Grandmom closed the cabinet door where she'd taken down some cups for their tea later and gave Carlyn a surprised look, as if she'd expected her to say something different. "I'm glad I'll get to see your play, too. I'm proud of you, dear. You're very talented. Maybe a big-name Broadway producer will come to the show and you'll be discovered."

Carlyn laughed. "That only happens in the movies."

Her grandmother wagged a finger at her. "Don't be so negative. Have faith. You're talented. You'll be discovered."

Carlyn kissed her grandmother on the cheek. "Thanks, Grandmom. Let's go into the living room and watch TV." Carlyn needed to change the subject. The only way she would be "discovered" was to send her plays to agents. Scary thought! Fear of rejection loomed large whenever she considered submitting.

As they started for the living room, Carlyn heard the door to Wolf's apartment open and close. She hoped that signaled he'd come home and not gone out. "Choose what you want to watch, Grandmom. I need to go talk to Wolf."

Her grandmother put a hand on her hip. "It's about time. You've been moping around here like you lost your best friend. I ran into Wolf in the hall the other afternoon, and he looked as gloomy as you. Get over there, girl, and make things right."

A few seconds later, Carlyn stood in front of Wolf's door fighting her nervousness like an actor battling stage fright. She'd always hated confrontation, but she owed Wolf an apology.

She knocked several times before he answered. His eyes widened when he saw her. Dressed in jeans and a black T-shirt, with his thick, straight midnight hair loosened to brush his shoulders, his appeal made Carlyn want to throw herself into his strong arms.

He held his cell phone in his hand. He lifted the phone to his ear and spoke into it. "I'll call you back." Disconnecting the call, he met her gaze. "Carlyn? What are you doing here?"

With an effort, she found her voice. "Can we talk? Or are you busy?"

He moved back to let her pass. "Come in."

Folding her arms across her chest, she entered the apartment. When he'd closed the door, she whirled to face him. "I knocked on your door a few times over the weekend and called you. I didn't get a chance to speak to you at rehearsals. I hope everything's okay."

"I had some things I needed to work out." He didn't move from the door. "I walked around the city, took pictures, had dinner with a photographer friend in town for a few days. My sublet will be up soon and I have some decisions to make. When you knocked, I was on the phone with an editor, lining up my next overseas assignment."

The pain of his leaving sat like a rock on her chest. "You're going."

His dark eyes bored into hers. "I have nothing to keep

me here."

She winced at the hurt in Wolf's voice. His leaving would put a hole in her heart she feared would never heal.

His gaze made a leisurely scan of her body, coming to rest on her mouth. His lips thinned into a rigid line. "Have a seat." He pointed to the overstuffed sofa. "How about a glass of wine?"

She sank into the soft fabric and nodded. The coldness in his voice and the tightness of his features made her want to flee to the comfort of her own apartment and Grandmom's arms.

I can do this, she told herself while she waited for Wolf to come back with the wine.

He handed her a glass of cold white wine, then settled into the velvet-covered chair facing her. Holding up his glass, he said, "To us, to what might have been."

She took a large, fortifying gulp of her drink.

He leaned back and stretched his long legs in front of him. "What did you want to talk about?"

She wrapped her hand around the stem of her glass and met his eyes. "I came to apologize. I misjudged you and said hurtful things and I'm sorry."

"I'm a big boy. I can handle it."

"I judged you without knowing you."

He chuckled, and his stern features softened. "You should have waited to know me, then you could have hated me."

"I don't hate you."

He shrugged. "If you did, you wouldn't be the first woman." He stared into his glass as if the answer to something lay in the sparkling liquid.

"I'm sorry," she said again.

He focused his attention on her. "So what changed your mind about me?"

She ran her fingers over the droplets of condensation on the outside of her glass, buying time to choose her words. "I read the news account of how you saved that little Iraqi girl. You're a hero."

Features taut, he set his glass onto the marble-topped table in front of them. "I'm no hero. I promised her I would save her family, and I couldn't. "

Carlyn set her glass next to his and leaned forward with her hands on her knees, resisting the urge to go to him and gather him close. The stiffness of his body told her he'd rebuff any comfort from her.

"You saved that little girl's life, Wolf. It wasn't your fault you couldn't save her family. You need to stop beating yourself up over that."

"That's what they tell me." Sadness tinged his voice.

"What happened to the girl?" Carlyn asked softly.

"Other family members took her in."

"You gave her a chance at life. Be proud of that."

He raked fingers through his hair. "I'm trying."

"You risked your life for her. You're a brave and honorable man, Wolf Martinez."

To her surprise, he tensed, anger evident in the harsh lines of his face. "You didn't decide I'm a decent guy on your own? You read I'm a so-called hero, so you figured I'm okay."

Crap. This wasn't going the way she'd hoped. Carlyn pushed up from the sofa and walked over to him, placing her hand on his shoulder. His muscles flexed under her fingers, but he didn't move away.

"I'm doing this wrong. Reading about what you'd done

for that little girl and for the other children you've helped made me realize how narrow-minded and judgmental I've been." She stepped back, releasing her hold on him. Hugging herself, she walked to the window to stare out at the darkness. "I used my broken heart as an excuse to push you away. I convinced myself you couldn't be trusted because you were too brash, too sexy, too sure of yourself. I've allowed past hurts to color everything I do."

She strode toward the door. She'd offered her apology. With her hand on the doorknob, she turned. "For the record, before I read that article, I'd already decided you're a decent, good man. I regret it took so long for me to realize that." She turned the knob.

"Carlyn, wait."

Wolf's words halted her. He closed the distance between them and grasped her shoulders to turn her around to face him.

He caressed her cheekbones with his thumbs. His features had softened, and sadness reflected in his eyes. "I owe you an apology. I pushed you away, too. I told myself it was for your own good. I'm learning to deal with my feelings of loss and guilt. I've been attending a support group for PTSD. It's helped. I love my work, but it takes me to all the world's hotspots. I could be killed at any time. That wouldn't be fair to you."

His intense gaze held hers. "Brashness and arrogance are my way of keeping people, especially women, at arm's length. I couldn't do that with you, Carlyn. You're special. I've fallen for you, but I'm no good at love, and I'm no good for you."

She gripped his forearms. "Let me be the judge of that."

He gave her that seductive, sexy grin of his. "I want you,

but I won't hurt you. I'll be leaving shortly to go God-knows-where."

She stood on tiptoe and touched his face. "Then let's not waste any more time."

He captured her lips in a gentle, sweet kiss. She opened to him and wound her arms around his neck, wanting him, letting go of her fears, pushing aside the future. His kiss became hot, more intense. She wanted all of Wolf, body and soul, for as long as she could have him.

He pulled free and ran his palms down her arms to grasp her hands. "You're sure about this?"

The slight tremble in his voice filled her with feminine pride. "Very sure."

Taking one of her hands, he led her toward the bedroom. Her stomach clenched with the desire that pooled deep within her. Nothing else mattered but this moment with this man.

As dawn painted the city in golden lights, Carlyn let herself into her apartment. She'd gotten no sleep. Rather than feel tired, she felt energized, sated, happier than she'd ever been before. Until Wolf she hadn't known real love.

She froze halfway to her bedroom. Wolf would leave soon, and she might never see him again. She squeezed her eyes shut against the pain. When she opened them, a shaft of rosy gold light illuminated a path to the snow globe. Red Riding Hood stood, as always, with the black wolf behind her.

Trust the healing power of love to find you, the eccentric woman who'd sold her the globe had said. Carlyn and Wolf had both needed healing. They'd found each other.

Her step lighter, she headed toward her bedroom.

They'd find a way to be together.

◇◇◇

Later that day when Wolf showed up at rehearsal, the air around them crackled with sexual energy. Carlyn wondered if the others in the small theater noticed, but the actors and crew were too involved with their jobs.

As they were wrapping up, Mr. Henninger came in carrying a large box. "We got the playbills and the brochures for the play." He beamed at Wolf. "Your pictures make our production look like something on Broadway."

Wolf nodded at Carlyn. "Carlyn's play and her directing are as good as anything on Broadway."

Gratitude flowed through Carlyn and she smiled at Wolf.

"Yes, of course." Mr. Henninger pulled a few playbills and leaflets from the box he'd set on the floor and handed them to Carlyn and Wolf.

"Everyone, come here," Carlyn shouted to the others on the stage. The actors and stagehands clambered down the steps and surrounded them.

Wolf handed out the papers to the kids, who exclaimed excitedly as they scrutinized them.

Carlyn stood to the side to read. The brochures and playbills were as well-done as anything she'd seen on Broadway. Wolf's photos leapt off the pages, their authenticity and richness perfectly capturing the essence of her story.

"What do you think?" Wolf said, coming up to her.

She blinked back tears. "Your photos are amazing. You're one of the most talented photographers I've ever seen."

He put an arm around her shoulders and drew her close.

"You're a gifted playwright."

"Thank you."

"You deserve to be on Broadway."

She stepped back. "I'm not that good."

"You are. Stop selling yourself short. Have you submitted to agents?"

"No. My plays are like my children. I'm afraid I couldn't handle the rejection."

He took her free hand in his. "You're strong and you can handle whatever rejections you might get. You'll never know unless you put yourself out there."

Put herself out there. She'd done that by falling in love with him. Maybe she had the courage now to pursue her career dream.

Her thoughts were cut short by her students crowding around her, talking excitedly about the play and how they were all going to be famous thanks to her and Wolf.

CHAPTER FIFTEEN

Opening night. The very words shredded Carlyn's nerves and had her stomach churning. She'd barely eaten all day. Ten minutes to show time, she stood backstage, script in hand, and tried to maintain a façade of calm for the sake of her actors. Stagehands bustled around her, adjusting the lighting, making sure the props were in place and the scenery panels ready.

"Ms. Cameron, where does this go?" Ryan, her student in charge of props, approached her holding a large vase of pink roses.

Carlyn frowned. "That's not part of the props."

Giggling burst around her. She whirled to find herself surrounded by her actors and crew.

"Read the card, Ms. Cameron," Stacy said.

Fingers trembling, Carlyn removed the card set in a holder with the flowers. She read, *To Ms. Cameron, the best teacher ever. Thanks for your hard work. This is a great play.* It was signed, "The cast and crew of 'Amy's Choice.'"

Blinking back tears, Carlyn raised her head to the eager faces of her students. "Thank you all. I couldn't have done this without any of you. You're an amazing group."

"You should be on Broadway," Ryan said. The others

nodded.

Smiling, she said, "Who knows? Maybe that will happen." She'd begun to believe in herself. Wolf had done that for her.

"Five minutes, everyone," Ryan shouted.

Carlyn swiped at a tear. "Showtime. Let's break a leg, people."

Ninety nail-biting minutes later, the play finished to thunderous applause. Carlyn leaned against a wall backstage and let the tears flow. She'd done it. Her students had done it. They and the play were a rousing success.

The cast took several curtain calls, then they called her to the stage. Carlyn held hands with the others and took bows. The headmaster, grinning, walked onto the stage holding a large bouquet of red roses. He handed the flowers to Carlyn and said loudly enough for the audience to hear, "Thank you, Ms. Cameron, and your cast and crew, for putting on a tremendous play. You've done Wilbur Academy proud."

More clapping and shouts thundered through the small auditorium. After one more bow from those on stage, the curtain dropped. They would give two more shows over the next two days, and Carlyn had confidence those performances would go over as well as tonight's. Thanks in part to Wolf's photos, they'd sold out each performance.

When she went backstage again, she found Avery and Josh, Bella and Chad, and Grandmom already there. A large basket of fresh fruit, a gift from them, waited for her. Her heart swelled from all the thoughtful gifts. She scanned the area, searching for Wolf. A wave of disappointment hit her when she realized he wasn't there. After hugging the others and accepting their congratulations, she said goodnight to her students and headed out with her friends and Grandmom for a celebratory dinner. Josh put the flowers and fruit in his SUV. He and Avery would drive Carlyn and Grandmom home later.

"Where's Wolf?" Carlyn asked as she climbed into the vehicle.

Avery twisted from the front seat to look at her. "He left as soon as the play ended."

Carlyn pressed her lips together, fighting her hurt.

When they arrived at the nearby restaurant where they'd made reservations, they were ushered into a private room on the second floor. A large round table covered with a white tablecloth dominated the room, richly decorated in shades of gold and white. In the center of the table stood a cut-glass vase filled with purple orchids. Crystal glasses and beautifully appointed china, along with silver flatware, adorned the table.

Carlyn turned to the maître d'. "We didn't reserve a private room."

"Your friend here did."

Wolf stepped into the room. Carlyn's heart leapt. Like her heart, she wanted to leap into Wolf's arms. Feeling the stares of the others, she restrained herself.

Wolf kissed her on the cheek and took her hand. "I hope you like this. I've arranged for a special dinner, on me, for the newest up and coming playwright in Manhattan. Your play is amazing." He pulled a business card from the inside pocket of his suit coat. "He thought so too."

He handed Carlyn the card. When she read the name of a well-known theatrical agent, her insides began to tremble. "He was there tonight?"

Wolf nodded. "I know him personally, and I invited

him. He wants you to send him your plays. He says you've got a real talent."

"Oh, Wolf. This means more to me than I can ever say. Thank you."

"Drinks all around," Grandmom shouted to laughs and claps.

In a fog, Carlyn allowed Wolf to lead her to the table.

A small silver jeweler's box capped with a red bow waited for her at her spot. Frowning at Wolf, Carlyn sat and pulled the box to her. She lifted the top to reveal a ruby-crusted charm of Red Riding Hood, hung from a thick gold chain.

Wolf leaned in to whisper in her ear. "To my own sweet Red Riding Hood. This Wolf wants your heart."

"He has it," she whispered, her throat thick with tears.

"Do you like the necklace?" he asked.

"I love it. Thank you, Wolf."

He gave her a gentle kiss before releasing her. "My Red."

"Don't call me that, wolf in Armani," she said with a laugh

Bella held up her champagne flute, glancing at Chad, Avery, and Josh before her eyes settled on Carlyn and Wolf. "A toast. To magic snow globes."

With confused looks on their faces, Wolf, Josh, Chad, and Grandmom lifted their glasses.

Avery, Bella, and Carlyn laughed together. "To magic snow globes," they said in unison.

CHAPTER SIXTEEN

Manhattan, three months later

An enthusiastic crowd of art lovers and curiosity seekers surged through the Lancashire Gallery, anxious to view the display of photos from world-renowned photojournalist Wolf Martinez. The gallery doors were open to let in the warm May air. Laughter, talking and clinking of glasses added to the cheerful atmosphere.

With Wolf busy talking to a group of art critics and admirers, Carlyn used the time to get off her aching feet. She sank into one of the upholstered chairs set around the sophisticated gallery. As soon as she sat, Bella and Avery approached her. Bella held two glasses of champagne and handed one to Carlyn.

The other women sat on chairs flanking her.

"You and Hugo have done a wonderful job of showing Wolf's photos," Carlyn said, raising her glass to Bella.

"We had something great to work with," Bella said. "Wolf is one of the most talented photographers to ever come through our gallery. Thank you for convincing him to show here."

260

Carlyn sipped her cold drink, enjoying the cool slide of it down her parched throat. "I needed that," she said, gripping her half-filled glass. "Wolf has a rare gift. He'll be off to some war-torn part of the globe soon. He would have gone long before now, but he stayed for me, then this exhibit." She touched the jeweled Red Riding Hood necklace she wore, as if the mere act of rubbing it would keep Wolf at her side. "I'll miss him, and I'll worry about him."

Avery patted her hand. "We know you will. Any time you need to get away, you're welcome to come to Vermont and stay with Josh and me."

"Thanks, Avery."

Carlyn glanced around the room as stirrings of dread and regret mixed an uncertain brew in her stomach. She knew how much his career meant to Wolf and she'd never ask him to give it up for her. A part of her wished he loved her too much to leave her.

She shook away the thought. For the past three months, they'd been inseparable. Soon after Grandmom left to go back to Maine, Wolf moved in with Carlyn. They shared laugh-filled days and passionate nights. She knew he loved her, but he never said he would stay.

And she never asked him to.

Sometimes when he thought she slept, she'd hear him on the phone and assumed he was lining up assignments. She wondered what dangerous country he'd travel to soon.

Wolf entered the room where the three women sat. His gaze met Carlyn's. The air between them thickened. As always, when she saw him, her pulse jumped a few notches and her insides warmed. Magnificent as always, tonight he did indeed look wolfish, dressed in tailored black pants, black dress shirt, worn tieless, and with his ebony hair tied back. Her wolf in Armani. She loved him so much.

With the lithe grace of a timber wolf, he headed toward the women. Smiling at Avery and Bella, he said, "Mind if I steal Carlyn for a while?"

"She's all yours," they said.

Wolf held out his hand to Carlyn. She slipped her hand into his large one and stood. He cupped her elbow and led her out of the display rooms into the back of the gallery and down a dimly lit hallway.

"Where are we going?" She tugged on his hand.

"You'll see."

They stopped in front of a door marked with Bella's name. Wolf pulled a key from his pocket and unlocked the door.

"Bella's office?"

"It's okay. She gave me the key."

Wolf switched on the overhead lights, bathing the room in brightness. On Bella's large oak desk rested a crystal vase filled with yellow roses.

"The roses are for you," he said.

Carlyn met Wolf's eyes. "They're beautiful." She strode to the desk and bent to inhale the sweet fragrance of the flowers. She plucked the gift card with her name and read it with tears in her eyes.

To the woman who makes me a better man, the woman whose love healed me.

Wolf came up behind her and pulled her against him, circling her waist with his arms. Her eyes moist, she turned. He cradled her against his chest.

"Thank you for the flowers and for what you said on the card."

He gently set her away from him. "There's something the card didn't say."

"What?" Her voice trembled.

"I love you, Carlyn Cameron. More than I thought possible to love anyone. I fell in love with you the minute I saw you in that church." He twisted strands of her hair around his finger. "My Red Riding Hood."

She stroked his face. "I love you, my big, not-so-bad Wolf."

He took her hand and led her to the small sofa. He kissed the tip of her nose before he sat and settled her against him, with her back pressed against his firm chest.

She snuggled in the crook of his arm, feeling the contentment and peace she'd once thought lost to her.

"Do you remember what I said the first time I saw you?" he asked.

"How could I forget? You said I was the woman you would marry." She twisted around to look at him. "I thought you were an arrogant jerk."

He grinned. "I might have been." He gathered her against him again and rested his chin on the top of her head. "It wasn't a pickup line. As soon as I saw you, I knew you were special. But when you rebuffed me, I figured maybe I was out of your league."

Frowning, she slid free and faced him. "Out of your league? What are you talking about?"

"You're not like most of the women I've been with." His lips tilted in a self-deprecating grin. "You were too smart to fall for my lines."

"I kind of did fall for your lines."

He laughed, then his features grew serious. "Because of my gypsy lifestyle and some of the women I've been involved with, people assume I'm something I'm not."

Heat crept up her neck to her face. "I'm guilty of that, too. With your looks, charm, and worldliness, I'd assumed you were full of yourself and not trustworthy." She touched his face, running her fingers over his sharp cheekbones. "I'm ashamed I was so judgmental."

He settled her close again, wrapping his arms around her. "Most of my bravado is a sham, something I learned early on to mask my insecurities. Later, I found it helped me stay alive in all the dangerous places I traveled to."

"You had insecurities? I find that hard to believe."

He laughed. "Hard to believe, huh? A nerd in school, I got teased a lot. My parents worried about me. My mom enrolled me in art classes, hoping I'd find something I liked. The first time I held a camera, I knew I'd found my future. Photography took me out of my shell. Deep down, I'm still that nerdy kid. I perfected my arrogance. It seemed to go with my profession."

He kissed the top of her head. "I've never before told a woman I was going to marry her. It took a while for me to realize I needed you in my life. I almost blew it though. I'm glad you decided to take a chance on me."

"So am I."

He set her away from him and strode to the desk. Opening a drawer, he pulled out a tiny jewel box.

Carlyn forgot to breathe.

He knelt on the floor in front of her and opened the box. Inside, nestled on white satin, sat an exquisite pear-shaped diamond surrounded by smaller diamonds.

Carlyn began trembling.

"Carlyn Mary Cameron, will you marry me?"

She gazed into Wolf's velvet brown eyes, the eyes of

the man she would love forever. "Yes, Wolf, I'll marry you."

He slipped the ring on her finger. It fit perfectly. She tilted her hand back and forth, letting the overhead light play on the facets of the stone. Tears streamed down her face. "It's beautiful. I've always dreamt of a pear-shaped engagement ring. And it fits me perfectly."

She met his eyes again. "How did you know what type diamond I like, and my size?"

He sat on the sofa and cupped her face between his hands. "Avery and Bella told me about your love of pear-shaped diamonds and your grandmother told me your size."

"Grandmom and my parents. I have to call them."

He chuckled. "They know. They'll be here. Later, we'll call my parents."

"You thought of everything." With a teasing grin, she tilted her head. "Pretty sure of yourself, aren't you? What if I'd said no?"

He grinned. "You wouldn't."

She hugged him. "That's the arrogant guy I fell in love with."

He kissed her, showing his love in the gentle touch of his lips. Releasing her, he said, "You once told me you no longer believe in happy-ever-after. Do you believe now?"

"Yes, love, yes. For now and always."

A thought hit her, dousing her joy. "You travel to terrible places. I couldn't take it if something happened to you."

He took her hands in his. "That's about to change."

"How?"

"I'm committed to this last overseas assignment. It shouldn't take more than a month, then I'll be back here. For good."

Giddy joy made her want to jump up and do a little dance. "You're coming back? For good?" She squeezed his hand. "Wolf, I know how much your career means to you, and you're so very talented. I want you to be happy."

"My career does mean a lot to me, but you mean more." He skimmed a finger down her face to her lips. "You didn't think I'd give you up, did you?"

"I'd hoped not. What will you do?"

"The editor of one of the magazines I freelanced for is now a department head at a small college in New Hampshire. He's offered me a job teaching journalism and photography. I want to take it, but only if you're okay moving to New Hampshire. I won't do anything you don't want."

Elation made her heart race and warmth radiate through her body. She gripped his upper arms. "I love New Hampshire. I'll have to come into Manhattan from time to time to see how my play is progressing."

He frowned. "Your play?"

She rubbed her hands together. "I have an announcement of my own. I'd planned to save it for later. I submitted one of my plays to the agent who came to the school play. He loves it. He's found backers, and we're going to produce it. Off-off-Broadway, for now, but it's my start, what I've always dreamed of. You did it for me, Wolf. Because of you, I put aside my fear of rejection."

He hugged her, then took both her hands in his. "Congratulations, sweetheart, but I'm not surprised. You deserve all the success you can get." The love that shone from his eyes wound around her heart. "You've done something for me too, Carlyn. Loving you has given me the courage to go on, to fully live my life."

Trust the healing power of love to find you. The words

of the eccentric woman who'd chosen her Red Riding Hood snow globe floated through Carlyn's mind. Chills raced up her spine. "We healed each other," she whispered.

His gaze, hot and dark, locked with hers. "My first words to you will come true. You are the love of my life, the woman I'll marry."

His tender kiss sealed their love with the promise of happy-ever-after.

Later, they went back to the gallery where Carlyn's parents, brother, sister-in-law, and Grandmom, along with Avery, Josh, Bella, and Chad, waited with expectant looks on their faces.

Laughing, Carlyn held up her hand to show her engagement ring. After hugs and kisses, they toasted with exquisite champagne, a gift from Bella's boss.

Grandmom took Carlyn's arm and led her aside. "I told you Wolf was a good guy. I'm glad you finally listened to me. Grandmom knows best."

Carlyn kissed her grandmother on the cheek. "You certainly do. I'll never doubt you again."

As the crowds in the gallery began to thin, Avery, Bella and Carlyn sat at a small table nibbling on appetizers and sipping ice water.

"Can you believe it?" Avery asked. "The three of us happy and in love."

"I can hardly believe it myself," Bella said in a dreamy voice. "Soon Chad and I will be married."

"You were the cynical one, Bella," Carlyn said.

"Chad changed all that," Bella said. "Thank God."

Avery turned to Carlyn. "And you were the romantic."

Carlyn laughed. "Until I wasn't. I believe in happy-ever-after again."

"I judged men by their ambition," Avery said, smiling as she looked at Josh. "Josh showed me real love and gave me what my heart truly needed."

Bella glanced over at Chad, deep in conversation with Josh and Wolf. "I wanted a frog, but I got a prince."

"I wanted a guy like the romance heroes in the books I love," Carlyn said, her gaze on Wolf. "He's my hero, in so many ways, only I didn't know it at first."

When a waiter walked by with a tray of champagne flutes, each woman took a glass.

Avery lifted her glass. "To the orange-haired woman who knew exactly what we each needed."

"I never believed in magic, yet there was magic in my snow globe," Bella said.

"In all our globes," Avery said.

As the women clinked glasses, a gentle breeze, bringing the scent of a springtime meadow, blew over them. They turned toward the gallery door. The elderly woman who'd chosen their snow globes stood in the doorway. Dressed in a bright orange coat that matched her hair, and wearing gold high-topped sneakers, she carried a large plastic shopping bag covered with flowers.

With a wave of her hand, she grinned and slipped through the open door, disappearing into the night.

Carlyn stared at her two friends. Their eyes were wide, as she knew hers were. "Yes, there was magic in those snow globes."

***

*Thank you for reading *Snow Globe Magic*. I really appreciate your purchase.*

Books by Cara Marsi

A Catered Romance
A Cat's Tale & Other Love Stories
(All stories in this anthology are available separately)
A Cinderella Christmas
A Groom for Christmas
Accidental Love
Capri Nights
Cursed Mates
Her Forever Husband
Her Snow White Christmas (Snow Globe Magic Book 1)
Her Frog Prince Holiday (Snow Globe Magic Book 2)
Her Red Riding Hood Valentine (Snow Globe Magic Book 3)
Snow Globe Magic Boxed Set
Logan's Redemption (Redemption Book 1)
Franco's Fortune (Redemption Book 2)
Luke's Temptation (Redemption Book 3)
The Redemption Series Boxed Set
Love Potion
Loving Or Nothing
Murder, Mi Amore
Storm of Desire
Sweet Temptations
Sweet Temptations Boxed Set
The One Who Got Away
The Ring
Wedding Dreams Boxed Set

Read excerpts at www.caramarsi.com
All books available at online booksellers

A Catered Romance, A Groom for Christmas, Capri Nights, Cursed Mates, Franco's Fortune, Logan's Redemption, Loving Or Nothing, Luke's Temptation, Murder, Mi Amore, and Snow Globe Magic Boxed Set are also available in print

***

All about Cara Marsi

An award-winning and eclectic author, Cara Marsi is published in romantic suspense, paranormal romance, and contemporary romance. She loves a good love story, and believes that everyone deserves a second chance at love. Sexy, sweet, thrilling, or magical, Cara's stories are first and foremost about the love. Treat yourself today, with a taste of romance.

When not traveling or dreaming of traveling, Cara and her husband live on the East Coast in a house ruled by two spoiled cats who compete for attention.

Read more about Cara's books and sign up for her newsletter at her website CaraMarsi.com. She's on Twitter, Goodreads, Facebook, and Pinterest and is always interested in meeting new friends.

***